# The C



E. Barrington

**Alpha Editions**

This edition published in 2021

ISBN : 9789355116956

Design and Setting By
**Alpha Editions**
www.alphaedis.com
Email – info@alphaedis.com

# Contents

# PREFACE

"THE CHASTE DIANA."

This romance of "The Beggar's Opera" introduces many real persons but all imaginatively treated. Lord Baltimore, "The American Prince," as he was called at the time in society, has come down to us with a reputation for heartlessness of which I have made the most, and it would be difficult for any novelist to exaggerate the whims of the famous and beautiful Duchess of Queensberry—or Queensbury, as I have preferred to spell her title, that being her own and (generally speaking) the contemporary method. The Duke of Bolton's marriage I have antedated. My picture of the Royalties is fully sanctioned by history. As to the charming figure of Lavinia Fenton, it offers a wide field to the imagination, and will doubtless from time to time be filled in according to the man that draws it and the mind that conceives it, for there are few records. But what is known of her story is compatible with the picture I present.

E. BARRINGTON,

Canada.

# CHAPTER I

IT was the winter season of the year 1727 and the great Mr. Rich, patentee and manager of the playhouse in Portugal Street, Lincoln's Inn Fields; was seated in his own parlour where he received the budding players of both sexes and made and marred careers like a very Fate. To Portugal Street come trembling beauties whose voices die in their throats as that piercing eye falls on them appraising every feature with no thought but how many guineas are like to be made on the strength of it. To Portugal Street, Lincoln's Inn Fields, come also the anxious dramatists from Grub Street, some with a cheap swagger that Mr. Rich quells on the instant, some with lank cheeks and threadbare cuffs and an entreaty for a hearing which is apt to provoke the great man's ire and contempt as he sits to receive his courtiers in a velvet coat and breeches, sober enough, but with a good bit of lace at the throat, and a wig handsomely curled about his shoulders. For whatever may be the standing of player-folk, and God knows it is none too high, Mr. Rich is minded that their manager shall win respect. What! hath not Mrs. Oldfield been received at Court in spite of blots on the scutcheon in the shape of two gentlemen—Mr. Mainwaring and his successor General Churchill, setting aside certain passages with Captain Farquhar, the gay dramatist, which might or might not be censurable? Yet, notwithstanding, the lady went where she would, and the Princess of Wales (willing to oblige this charming person) informing her that she had heard she was the wife of General Churchill, Mrs. Oldfield did but sweep the prettiest curtsey and reply, "So it is said, please your Royal Highness, but we have not owned it yet."

An example of coolness, thinks Mr. Rich, for all who would exalt the profession to follow. So there he sits, a gobbling turkey-cock of a man when crossed, kindly when humoured, his eyes very shrewd and keen between their layers of flesh. A choleric, genial, short-nosed man, himself the unrivalled Harlequin and a player after a fashion, he falls a little on the side of rudeness to inferiors lest he slip into that of servility to superiors, an uneasy matter but always to be kept in view.

On this evening he had done his day's work and routed not a few miserable pretenders to parts in the new raree-show shortly to be produced to the public. He had two companions—fine, careless easy gentlemen both, and almost as much at home behind the scenes as himself.

The one, lounging in an armed-chair was a young man of almost effeminate beauty. Disguise him in paint, powder and hoop, and you had a charming Lady Easy, with the absolute manner of bon ton, and should The Careless Husband be needed to play up to her Ladyship, as in the comedy of that name, the other young man dangling a pair of handsome legs from Mr.

Rich's table was your very fit! None better! and in real life as careless a husband as any that ever trod the boards, perhaps not altogether by his own choice.

Permit me to present the first—fair, blue-eyed, and slender, a pretty man indeed, though with not too many inches to spare. Prodigious fine in velvet and embroidery, yet steel and fire under the graceful mask of languor. 'Tis the American Prince as they call him about town—my Lord Baltimore, a potentate after a fashion, since he holds by due succession the patent of Maryland in the New World, paying yearly as fee two Indian arrows at Windsor Castle every Easter Tuesday, and the more substantial rent of a fifth part of the gold and silver ore therein found. A very great gentleman with his American principality, and the most fascinating bachelor in London, an arrant rake and favourite in all the boudoirs. Scarce a fine lady but aspired to be the American Princess.—But this tale will show his Lordship as he was and more words are not now needed.

The more masculine looking beau—a handsome grave brown man, is his Grace the Duke of Bolton, unwilling husband to my Lord Carberry's daughter and heiress, a lady as homely and sour as a withered crab-apple, and indeed 'tis more than rumoured that the ill-matcht pair parted after the wedding feast and a few ceremonies to mislead the public. It follows that his Grace is a mighty patron of the playhouse, whether at Lincoln's Inn Fields or in the Haymarket, and there is scarce a man in town whose judgment Mr. Rich would more willingly accept of the promise of a new tragedy or comedy Queen. Indeed he seeks that judgment at this moment.

And so my story begins.

"You will observe, your Grace," said Mr. Rich, with an anxious brow, "that I stake not only my reputation but a vast deal of money on this venture. Stap my vitals, if I know whether I do well!"

" 'Tis certain, Rich, you've done so ill of late," says the American Prince, yawning over his gold snuff-box—"that you can scarce do worse. The farces you have gave us of late were more funereal than a dirge, witness 'The Capricious Lovers' that only Mrs. Mincemode saved from damnation the first night, and when you followed with 'The Female Fortune Teller' and capped it all with 'Money the Mistress'—Lord save us, man, you left not a leg to stand on to your warmest friends."

" 'Tis very true," interrupted his Grace of Bolton, "and were it not that Drury Lane was as dull as a Friends' ranting house and so no rival, you had sunk altogether. But tell us, Richie, what like is this new stuff you have in hand? Has it ever a laugh in it or is it all snuffle?"

Mr. Rich, wincing somewhat at the "Richie," pulled out a roll from his scrutoire and laid his hand upon it.

"Why, your Grace and your Lordship, there's the point. I would to God I knew. 'Tis a case of triumph or calamity—no halfway house, for 'tis so damned unlike anything yet seen, that I can't for my life tell whether I'm a fool or a wise man to have to do with it."

"The author?" enquired my Lord Baltimore, scarce raising his eyelashes, long and golden as a girl's.

"Why the author is Gay, my Lord, and 'tis writ under the influence of spite and disdain, a sharp enough pair of spurs to knock out what mettle is in a man."

"Aha! I know the inmost of that business," his American Highness laughed musically. "I'll tell you the story, Rich. 'Tis worth a laugh. 'Twas his seeking preferment at Court and getting only the office of nurse-tender, bear-leader, call it what you will! to the youngest royal children, that put him out of love with the nobility and gentry. What hath he done for vengeance?"

"Why, my Lord, 'tis hard to describe. He hath writ a very droll—what shall I call it?—a farce, no!—a comedy? Yes, but 'tis more of a kind of an opera, so full of songs, only that the hero is a highwayman, and the ladies—why, the less said about the ladies and their honesty the better. Newgate wenches at best. 'Tis at least very original."

The Duke sat bolt upright.

"Original? Why that was Swift's notion," he cried, "Why, Richie, you must remember that Dr. Swift said the town was sick of Amorets and Bellarmines and all those brocaded perfumed cattle, and that if a manager had luck and courage and would stage a Newgate pastoral, the world and all that therein it would be a rabble at his heels applauding and pouring gold into his fists. Didn't he say that, and didn't I hear it with my own ears? And d'ye mean to tell me Gay has cribbed the notion?"

"Not a doubt of it, your Grace. But the fellow—stap my vitals if I can help laughing at the rogue! hath done it so arch—so comical—I don't know what I would say!—that I dare swear Swift himself will forgive him, and then rather that it would ill become his gown to set some of the jests on the stage, though he is not too retiring in his writings."

Lord Baltimore raised his fine-drawn eyebrows:

"Smutty, then, Rich?"

"Well, as to that,— So-so, and yet not too much, so, your Lordship. You are aware that the public demands a certain license and His Majesty rebuked his players for what he termed emasculating a comedy not so long since. 'Tis very hard to steer between Scylla and Charybdis, my Lord. But I think there's enough to please his Majesty and the public without disgusting the prudes."

"Have you the words handy?" demanded his Grace, "I'm not of those that believes smut takes the *pas* of wit. I know not how it is but there's something in these brutalities sickens my stomach especially when a pretty woman's called upon to speak them."

"We don't find they rebel, my Lord Duke. In fact I've known one or two ask a little more pepper and mustard to season her part."

"Poor devils, they rant for their living—what can you expect?" says his Dukeship with easy contempt.

"Not altogether—as I think your Grace knows as well as most," says Mr. Rich with a somewhat gross twinkle in his eye, then hastened on as the Duke stiffened a little. "Be that as it may, we can't do without 'em, and God knows I'd sooner manage fifty men than one haughty slut like Mrs. Oldfield or Mrs. Cibber. But I think there to be little question that if my cast is what I desire, this venture of Gay's may take the town. Can either of your Lordships oblige me with a seductive Polly?"

"Pretty Polly!" mocked the American Prince, "Why I know a brace of pretty Pollys, Rich,—but they don't warble, no more than their namesakes. I take it your Polly must be tuneful?"

"Lord, Yes! your Lordship. She must have a voice like a thrush and the face of an innocent angel new strayed from Eden, and the heart of a little devil ("That should not be hard to find!" interpolated his Grace), and the abandonment of 'The Country Wife,' and the archness of Millamant, and the demureness of a cat after cream, and——"

"And in short the paragon doesn't exist." Lord Baltimore was yawning again, and flicking imaginary dust off his smoke coloured velvet. "Can't you dispense with her, Richie?"

"Why, I have sent a hue and cry through the provinces, and even through the purlieus of Drury Lane and St. Giles's."

"Faugh!" says his Lordship, "Well, I was ever obliging, Richie, and if I hear tell of a Venus with the appearance of Dian and the voice of Polyhymnia you shan't lack for information. Are you for Lady Lansdowne's drum, Bolton? There's a fair widow there— Ah, Richie,—if beauty and rank and every elegant accomplishment would take the boards, you might find your heroine yet."

Rich grinned:

"They take 'em at second-hand, your Lordship, running after our handsome players. But if you will deprive me of your company will you look in tomorrow about this time to know if I have trapped my quarry? If not, we must hang up the play for a better season."

"What does Gay call his stuff?" asked the Duke, leisurely descending from the table.

"Why, 'The Beggar's Opera,' your Grace. The name's original too, if it do but take. There's much in a title. If I can better it, I will."

"You can't better it," says his Grace. " 'Tis saucy, provocative, and runs off the tongue. What would you have more? What's the heroine's mellifluous name? Lindamira? Amoret?"

"Why no, your Grace—Polly Peachum. It hath a common or village sound to my ear. I doubt it takes!"

"You're an old fool, Richie," said the Duke. "Its commonness is its recommendation. Don't all the fine world *s'encanailler* nowadays? There are as vulgar trollops at Court as any——"

"In St. Giles's," finished the American Prince. "True, O King,—and now, Richie, have our chairs called, and may the gods be good to thee and give such a Polly Peachum to thy embrace as ever the world hath seen. O the sweet name! I protest it tastes of peaches hot in the sun. I can see her lips like two cherries—her eyes blue as summer seas, her voice like the gurgling and purling of a brook, her arms round and smooth as Parian marble. O Richie—Richie, you old devil, what images have you raised! If you find her not, I'll go search her myself."

"Your Lordship hath but to sit still and whistle," cries Rich, "to have all the pretty charmers come running to you like a flock of hens! There's a scene somewhat like it in Gay's opera, where Macheath the highwayman—who needs not even to whistle, has them running all about him, and each with a baby on her arm."

"That's comical!" says the Duke laughing, "and does pretty Polly pipe her eye to see it?"

"Not she! your Grace! A delicate—or indelicate regret is all the stage directions admit of. She's a fine pliable girl and after a little tiff with Lucy Lockit comes to heel like a spaniel."

He began humming in a rich throaty voice—

"Lucy Locket lost her pocket,

Kitty Fisher found it."

"Kitty Fisher!" Both gentlemen burst out laughing.

" 'Tis topical then, Rich!" says Lord Baltimore. "Why I guarantee it success, if so. Didn't Aristophanes bring down the house, or was it the Acropolis at Athens, by laughing at all the wits and holding up the mirror to the pretty Aspasia? They'll run in their thousands to look into a mirror whoever holds it, were it their father the devil."

Rich was all smirks and bows as they cloaked themselves to depart. He knew, none better, the value of the countenance of two such men—the very pink of fashion. Fashion is a capricious jade. Her aureole may or may not enhalo the head of rank. There were peers whom apart from their purses Mr. Rich might well afford to neglect, but not these two. What Lord Baltimore said the ladies would swear to, and were his Grace of Bolton to favour the production with his approval the play was made. Yes, even with the gallery, for so liberal were both these gentlemen in scattering their gold that there was not a chairman or footman or a gentleman's gentleman in London town but had a lavish word for both, and doubt not that a gentleman's gentleman also hath as much influence in certain circles as their Lordships in St. James's. The manager himself escorted them to the door and stood there bowing obsequiously until they turned the corner. You might think there was not a care on his periwigged brow, so honeyed were his smiles. But 'twas very visible as he turned back to his parlour. The world had not used him well of late, nor could he forgive it unless 'twould send him a paragon for his Polly. He swore a little under his breath as he sat down again, running over in his mind the women available and their failings. 'Twas infinitely distressing, for in spite of his doubts to the two gentlemen he had little in his own thoughts but that here was a prize. 'Tis very seldom a manager himself is tickled by a jest or moved by a situation, yet sure enough Gay had performed this miracle with Rich. But the woman—curse her!—the woman! He sat down heavily—the corners of his full mouth drooping into the turkey-wattles of a lace cravat.

'Twas then a knock came to the door, and entered to him Mrs. Scawen, the lady whose office it was to keep his parlour sweet and clean, and announce and dismiss claimants to his attention.

"Not now, Mrs. Scawen,—not now! I'll not see another incompetent this night if I die for it. Lock the door and fetch me a pot of porter and oysters and send the fool to the devil."

"But your Honour—your Worship!" cries Mrs. Scawen holding the door and intruding only half her stout person within it. "It isn't a fool, as I hope to be saved! It's a woman!"

"A woman and no fool!" says Mr. Rich, pulling out papers from his scrutoire, and indifferent enough, "Well, you should be a judge, Scawen, after all the fools you have seen come in at this door. None the less, send her to the devil. She won't have far to go."

Mrs. Scawen advanced herself a step further and looked round the corner of the door.

"Why, your Honour, 'tis true I should know a fool by now and I give your worship leave to call me one if I don't. But this one is all obligingness and hath so pretty a way with her, and lips like cherries and a voice like a thrush or blackbird—"

His American Highness's description, you see, exact! Mr. Rich looked up.

"What did she give you to say this, you old harridan?"

Mrs. Scawen turned out her pocket—

" 'Tis as bare as charity, your Honour, but for my huswife and the nutmeg for my mulled ale. No, 'tis the truth. Lips like cherries, and a voice like a thrush, and hair——"

"What like was her hair?" cries Mr. Rich "Cobwebs of gold— O, stow this rant, old woman, and get you gone and dismiss her. I'll not see her. I'll not see Helen's self this night. Go, get the oysters."

Mrs. Scawen curtseyed.

"They're here, your Honour. Don't I know your blessed habits by now? I don't know who Mrs. Helen might be, but I know well that this young person is as pretty as her ladyship and to spare. She'll draw all the gentlemen at the tail of her petticoat—no question but she will. 'Tis worth your Honour's while to have a look."

" 'Tis worth my while to do and suffer anything to stop your tongue, Scawen. So have her in, and if she falls an inch short of your perfections I'll dock you half a guinea next pay-day."

The door closed swiftly, and there was a moment's peace during which Mr. Rich helped himself to snuff and surveyed his silk hose with some satisfaction. He had no expectations about the coming applicant, but 'twas worth while to keep old Scawen in tune—she was a conveniency at all times and no end to her obliging compliance where he was concerned.

Female voices, one very low, were heard coming along the grimy little passage. The door opened and Mrs. Scawen flattened herself against the wall to give passage to a cloaked figure.

"Mrs. Diana Beswick," she said, and took up her own post behind her master.

# CHAPTER II

NOW this is the story of this woman—Diana Beswick,—who would have told her own story if she could, and indeed had the zest for it, for she pondered often over her life, finding it more strange than any written in any book. But 'tis to be thought she knew either too much or too little of her charming subject or had not the words at command. Let me set down her qualifications as a truth-teller and on these let her be judged.

*Item.* She was beautiful, and not beautiful only as a statue formed to excite admiration rather than love. Truly she wore the girdle of Venus for she was adorned with a thousand indescribable charms and graces as when a landscape is bathed in sunshine and all the pretty warblers sing and every flower spreads its coy bosom to the sun.

*Item.* She was an actress the most finished, and where she captured all opinion and led it whither she would, may it not be argued that such a lady was sometimes her own dupe also?

*Item.* From her skill in portraying the emotions of others, 'tis to be allowed she was certainly skilled in the art of fiction.

*Item.* She had the gift, with her eyes of sunshine and voice of music to make all believe her true as Truth's self even had she vouched for the Impossible.

I ask therefore, can such a woman tell the truth about herself even if she would? I leave it, as I said, to the world's judgment. But because her history is very moving, entertaining and marvellous, 'twere pity it were not set down.

For this was no honey-sweet beauty of April smiles and tears and fond abandonments and compliances. 'Twas this at times certainly, for every mood was natural to her and she adorned them all. But she wore each as she might put on her satin manteau and lay it away when it had served its turn. At other times you beheld a Dian, austere and chilly—"severe in youthful beauty," and desire was quenched in the frosty sparkle of her eyes and scorn winged its shafts from the bow of her lips smartly enough to disconcert not a few of the idle gentlemen who swore and drawled about her. And when she had them daunted—suddenly her Goddess-ship would slide down from her pedestal, and 'twas a young girl all hopes and fears and a dewy tremble on her eyelashes looking up into your face for encouragement and approbation. She was then perhaps most dangerous, for 'twas a natural movement to lay love at her tender feet for a stepping-stone amid the quagmires of life.

And here is the story of how two gentlemen did this, and their reward.

’Tis to be seen that a surprise awaited Mr. Rich when that hood should be lifted, for she wore it muffled about her face. She came up beside him and dropped her curtsey, and he bowed sitting and rather on the careless side, a way he affected with his suitors and suitresses. To Mrs. Oldfield and her like, who had made their way and topped their parts he could be deferential, otherwise he wasted no civility.

Seeing he awaited her speech, a low voice, sweet as dropping honey, emerged from the hood.

“I venture to present myself, Sir, in hopes you might have a small part unfilled in whatever new play you might think to produce shortly. My ambitions are humble. ’Tis so needful I should place myself.”

Mr. Rich sat up somewhat straighter because ’twas the voice and accent of no Drury Lane hussey, but of a gentlewoman. Here his first surprise lay in wait for him because it was by no means a common thing that a young gentlewoman should find her way to his parlour. I own him curious as he provoked her to speak further.

“Ambition should never be humble in this profession, Madam. ’Tis a fair field and no favour, and if an actress wins the public there’s nothing beyond her hopes.”

“True, Sir. I doubt if you would find me humble later, but I can scarce expect a gentleman of your experience will admit me at my own valuation.”

An astonishing admission. His heavy eye lightened a little. This resembled not the modesty, mock or otherwise, of the cringing suppliant that was his usual fare in that place. He dallied a moment with the surprisingness of the thing.

“Then you value yourself high, Madam. Doth your experience warrant it?”

“Why, as to experience, Sir,—’tis not much to vaunt myself on. You may recall that in the playhouse in the Haymarket a year since there was a few performances of a few plays. Nothing fixed.”

“I recall. They gave ‘The Beaux’ Stratagem’—I forget what else.”

“ ‘The Orphan,’ Sir. I was presented as Monimia in ‘The Orphan,’ and Cherry in ‘The Beaux’ Stratagem.’ An understudy. For four nights.”

“Indeed. Both parts warrant me in supposing a pretty face. Throw back your hood, child.”

She untied a ribbon at the throat and threw it back with a quick gesture. And here was Mr. Rich met with his second surprise.

There hung behind her the looking-glass wherein he was wont to adjust the elegance of his wig and cravat. 'Twas a good one, for he valued his appearance beyond expense. Now it reflected her graceful shoulders and the creamy pillar of a swan throat, atop of which percht her little head with the knots of black silken hair disposed about it very simple and unlike the *curley-murley* style then the mode. She carried the said head high—could not indeed do otherwise, for the throat was stately, but it gave her the carriage of a princess. Her eyes, meeting his with anxious candour, were the deepest blue running on the violet side and veiled with the most expressive eyelashes in the world. An Irish combination 'tis true, but come by right, for her mamma sprang from the noble stock of the Maguires of Ballyinch, though she had never set foot on Irish soil. For the rest, the low broad brows and heart-shaped face, and even the bow of the arched lip raised over the little pearls within were beautiful. Nature, that is but a niggard stepmother with most of us poor mortals, gave with more than maternal tenderness to this darling, perfecting her picture with little touches, not to be described, such as the great Kneller lays upon a picture he loves. These made her every look an allurement, her every movement a favour to those who saw.

All this Mr. Rich could perceive, yet knew not the mere alphabet of the charm that made her what she was. How shall a man see if he be blind or hear if he be deaf? How shall a man with little mind and no sensibility perceive what the play of both may add to the power of beauty? And moreover she naturally did not set her illuminations alight for him. She was too frightened indeed. But he saw before him a fine young woman of what his practised eye detected for an excellent stage presence, and spoke to that.

"Why, I must own that I commend the choice that made you Cherry, child. But the experience is no experience at all—if it be not a something gained in facing an audience. And these are speaking parts. The ladies I engage for what I have in view must also be little warblers for there is a chorus to many of the songs. I conclude you no singer since you was chose for such parts."

A slight smile raised the corners of her fair lips.

"Sir, I did not know 'twas required, but— Yes, I can sing."

"A ballad over your needleworks, child? Well, but I need somewhat more."

"Somewhat more I can do, Sir," she said modestly, "I have had lessons."

"Can you sing me a lesson now?"

'Twas a hard test and Mr. Rich knew it, but the girl invited tests. Two she had past triumphant, but the third was the hardest. 'Tis to be said however that he already saw her in his mind's eye in the chorus, was it but up the stage or in the wings. That face would stir the gallants, he dare swear.

Bending over his scrutoire he took out a sheet of music very neat written,

"This here's a song in the new piece. You would not have this song for 'tis the first woman's. Still, since we can't ask you for a chorus, 'twill give me the notion of your voice, Mrs. Beswick. Will you try it—you can read the music?"

"Certainly, Sir," she replied with a little curtsy, and a sort of assured modesty very pleasing. "You will make allowance for my situation, I am certain."

He composed himself in his chair as she took the music in hand, and stood up like a young poplar by the candles to get the light on the sheet. A few minutes past while she read it down slowly and carefully, the paper shaking the least in the world in a somewhat trembling hand. Then she began:

"Cease your funning,

Force and cunning

Never can my heart trepan.

All your sallies

Are but malice——"

Mr. Rich made a start here that completely overset her and she dropped the music outright and put her hand quick to her heart.

"O, Sir," she fluttered.

"Hush, hush, my child. Compose yourself and proceed. Begin again." For here came the third surprise! Heavens, what a voice! Not grand, massive, commanding like Cuzzoni's—not a voice to storm the town in grave opera or in the great Mr. Handel's oratorios, but fresh, clear and sweet as a linnet's at dawn.

"O Lord, the pretty innocent!" cries Mrs. Scawen from behind her master's chair. "Sure she trips up the notes like a lark running up the sky. Was ever anything so uncommon! Sure she fetches the tears and I don't know why."

"Be quiet, woman. Be not a chatter-chops!" says Mr. Rich, as stiff as a magistrate in his chair. "Continue, Mrs. Beswick. To the end, if you please."

She did so, less fluttered now that she perceived the start was not fury. Indeed she sang it charmingly. She hit every note in the middle true as a silver mallet. Never was such effortless singing. 'Twas art concealing art. It might be supposed the fair creature had never sung a lesson nor a scale nor had human teacher, but sang as a bird does on a flowery branch for mere delight in the sound of her own most delicious voice—a singular high soprano, clear as crystal and as little impassioned. But that might in part be owing to the circumstances which certainly did not invite passion. He was about to speak when she interrupted, but modestly:

"Sir, your discernment will tell you 'tis impossible I should do myself justice in a lesson of music I know not. If you was at the music in honor of St. Cecilia some months since at the Crown Tavern you might recall the song "Pur dicesti," which Madame Faustina sung there. Have I your permission to sing a passage or two?"

Mr. Rich had not been present nor was skilled in music further than as his trade used it, but as in a kind of dream he gave his august permission, and the room rippled to the sweetest trills and melodious cries of the Italian master. He could contain himself no longer. He broke in upon the woven enchantment. He leaped up.

"Say no more, child. Sing no more. I'll search no further. You're the cordial drop heaven in my cup has thrown. You're my Polly!"

For one second she looked scared and shrank, his face being so masterful. Then she saw his drift and her gravity broke up into dancing smiles of delight. He caught her hand and they stood linked a moment—Youth and joy at one.

"Polly!" she cries. "Is Polly her name? Then indeed 'tis something new. Trust me, Sir, and I'll make you the agreeablest Polly in all the world!"

"You will, my girl, you will, for you can't do otherwise. You have but to look and sing and if you were the veriest stick that ever trod the boards, you'll have the town at your feet."

"Me a stick!" she cried, highly offended. "Why, Sir, my 'Cherry' was adorable. There wasn't a man saw it but said so, and you know 'tis an arch part. I hope I'm no fool if I *do* look one. Hear me do a speech of Lady Betty's in 'The Careless Husband.' "

She dropt his hand, and advanced, tripping with the ease and grace of a fine modish woman:

"O, my dear! I'm overjoyed to see you! I'm strangely happy today. I have just received my new scarf from London, and you are most critically come to give me your opinion of it."

Falling into her vein, Rich, laughing, took up Lady Easy's part. He knew every line.

"O, your servant, Madam. I'm a very indifferent judge, you know. What? Is it with sleeves?"

(She languished and pouted at him)

"O, impossible to tell you what it is. 'Tis all extravagance both in mode and fancy, my dear. I believe there's six thousand yards of edging in it. Then, such an enchanting slope from the elbow—so lively, so noble, so coquette—"

She broke off laughing.

"*Now*, am I a stick, Lady Easy?"

"My dear, you're perfection's self!" cries Mr. Rich. Then cautiously recollecting himself, because this might count in the salary, he said:

"Consider yourself bespoke for Polly, Mrs. Beswick. And I would have you meet Mr. Gay tomorrow and consider the part with him. For though authors be very blundering in stagecraft, expecting the impossible and indeed a general hindrance, still they can't be altogether set aside. Be pleased therefore to be here tomorrow at the hour of eleven in the morning when the conditions shall be adjusted to your satisfaction and mine."

She clasped her hands and looked at him in a kind of ravishment.

"And is it really true? Sir, what shall I say to you? O, I will play as you never saw woman play yet—no, not even the great Mrs. Oldfield. You see me now but in hood and cloak, but when dressed to advantage, my hair curled and frizzed about my face in the mode, I trust you will admit my person not negligible. Indeed I won't disappoint you and to the last day of my life I will murmur to myself— ' 'Tis to Mr. Rich I owe all I have and am!'

" 'Tisn't, my dear!" says he, surprised into candour. " 'Tis to an uncommonly lavish nature you owe it and not to an curmudgeon like me. But I'll be a true friend to you so long as you deserve it. Perhaps longer, if I look into your eyes. But a word on that. My own orbs are spectacled with good sense and a fine woman doesn't strike the youthful fire out of them as once she did. Come—in your ear. Other and younger eyes will kindle at yours.— Are you an honest girl, child? or is there any gentleman behind you to put you forward and live on your earnings?"

Instead of flushing and anger, she laughed the clearest laughter in the world.

"Gentleman, Lord bless you, Sir—what have I to do with gentlemen? 'Tis to get away from one, I'm here. My stepfather. And as to gentlemen, I'll have none of them,—let them stick to the audience, and I'll stick to the boards. I want but one lover, Sir—the public. That's the heart I would win and for any other I have no use. And as to matrimony—what! to bear the uneasiness of a man's temper and the fret of babies and the bearing them, and the dull life of a wife whether she be a slut or a lady of quality! No, Sir, indeed I am all yours and my profession's."

She was but a girl. Relieved of anxiety this showed most charmingly and touched a paternal vein in Rich neither he nor any other knew he possessed. He sighed a little looking at that fresh sparkling beauty—all cream and roses, and the sweetness of a May hawthorn.

"Why, child, you speak brave, but you're not to learn there are dangers here—men——"

"I give but a snap of my fingers for them, be they who they will!" she cried, and snapt her fingers to suit the words. "I'll take care of myself, Sir, and if I can't, I'll ask you for your protection."

"I will be at your service," he said, somewhat more grave than his wont. "Your age, Mrs. Diana?"

"Eighteen, Sir, last June. My mother is Mrs. Fenton, wife of the gentleman who keeps the Savannah Coffee House in Charing Cross. My father was Mr. Beswick, a lieutenant in his Majesty's navy. He is dead three years. And for his sake, Sir, I entreat you give not my real name to any concerned till I shall decide by what name I would be known. It shall not be my own, for reasons."

Mr. Rich assenting, noted all particulars in his pocket book, then took up her cloak and put it about her, drawing the hood over her face.

"Let us quench the moon in clouds. There are too many peepers about!" says he. "And now, Scawen, fetch a chair and put this young lady in it and tell the chairmen they are answerable to me for her safety. My dear, go to your home now, and tell your mamma what hath been done, and conduct yourself with gravity and discretion and I doubt not but much success awaits you."

Mrs. Scawen called the chair, but 'twas Mr. Rich himself who placed the hooded lady within and laid stern injunctions on the chairmen, who knew him well. He stood watching a moment as they swung off with the treasure—a treasure indeed to him.

" 'Tis a fair creature and my very Polly!" he said to himself, and later, with a sigh, "God be good to the poor child!"

'Twas not wholly selfish at heart.

# CHAPTER III

MRS. DIANA had much to consider as the chairmen bumped her along the ill-lit streets leading to Charing Cross. To be candid, she had been swayed by an impulse in thus presenting herself and the matter remained to be broke with Mrs. Fenton. She was a good girl to her mother, and her father counts not, though if good looks and a certain seductive way be reckoned, she was the more indebted to him for her inheritance. In these qualities her mother was not preeminent and it is a melancholy consequence that Mr. Beswick, retiring from the Royal Navy, betook himself to the American colonies and the society of a lady who pleased him better in those respects. He returned however once or twice on business and expected notwithstanding to be received with the veneration due to a husband and father, and oddly enough was so received and appears to have excited a romantic interest in young Mrs. Diana's tender bosom. 'Twas something to have a parent who sinned in the high sentimental strain and not with the creeping hypocrisy of other people's parents who indulged their vices under the guise of all that was respectable—as was very well known to Miss. She even entreated him on his last visit to take her with him to the colonies and doubtless imagined herself a fair Pocahontas in moccasins and wampum chasing the flying deer. Mr. Beswick, however, who had some humour, did but laugh consumedly at the pretty picture and recommended attention to her sampler. 'Tis to be thought he might prefer a duo to a trio. In any case he returned to the deputy ruler of his heart and his wife and daughter saw him no more.

In a year his relict married Mr. Fenton, of whom more hereafter, and thus became Mistress of the Savannah Coffee House. It had been a prosperous business and a resort of many wits and beaux—such famous dramatists as Wycherley, Congreve, Farquhar and many more. Sir Richard Steele had leaned frayed velvet elbows on the table, while he argued, half maudlin with wine and good-temper, and Swift drew his harsh eyebrows together and felled his flimsiness with a word.

But Mr. Fenton drank to excess and there was an ugly scandal one night when he drove a bottle at a guest he had insulted and the watch was called in, and it got about and men fought shy of the resort and betook themselves to pastures new. 'Twas a very inferior set of persons came there now, and had Mrs. Beswick enquired into the circumstances as narrowly as became her prudence she had never become Mrs. Fenton.

A good easy woman, it perhaps weighed with her that Mr. Fenton was so cordial in welcoming her daughter and she stayed not to consider his motive.

" 'Tis Di for a good song," says he, sitting with his arm about her and his glass and churchwarden at his elbow, "and a pretty face into the bargain, and if custom is lacking here, which is certainly not the case, her face at the windows would do the trick in a jiffy. Bring her then, Lavinia, to a kindly welcome and a cut at my mutton for so long as the rakehelly gallants leave her with us—which I dare swear won't be long."

This speech might have gave Mrs. Beswick pause but did not. Perhaps she saw the matter plainer when she became Mrs. Fenton, for it is certain she then was a very dragon of propriety and therefore though certain men, by courtesy called gay and gallant, still frequented the house, 'twas much if they caught a glimpse of Diana vanishing up the stair with a Parthian dart of a lovely ankle beneath her hoop, or heard a voice carolling above like a lark in the clouds. Indeed 'twas more reasonable to hope for a word with Her Royal Highness at St. James's! And so it stood, in spite of Mr. Fenton who saw his hope of a lure melting from him.

Mrs. Fenton's tail was pinning up for a visit to a neighbour when Diana entered the parlour, and, seeing her mother preparing to go out, drew back at the door. It fell unlucky for 'twas now or never, and even her young courage was somewhat daunted at her own action, and the disclosing of it. But she was desperate. Suppose Mr. Fenton should come in! Suppose her mother should hear some rumour—for it seemed such news must be striding the city already on every tongue! So with a hundred supposes trembling in her heart, she ventured to accost the lady so busily occupied with festooning her ample skirts over her hoop.

"Will my mamma be so obliging as delay going out until I venture a word with her?"

"Why, Di, how can I? 'Tis most unreasonable when well you know I'm bespoke to Mrs. Clayton for a week. Come hither and help me."

The beauty knelt on one knee and took the corking pins obedient. Then paused, and looked up pleading.

"If my mamma did but know the good fortune that hath befallen me, I should not ask in vain."

"Good fortune!" cries Mrs. Fenton, throwing up her hands. " 'Tis many a day since that came our way. Is it an offer of marriage, child? O how shall I delight to trumpet it at Mrs. Clayton's—the proud hussey! Why her Bell hath but taken up with a haberdasher! Who is he, my heart's delight? Not one of these ranting officers I trust that wears all his fortune in his regimentals! Or is it young Crosby, the alderman's son? I noted the sly rogue had many errands here of late. Now, perhaps, Di, you'll thank your mamma's care that kept you secluded from all their impertinences."

"I thank my mamma for more than that," says the charmer, "and 'twill add to all I owe her if she will delay but one half-hour. Sure Coppet can run with word to Mrs. Clayton."

'Twas the thought of marriage fixed Mrs. Fenton. She could not desert that enchanting topic, and leaning over the stair-head she summoned Coppet to his errand, while Diana laid her cloak and hood aside with an anxious brow.

Returning, Mrs. Fenton plumped into her armed-chair and desired Diana would shut the door.

"And now are we private, my bird, and I would have it all. I will see Mrs. Clayton later. She grunts mightily with her cough, poor woman, and 'tis a kind heart, all said and done! So I'll go, but later. Now, child!"

She drew up a stool to her mamma's feet and leaned her arm on the maternal knee, looking up with her smile angelical.

" 'Tis not marriage, my mamma, but something much more desirable."

"What? What? Not marriage? Sure there's nothing more desirable than marriage for a girl," cries mamma, her face falling.

It came a little foolish from poor Mrs. Fenton who had certainly not been blest either in her first venture nor her second. Her daughter shot a glance at her from those dangerous long eyes of hers.

"Need we pretend when we are alone, Mamma? Sure I know very well you were not happy with my father. How could you be and him in the colonies? 'Twas scarce to be called marriage. And Mr. Fenton——" she paused expressively.

"O my child," cried Mrs. Fenton, dissolving into facile tears, "what do you know of such horrors, and why is my unhappy fate to be yours? Sure there are good honest men in the world that love their wives and have never an eye for any man's else's."

"If there be, I've not seen them. They never come my way," replied Diana sombrely. "Men! I loathe and detest them. Ever since I grew up and comprehended their aims I've feared and hated them."

"Lord, how unnatural! You that's all beauty and sweetness and that they would die to please, how can that be? Alas, child, you take neither after your father nor your mother. Sure you can't propose to be an old spinster woman with a cat and a parrot and all according! Defend us!— Sure that's never in your mind."

A moment's silence and the lady resumed.

"And I can tell you this, Di, marry you must and whether you would or no, for needs must when the devil drives, and I know no devil like an empty purse. Things are going down child, down! You know we scarce have visitors now, and none but those to be ashamed of,—and listen in your ear—(she glanced fearfully at the door) 'twas but last night when you was gone to bed that Mr. Fenton told me plump out that things were slipping from bad to worse. And, says he, if Di's pretty face is to be shut away from my customers that's left I won't be answerable for the consequences! He did so, child! and when I asked his meaning, says he— 'I would have her come down and sing for my customers and be pretty-behaved with them, and there's no harm to her and gain to me that may keep us all off the parish.' I cried, Di, indeed I did, child, but he took no heed."

Mrs. Diana's fine dark brows were drawn together and her lips in a stern line above her pearls of teeth. Perhaps these news did not come so surprising to her as her mamma might suppose. But she said nothing. Mrs. Fenton continued—her handkerchief to her eyes, her ample bosom heaving with sobs.

"So you see, child, well may my thoughts turn to marriage and a good home for you, where perhaps there might be a knife and fork laid for your poor mamma if things go from bad to worse, for I won't have my child made a decoy, so I won't! No, not to please Mr. Fenton nor any man on earth. What would your dear father have said that had such high notions of honour? Why, don't I remember his saying last time he went—'Lavinia, if when I come next I find my girl come to any harm 'tis you are answerable and I'll have your heart's blood if I swing for it!' Ah, 'twas him for handsome uplifted notions of honour. I can hear him say it so fine!"

'Twas bewildering certainly for a young girl still in her teens to adjust the rights and wrongs in such cases. Our poor girl could scarce have made a worse choice of parents all things considered. And besides all this she had herself to contend with, and she so young! Even the blossom was not set, much less any show of fruit. Indeed she was helpless in the face of her own emotion, ignorant but passionate and slave of the desire to express herself in some form that would catch the world's approval. And 'tis true she hated such men as came her way, plumbed their shallows, (for deeps they had none) and then scornfully passed on. She saw no help in any but her own powers. In a certain fashion however her mamma's words now gave her courage. But let her speak for herself.

"I wish my mamma to know I am resolved to leave Mr. Fenton's house."

She leaned upward affectionately and put her arms about her mother, and would have said more, but was violently interrupted.

"Leave Mr. Fenton's house! Lord, what words are these? And not to be married? For what reason?"

Diana might have run off many to non-suit her mamma's unreason. That he drank, diced, betted, that he was almost openly unfaithful to his obligations, that on her mother's own assertions he proposed to make use of her face as a decoy to his unworthy companions. But she summed all up in one phrase.

"Because he is intolerable, Mamma. Because whichever way I turn his figure blocks the road. Let us speak freely. I'm in danger here and you know it."

"Danger! With your mamma to watch you! 'Tis a poor compliment to my wisdom. My heart's almost broke to hear you, you undutiful child! And if not marriage, then what? You're a scatter-brained little fool, and I doubt but you will end as some fine gentleman's Miss instead of an honest man's wife! Good Lord, how shall I get to Mrs. Clayton's and the street all floated with rain. Hark to it! I'll hear no more folly."

But the two arms about her person held her fast and two eyes that had softened a stone looked up at her.

"My mamma must hear her girl. Who have I, if not you, Mamma? I have been a great studier of music and you know my voice hath been commended. 'Tis my intention to be beholden no longer to Mr. Fenton, but to go on the stage. For good."

The murder was out.

"The stage!" screamed Mrs. Fenton, violently unloosing the arms. "That I should live to hear it. The stage!—where every woman is a hussey and every man a knave. If you go on the stage in a year from now you'll be a mincing wanton that a decent man will flout."

"And what shall I be if I stay here, Mamma? What has yourself said? Don't I know Mr. Fenton hath been pleased to borrow your little capital for his pleasure? Don't I know we are all living on credit? We shall see the inside of a debtor's prison before long, Mamma, and what then?"

"Di," cries the other, exerting herself feebly, "you had always the horrid skill to make the worse appear the better reason. I can't debate with you—I never could from the day you was six, but I bid you on my blessing to consider, and I say that the example I set you when Mr. Beswick run off to the American colonies is the only safe one for a young woman to follow. Shut your eyes and your mind to what's disagreeable in the present and be patient."

Diana showed her little teeth in a smile that was not gay.

"Surely the men invented that commandment. But in your case, Mamma, be pleased to remember you had a husband, and, thank God, I'm free. A girl needs not ruin her life for her stepfather. 'Tis certainly not in the Church Catechism."

A few tears ran down the poor lady's cheeks and her girl made no motion to dry them. She stared above her mother's head at the print of the fair Mrs. Oldfield as Lady Betty Modish which graced the wall. That was her own possession; her father's gift, and perhaps it had set her thoughts in that train. She said nothing but indeed followed her dream as her mother rambled weakly on, till she happed on the phrase that the child had food and roof and sure that should content her. Then Diana flamed indignant, towering above her.

"Food and roof? But it does not content me. How should it? I need more. Eighteen!— 'Twas my birthday a week since, and what happiness or good has one of the eighteen years brought me? That man feeds on us, lives on us, sponges on us, and would do worse. He will suck us dry as a China orange. No—I have my chance and tomorrow I go."

"Good God, and where?"

She condescended then on explanations, and added that she knew a good old woman who would give her lodging and that the fine salary she expected would make all easy. The old woman in her head was Mrs. Scawen for she knew no other, and 'tis to be seen how wild and insubstantial were all her plans. Indeed her mother was not wrong in scenting much danger, and equally the girl was cruel enough, in her young rebellion, to these anxieties. But there it was, and if anything was needed to clinch her resolves it was when Mr. Fenton swaggered into the room in his spotted and blotched cloth coat, carrying his bloated face without shame and garnishing every sentence with a deep oath. The courtship had been short, or sure poor Mrs. Fenton had discovered what like he was in time to save her and her child.

The two women hushed their talk like birds before a storm when he flung himself into the creaking armchair and came out with a proposal that the girl should dance and sing at a roister to be held at the coffee house in a week's time.

"There's money in light toes and a pretty face, Lavinia," says he, "and when I hear talk of these foreign beauties coming to twirl the money out of poor English pockets I think I know as pretty a girl at home and I'm much mistook unless she sits by me now."

Mrs. Fenton made an exclamation of horror.—A dancer! then silenced herself because Diana sat rigid. Thus they endured until the horrid man took himself off to his bottle below, and then the poor lady flung herself weeping into her girl's arms and owned she could see no hope of better things.

"But promise me, promise me, Di," she cried, "that you won't drag your father's honoured name in the dirt of the stage. Sure you don't forget his father was a landed gentleman in Sussex if he hadn't diced his all away. Promise me this."

Diana promised, with a glitter in her eyes. "You have my word, Mamma. I'll take a name that no dirt can soil because it's so black already. Fenton. I'll be Mrs. Fenton. And for Christian name—O, my mamma, lend me yours that I may have one thing at least clean about me where I go. Let me be Lavinia because 'tis your name. Lavinia Fenton! And if I make my fortune you'll come to me, and we'll have rooms where that horror can't pursue us, and some happy day to come, you'll bless your Lavinia Fenton!"

So her heart softened when she saw her mother's grief, and it well became her.

The two passed the evening together talking and weeping, clasping each other's hand, and trembling each in her own way at the coming dawn and its events. They slept in each other's arms also, if sleep it could be called, with Diana huddling against her mother like a young bird that quakes to leave the nest maternal, yet knows her wings are fledged. And such indeed was her pitiful case.

So she saw the morning dawn wet and dismal behind the curtains, and clung the faster to her one refuge.

# CHAPTER IV

"THE fair widow," as my Lord Baltimore had complimented her, the Lady Fanny Armine, sat next morning in *negligée* in her fine boudoir in Pall Mall, surrounded by all the fashionable frippery of the finest of fine ladies whose gold is as bright as her eyes. Porcelains from Nankin, china gods and monkeys of equal grinning ugliness, chessmen from India in cherry and white ivory, adorned the costly Japan cabinets. Toys from the ends of the earth to please my Lady Fanny—and 'tis to be thought they failed to please her for she never looked their way, but writ and writ, heedless also of the letters and billets that strewed the carpet about her. For this lady might have said with the fair Millamant— "O ay,—letters. I am persecuted with letters. One has 'em one does not know why. They serve to pin up one's hair." Indeed she put them to little nobler use than this, or the voider beside her desk. Love-letters, you perceive! But 'twas no love-letter she writ now, but one to a lady she loved—that never failed her in trouble or pleasure. In fine, a most unfeminine friend and cousin, in that she could be trusted with a secret, could give impartial counsel, and never grumble when 'twas not heeded, nor say "I told you so,"—when the inevitable result followed. In short an Irish pearl—her cousin Lady Desmond. But hear the letter. 'Tis revealing.

> "*My Kitty*, my heart's delight, as the song has it, here's the long-expected billet from your fond cousin. I was detained late at the Court last night whither I went after Lady Lansdowne's drum, and so could not seclude myself for a word with my cousin of cousins. But the merry morn is here, and here am I in negligée and my chocolate beside me, for a word with my Lady Desmond, my dear, dear Kitty. And Mrs. Clayton, who shortly proceeds to Ireland to join her episcopal husband and open all your eyes with her coach and six and yellow liveries, hath promised me to take this letter, and if she be not drowned in the crossing that vile water to place it in my Kitty's own fair hand.
>
> "Well, you would have the news, says you, and I won't fail. The first news is,—Kitty, 'tis good to be a widow! Don't pull a long face, Madam, but consider. You, 'tis true, love your Sir Richard. I was but sixteen when my uncle married me to the hobgoblin that swept me down to Cornwall and to a Castle Raggedy that the old miser had the money to set in luxury and would not. O Kitty, my life there!—I a blooming girl of sixteen and he *sixty*! If 'twas wrote in a book who should believe it? Didn't I cry so excessively that nearly all the blue was washed out of my eyes and left them the colour of skim milk? Lord, when I think of my days—and nights, and he as jealous of all the booby squires

about as though they were Sir Harry Wildairs—every man jack of 'em. Avaricious, my dear. If we had a chicken to our dinner, a roast was not allowed on the same table. My jailor—my tyrant, but surely no husband, yet I played him no prisoner's tricks. (That's known to you.) 'Tis no manner of good for you, Kitty, to say as you said before in your tender concern for me— And why would you take the brute? Ah, don't you recall my uncle and his pride and haughtiness, and when he commanded me what could I do but obey? Had I been a fortune—had I had any living soul to speak for me I had been Fanny Clavering still,—But Mr. Armine's interest in Cornwall was needful to my uncle's party in the House of Commons and I must needs pay the piper. Well, 'tis over now. I had but four years of it, but the great abhorrence I had for Mr. Armine made it seem like forty, and when I was left to my own guidance at twenty—two years since, I dare swear I felt myself a woman of forty in all but looks.

"Looks, Kitty! I see you laughing across the Irish Ocean. Well, without vanity I will own my looks passable. The American Prince last night at Lady Lansdowne's drum was so good as to say:

" 'Lady Fanny, here's poor Mr. Rich, the manager, ravaging all the town for a heroine for Mr. Gay's new piece to be produced in Portugal Street. For her qualifications he needs beauty of the sparkling order, an exquisite bloom like an apple-blossom in dew. Eyes like the sky above it, lips borrowed from the neighbouring cherry tree. Hair—he did not determine whether it must be spun gold or chestnut, but I am at this moment convinced that chestnut is the only wear. This paragon's bosom must resemble spring hawthorn in hue and fragrance——'

" 'In short,' says I, interrupting, 'she is a vegetable beauty, since all your similes are drawn from the garden. I imagine her not difficult to find on any farm. A country wench all curds and cream.'

" ' 'S'death! you laugh me out of countenance eternally,' says his Highness. 'But, for all your jibes, poor Mr. Rich is distracted and he swears the play that will delight the town is dead as mutton if he can't find the lady. Poor man! And here she sits before me radiant as Hebe—am I not blinded with her rays?—and as far out of the poor soul's reach as if in the heaven she's native to!'

"I took it, my dear Kitty, as a compliment to my clothes rather than myself, for I had on my white poudesoy embroidered with gold, and rose ribbons with pearl in my head, and 'twas acknowledged it became me very well.

" 'Not even to oblige you, my Lord, which must ever be my chief study,' I cried, 'can I consent to mince and flutter on the stage. I'm told that though you gentlemen do favour the company there, the ladies are—well, their morality is not highly starched, ('Is it here?' he interrupted laughing, and motioning at Lady Cranleigh in conversation with Lady Rose, but I went on regardless.) and the gentlemen are even more forthcoming than with us. I dare not risk my character as a staid widow in such surroundings. But what shall Mr. Rich do?'

" 'Probably hang himself, when I inform him that your Ladyship declines the part. 'Tis not however surprising that the chief actress on a stage like this, should disdain a lower.'

" 'Twas indeed a vast court, it being Queen Caroline's Birthnight—the men as splendid as the women, which says much. The American Prince had half the revenues of his kingdom on his back—I never saw him look better though he is a personable man always. His coat rose-colour velvet with diamond buttons of prodigious size and the long waistcoat, white satin embroidered by Mrs. Gilson's own hand (I know her stitch) in pink carnations and forget-me-nots. I heard the Queen remark the embroidery and ask who drew the pattern, telling him she was obliged to the company for the compliment of their Birthnight splendour. Indeed my Lord Baltimore becomes all he wears, though some prefer the graver, more manly features of his Grace of Bolton—his inseparable. So do not I, Kitty, though I love Bolton well.

"And now, now for a secret! What shall a woman do that wants a confidant? Reveal it to the butterflies here that will blurt it out to the next flower they perch on! No, forsooth— I am no such fool. But I am at this minute so sick of a secret that the mere pain forces me to be rid of it, and so I will send it across the Irish Sea, sealed in an envelope to my Kitty that hath known all my secrets since I was three years old and stole my first cake.

" 'Tis a heart now, Kitty,—not a cake—and perhaps not so sweet, and less wholesome. 'Tis my Lord Baltimore's. I think, I guess, I doubt, that his Lordship hath cast the eye of affection on a certain young widow—the Lady Fanny Armine. I *think*. I do not know. It is certain that he distinguishes me in every company, and that his words are— O, Kitty, honey, sugar—nectar perfumed with ambrosia! Indeed they are! But I would not build on that for indeed he is a male flirt if I mistake him not hugely. No—my girl,—words!—what are words? 'Tis his looks—a sort of—what shall I say? His fine eyes soften, he hesitates, dare I say he *fears* when he is in company with me, he whose looks never fall before the greatest sovereign in the world. When he's with another I find his looks seek me and hover about me, when—

"But how do you interpret all this, Kitty? For heaven's sake tell me! for I, who have dismissed—without vanity I may say as many lovers as any woman in London, can't trust my own judgment where my Lord Baltimore is in question. I dread to be most unfashionably kind to him. . . . I keep my eyes dropt lest he should read in them more than I mean, and for the life of me I can't tell my own meaning. What do I mean? Interpret for me. I would not be rash, Kitty. Do but consider my position. Free as air, a handsome fortune ('Tis as well perhaps to marry a miser since I am now repaid for all my Timon's economies!), the high world's admiration, cards, beaux, routs, drums, ridottos, masquerades. What more could he or any man give me? To be an American Princess—the Queen of Maryland? Yes, but, Kitty, what a figure should I cut among the savages! with half a dozen provincial ladies to dump curtseys to me? However 'tis not this, 'tis the sex—the sex! His Lordship makes an adorable lover that all the world envies. Indeed, I fear he is a better lover than ever he would be a husband. He is in my power now—Should I put myself in his? I took occasion to make some approach to this subject in regard to Mrs. Greville, married not long since:

" 'She had every good thing the world can show,' says I somewhat melancholy. 'And here she has made herself a slave to Mr. Greville whose temper is the shortest part of him (he measures near seven feet) and what's to become of the poor lady now? Marriage! 'tis to walk into a prison and shut the door on oneself. Who should know but I that have escaped by the skin of my teeth, as the Apostle says!'

"He unfurled my fan, smiling as if to himself.

" 'Why she has but engaged a new servant, Madam, the foremost and most heartfelt of them all. There's nothing of the devil in Mr. Greville. He has a heart as fine as his coat and a rent roll as long as his legs. He will not quarrel with his wife for a trifle. 'Twill be a scene of conjugal bliss from morning till night and night till morn. She has but to please him——'

" 'Please him!' cries I, 'Ah, that's the rub! And suppose she misses the way! And will he study to please her?'

" 'Some ladies need but be themselves to please universally and for ever. I know one!' says he, bowing.

"All very fine, my dear, at Court,—but at home, by the fireside! I would have said more, but Princess Emily past and stayed a minute. I never saw her look more becoming. She had a glorious stiff-bodied gown of orange and gold stuff with gold ribbons and diamonds in her head. My Lord Baltimore very gallantly got her a seat, we standing.

" 'I know I intrude,' says her Royal Highness very gracious, 'For whenever a gentleman is in talk with Lady Fanny he has the air of desiring to murder any third person who dares approach. Calm yourself however, my Lord, I design but a moment's stay.'

" 'I beseech it may be all night, Madam,' says I, 'my Lord Baltimore is dull. He sympathizes with poor Mr. Rich, the manager that can't find a player-woman for Gay's new piece, and such is his sensibility he can talk of nothing else. Mr. Rich is distracted.'

" 'Why, there are plenty and to spare of such wenches!' says the Princess.

" 'Indeed yes, Madam, but they're all so confounded ugly. Excepting only Mrs. Oldfield who is so engaged with her General at present that she won't look at Mr. Rich, there is not one handsomer than the Duchess of Bolton.'

"So saying he shot a look at that lady across the room and just then the Duke entered, very magnificent in purple velvet,—vastly grave and fine, and goes up to his wife, bowing low.

" 'Madam, how does your Grace? I trust I see you pure well?'

"The invariable ceremony! She rose and curtseyed,

" 'I thank your Grace. I do extreme well. I hope I see you the same?'

"He bowed and slid off to us. The strangest wedlock sure! Polite, but frosty as December. 'Tis thus and only thus they meet. I wonder would the American Prince and myself come to this favour after a year of wedlock? O Kitty, is not the risk too high for any woman? But supposing a woman loved him?—Supposing there was an emptiness in her heart every time he turned his back. Supposing she hated every woman under fifty that came near him! Kitty, I don't say 'tis myself I speak of, but if it were—what would you say?

"Well, the crowd was so great after this that we were almost drove apart, and I declare I had been smashed and buffeted and my manteau almost torn off my back had it not been that the two gentlemen put their arms before me. Later, Princess Emily came up past me again, very pretty in her orange and gold and whispers, 'When shall we give you joy, Lady Fanny? No question but my Lord Baltimore is caught and his fine wings clipt to some purpose. Half the world is chattering of those conquering eyes of yours. Give me the first news, your Ladyship!' She looked very whimsically upon me and would not stay one minute for my denial, but slipt on to where the Queen stood with Sir Robert Walpole beside her—the two of them so deep in affairs of state that neither had a look for the butterfly world about them. A gay surface, but much below it that catches not the eye. She has suffering in her face, too. I doubt we have her great mind with us long, and then for the foolish pepper-headed old King with that fool Mrs. Howard to rule him, and Sir Robert's day done! It sobered me a little, Kitty, in spite of my flutteration. Sir Robert's a great man for all his gross tongue and his insolence to my Kitty Queensbury.

"The night closed with his Lordship squiring me to my chair. He prest my hand, and once I was seated and the roof let down, he kissed it. I could feel his lips hot upon it. I leaned forward—I would have spoke, but the chairmen saved me. They broke into a trot and so I left him standing bareheaded, among the flambeaux.

"O, were he as good as he's handsome, Kitty!—and yet if he were, should I not weary of him as I should of sops and caudle. What do I want? I know not. I think I want a lover, but not aught so terrible as a husband. I should die of a harsh word from his lips. I want the brilliance of a bad man and the constancy of a good one. Arrant fool that I am!

"For news:—The King asked me how I had passed my time at the Bath, and stayed not for the answer. He was hobbling very gouty on a stick. The Queen had upon her half the di'monds she wore at the Coronation and was a blazing figure indeed. Lady Fanny Shirley had the prettiest dress at Court—a satin embroidered in roses—if 'twas not your humble servant's, as some were fond to say. And that's my pride, and here's Lady Carteret thundering at the door and I've denied myself.

"That makes my news, Kitty, my dear, and in return I require a full and true account of all yours, and desire you will speech it handsomely for me to your worthy Sir Richard and bestow a kiss for me on the little heir. May he grow up to resemble his dear parents in all that is worthy.

"But counsel me, Kitty.

"Your affectionate cousin and humble servant to command,

"FANNY ARMINE."

"He is called here among the topping ladies the Basilisk on account of his killing looks. In future when I write 'Bas' my Kitty will know my meaning."

This written, the beautiful Frances, spoilt minion of fortune, laid down her quill and looked about her at the room wherein she sat. Her white brow with the bright chestnut hair rolled back from it and a certain alertness in her eyes bespoke her however something better—a woman who could reflect with shrewdness, and speak much to the point, and all this was her seductive ladyship and more. She had a mind as well as a face and, as she began terribly to suspect, a heart as well as both, but what shall a lady do with a heart in a society which mocks at such a rustic possession? Indeed, as may be seen by her letter, she could scarce tell what to make of it. And ignorance may lead a woman into a sad quandary from which 'tis impossible to extricate herself. Was there a man in London to whom she had chose *not* to be attracted, Charles, Lord Baltimore, was that man? For why? Because Lady Fanny knew well that hearts hovered about him in hordes that he could scarce endure. His life was a hurry of gallantry, equipage, feathers, smiles, ogles, love and courtship. He was spoilt by women, if favours flung before his feet could spoil him. 'Twas said and believed his last voyage to his province was to escape the frantic pursuit of a lady whose rank shall make her nameless, and that relays of weeping charmers lined all the roads down to the port whence he sailed. He had fought three duels with jealous husbands and each time pinked his man, and got off himself for all three with a light thrust in the arm. His history might indeed be read by the light of sparkling eyes, and set to the music of sighs. And out of such charming flimsy stuff to make a good homespun husband! Fie!

No doubt but he distinguished Lady Fanny beyond any other, but O the helplessness of a woman! Was it dependable? What did his Lordship when he strolled off with the Duke of Bolton? Where did they go? How were his hours past? How shall a woman know? She sees what she sees, she hears what she is told, but what is behind the scenes so cunningly set, she cannot tell.

Unusual tears stood in Lady Fanny's blue eyes as she considered her case.

The door opened and her maid came in with a billet in her hand and a posy of flowers:

"My Lord Baltimore's gentleman left it, Madam, and enquired how your Ladyship had slept."

"Does he wait?"

"No, your Ladyship."

She laid the sealed billet by her lady and went off with a curious eye at it over her shoulder. Indeed Lady Fanny's hand shook a trifle as she opened it.

> "*Madam*, I purpose a water-party two days hence and it will be no pleasure to the host if you are not of the party. Therefore, I entreat you to reserve Saturday in my favour. If, as on the last occasion, you make conditions for acceptance, I need only say that that soft, that white, that all-commanding hand shall write its own conditions and I accept them unknown. You know very well that in your absence life darkens for me. When you come it is sunshine. If my tongue did not say it 'tis to be read in my eyes, the reflection of a heart that cannot lie to my lady. More I will not say because I am jealous of this paper that kisses your hand, but more, much more I will say when we meet, if I have permission to open my heart to my sovereign.
>
> "Your most humble obedient servant,
>
> "BALTIMORE."
>
> "P.S. Rich writes me word this morning that he hath found the paragon he sought, so my Lady Fanny Armine shall not be disappointed of her play. But the paragon is not so fair as my own choice, I dare swear."

She read the letter greedily, scarce heeding the postscript and knew not, poor lady, that the sting, like a scorpion's, lay in the tail.

"Is it love, is it love?" she murmured to herself, "or is it but the desire to insult his rivals and carry off what they call a prize? And for me—is it but the delight to see the heart that so many bleed for bleed at last for me? And could either of us endure the arrogance of conjugalities? Can I dwindle into a wife or he into a husband?"

She sat long musing, but when she caught up the quill again 'twas to accept of the water-party.

# CHAPTER V

THE scene is Mr. Rich's parlour once more and a trembling suppliant and a lenient judge, for Diana was all but on her knees to Mrs. Scawen without whose countenance she could scarce hope to establish herself in any decency outside Mr. Fenton's protection. Not only so, but her mother had made it a condition not to be evaded. During the performances in the playhouse in the Haymarket, Mrs. Di had kept her secret, appearing but four times, two in each week, and 'twas easy enough for her to slip in and out, Mrs. Fenton at that time nursing her friend Mrs. Somer through a congestion on the chest. Lord save us! had her mother known, what a hue and cry had there been! But now the matter was come to a head board and lodging must needs be found, and for the life of the girl she could think of none but Mrs. Scawen and her kindly rubicund face.

"For indeed, Madam," says she continuing, "your own good heart will tell you a girl of eighteen can't leave her mamma and live alone. What—O what shall I do, if your goodness fails me! I must refuse the part."

'Tis possible Mrs. Scawen might have an eye to pleasing her employer as well as the lovely suppliant who stood before her with clasped hands, her face shaded with a little gypsy hat over a cap and lappets tied under a chin with dimples the very sign-manual of Venus. 'Twas not an easy matter to refuse such a girl with the tears in her eyes.

"Why, Madam,—my dear!" (the last came out very natural from the good woman's warm heart), "I would not willingly refuse, but we're plain people, Scawen and me. We have our little house at hand in Prince's Place and it's true there's two little rooms going abegging, for we've neither chick nor child, more's the pity!—but plain, very plain. And you have the appearance of being used to comfort. I can't tell, I'm sure——"

"O Madam, Madam! Dismiss me not!" cries Diana. "All my hope is in you. Whatever the rooms may be, and the plainer the better, your goodness will light them up. You see me at my wit's end, and though I daren't suppose Mr. Rich would regret me if I slid out of engagement, still——"

"But a gay young player-lady," hesitates Mrs. Scawen, who had seen much of the sex under such-like conditions.

"I'm far from gay!" protested the poor player, now near weeping. "And I'll vow, dear Madam, that never a step shall cross the threshold but with your approbation. You shall be in place of my mamma who will run to thank you with all her heart for your goodness to her poor girl."

So 'twas finally settled and the two hurried off to survey the rooms before the meeting appointed with Mr. Rich and Mr. Gay. 'Tis true they were plain, but they served, and had the merit to be near the playhouse—no small convenience when the perils that beset a lovely face in London be considered. The bargain was sealed with a kiss, and then Mrs. Diana made for the parlour once more to face the ordeal, her whole heart a prayer for fortitude and mercy. She had as yet none of the confidence she was to gain later, and, had the two gentlemen been Grand Inquisitors and she a fair heretic, could not have trembled worse. Mr. Rich and Mr. Gay, the author, sat by the table—the former in a handsome sober suit of grey cloth, the latter in the uncommon garb of a big gown folded about him and a little cap. He had himself carried round in a chair from his morning meal which he took late and luxurious. Indeed a somewhat free use of the pleasures of the table had left its mark on him and he looked but sickly and peevish to Diana's thinking as she curtseyed low before her judges. She past as near Mr. Rich as she dared, breathing, "My name, Sir, is Lavinia Fenton." He nodded.

"I beg to present Mrs. Lavinia Fenton to your favourable notice, Mr. Gay," says Mr. Rich sedately. "You are aware, Sir, that your attractive conception of Polly is none too easy to meet and that I have been put to much trouble and in vain so far in the search. But last evening this young lady walked in carrying hope with her. Your own eyes will teach you, Sir, that her appearance is all we could desire, and my own ears vouch for a harmonious voice and neat manner of singing. You'll therefore——"

"Humph!" says Mr. Gay.

It fell a little chilling into Mr. Rich's periods, but he was used not only to Mr. Gay, but to the tribe of authors at large, and their irritability in face of their own precious bantlings, and laughed good-humouredly.

"Why, Sir, I know well that were Venus and Euphrosyne rolled into one they wouldn't fill an author's conception of his goddess. But yet——"

"The nose isn't sufficiently impertinent," says Mr. Gay, "and I would have the eyes more arch, more sparkling. Such as Bracegirdle's whom I remember in Millamant. Ah, there was a dish for the gods! Ah, Rich, Rich, where is her like?"

"If you would have this young lady's eyes sparkle, pay her a pretty compliment, Mr. Gay, as none can do so well, and I'll wager they outshine Bracey's. Come now! Bracey was a beginner once also! Cheer the young lady!"

'Twas kindly meant, but still Mr. Gay humphed.

"Her stature! I would have Polly an inch less—a dainty rogue a man may pick up betwixt his finger and thumb. I disparage not the young lady's appearance when I say I can figure her rather as the Mourning Bride than my bewitching Polly. There is a melancholy in her eye."

And 'twas at that moment that Diana, forgetting her own alarms in a statement so preposterous, broke into a roulade of laughter resembling a string of pearls, so round and mellow it fell from her rosy lips, and then, terrified, she stopt all of a sudden, and clasped her hands to her heart, fearing she had spoiled her chance.

"Again, again, child!" cries Mr. Gay eagerly. "That was my Polly's very laugh. If you can give us that for certain, I'll overlook the nose (—not but what your nose is very well otherwise!) and the inch too much. Laugh again, child!"

She did and naturally, for the queer man and his queer cap and gown so impressed her that 'twas no hard task. Mr. Rich looked on delighted as Gay cried:

"And your speaking voice, girl? Speak for me! My Polly is an arch rogue, but demure as a little Quakeress when she will. O a delicious slut! She hath a voice of music and can sidle and wheedle her way into a man's heart when most he closes it against her. Canst do that, child?"

She looked up beneath the veil of long eyelashes and smiled slowly, dropping a curtsey until her hoop settled low on the ground, and keeping her eyes fixed all the time on Mr. Gay as she rose again. She was no longer frightened. Trust a woman to know when her dart goes home. She clasped her little hands, and acted very passably for a beginner.

"O Sir, with a kind word to cheer me you shall see I am your very Polly. My nose, I cannot help it, though I pray its pardon if it offends you. And for my height— Do but look at my heels! Sure I can wear them flat if you will and there's your Polly—just so high as your heart. No higher!"

With her face all sparkling and beseeching like an April day, she raised her petticoats an inch and displayed a little foot adorably perched on a ridiculous high heel like a porcelain shepherdess. But Mr. Gay heeded not the foot though Mr. Rich marked it well.

"The voice—the air! Perfection's self," he cries, "I forgive the nose. Indeed of its kind 'tis charming, though I would have Polly's a little less correct in outline. But the voice! 'Tis as soft as a wood-dove's and assaults the senses like a rose perfume. She'll do, Mr. Rich. Your old discrimination is not run altogether to seed as I supposed. Let's pray she falls in love with Walker, though I hold him but a dull rogue for my Macheath."

"He'll do!" says Mr. Rich briefly. "But I'm content you're content, Mr. Gay. Indeed she's the right stuff, and so you'll say when you hear her warble. Not but what she wants training enough and to spare. 'Tis only in the fables that Minerva springs full armed from the head of Jove. But the stuff's there. Sir, we shall do."

"My dear," says Mr. Gay, snuffing and fumbling for his handkerchief; "Mr. Rich says right. You'll do. Be not too proud and perked up for teaching. Be docile, womanly and obedient, and you'll be the very rod with which I'll hit the court in the face and hold up its follies to the public. Go—you're a pretty girl and a good. I like you well. But stay a minute—" (and here he became awful) "No running after the fellows while the work's in hand. No junketing;—all sober earnest. This I condition for."

"She won't need to run after the fellows," cries Mr. Rich, bursting into a great laugh, "They'll do the running. Better instruct your Polly in the art of escaping, Mr. Gay. 'Tis that must be her study. Canst bridle, Miss Polly, when they become too ardent?"

She bridled charmingly and with the prettiest air of shy dignity. Indeed she was now at the top of her part, seeing that like a chaste Susanna she had the two elders on her string. An express then summoned Mr. Gay away to the Duchess of Queensbury who, having been at daggers drawn with the court, was all for Mr. Gay's company and was plotting reprisals with him. Mr. Rich, returning to business, fixed her salary at two guineas a week and one Benefit on the run should the play go over the month. She thought it riches and 'twas not amiss, Mr. Rich having favoured the great Mrs. Oldfield with but one guinea weekly when she appeared first as Candiope. At all events it left the girl overjoyed, knowing she could pay Mrs. Scawen and put something considerable in her pocket as well. 'Twas more than the wealth of nabobs, for 'twas freedom, hope, fame, and a many other glittering delights that rang to the tune of those two golden guineas.

She thought it due to Mr. Rich's consideration to mention her arrangement to share Mrs. Scawen's roof, the which he approved very kindly and with a sensibility beyond her expectation.

"I would not have you but under some sensible woman's wing that knows the risks, and since it can't be your mamma, you might seek further and find a worse than Scawen. She hath a good nature that does her infinite credit. Now, Mrs. Polly, if you permit me that liberty (that the secret of your name really be kept), come hither at four of the clock for the reading of the piece, and be not set back by the necessary fault-finding at rehearsals even though it seem rough. Nor yet by the jealousies of your fellow players, men and women. 'Tis the curse of the stage, but since 'tis human nature 'tis to be predicted 'twill outlast the stage itself. But fear not. The prize is great, and all shall be well."

'Twas surprising how the rough places smoothed themselves for this pretty creature. It gave her much hope and courage. She went tripping back to Mr. Scawen's whither her little baggage was brought by two hulking porters, and her mamma followed later to bestow her blessing and see Mrs. Scawen to implore her goodness for the girl and to be instantly summoned should any danger threaten.

"For I would have you know, Madam," says she feelingly to Mrs. Scawen, "that she's my all. I'm not so blest in my husband as I could wish, and if aught should go wrong with her I see not what shall become of me."

Mrs. Scawen vowed attention with many bends and curtseys, and then left them, Mrs. Fenton preparing to depart.

"My child," she said, embracing her, "Mr. Fenton hath tiffed all day about your going, and came near to strike me. But what he revealed in his anger justifies us, and there's no more to say but that I implore you to do me and yourself credit, remembering that your father came of an ancient and honourable family. Let it not sink in your hands."

"Be not low-spirited, my dearest Mamma," cries Diana, twining about her like an ivy to the parent tree. "Come often to see me and I'll work—Lord! how I'll work!—and then a little home for you and me and that bad man forgot."

So they parted, and the girl put her rooms in order, and then dined with Mrs. Scawen on a boiled chick neatly enough served, Scawen being absent all day on his business, and so to Portugal Street for the reading, all of a flutter, but winged by hope.

'Twas a strange scene to her in the green-room—rows of chairs set out for the players and a vacant space in front with two chairs and a desk for Mr. Gay and Rich, and candles beside 'em, for though still day the room was not overlight. Diana stood at the door a moment, looking timidly under her hat at the little crowd of persons not yet seated who were talking together till the two great men should appear. Their jargon was as strange to her as their faces. They looked her over carelessly and resumed their talk, each seeming familiar with all, and she the only stranger. This was the case truly, all being stock members of Mr. Rich's company. They might have made some little overture, she thought, but none did, and still she hesitated near the threshold.

Presently came steps behind her and the two gentlemen entered, Mr. Gay now extremely well drest in a snuff-coloured cloth suit in the latest mode and finely powdered peruke. He stopt by the door and made a sliding bow and flourish of his hat to the ladies, Mr. Rich following, the talk ceasing at once amid an avalanche of bows and curtseys. Mr. Rich said loudly:

"Ladies and gentlemen, the piece Mr. Gay is about to favour us with is so novel, so witty and humorous, with such strange unexpected turns as I don't doubt will distinguish us all very highly if justice is done in the playing of it. And 'twill doubtless add also to his own ever-green laurels. 'Tis scarce needful then that I bespeak your best attention to what follows. But before you are seated I beg to present to your good-fellowship Mrs. Lavinia Fenton whom Mr. Gay and I have cast for a principal part. I might indeed say *the* principal part were it not that she divides the honours with Mrs. Bishop who is chose for the Lucy Lockit of the production. But let no lady fear that she comes short of a humorous part and great occasions. Mrs. Slammikin—but I need not to continue. You will hear all presently. Ladies, Mrs. Lavinia Fenton. Mrs. Fenton, these are the gentlemen of our company."

All bowed, and curtseyed, with eyes of surprise and ('tis possible) jealousy on the newcomer. All, that is to say, excepting the men. For like one man they stared at the fair new planet swum into their skies and could not take their eyes off her. She wore her black hair fastened up with ribbons and drest in high rolls, and a handsome flowered chintz over a hoop of the top mode, and was, to be sure, a beauty confest, outshining all the rest, though Mrs. Bishop, the destined Lucy Lockit was a fine handsome sombre-eyed woman. For the excitement brought a lovely bloom to her cheek and made her eyes sparkle like purple wine in crystal. Mr. Rich shot her a glance of approval as he handed her to a chair on the right of the front row and did the same by Mrs. Bishop after.

'Twas a strange position for a slip of a girl. This must be owned. But Mr. Gay now began with his folio paper in his hand and a fine delivery from the chest, though a somewhat sawing action of the disengaged arm.

Beggars! The company stared upon one another wonderstruck. So engrossed were they that they knew not that a young man—beautiful as Apollo could he be dressed by the famous tailor Grimson in the latest mode, had come in softly by the door behind them, and sat astride his chair, leaning his arms on the back and his chin on them, and so continued through the reading.

So Mr. Gay proceeded, and, a very unusual circumstance in a green-room, the company more than once applauded, delighted at some rich and witty turn that caught their fancy. Walker—the destined Macheath, fairly roared outright at more than one speech to his credit, and at the first pause clapt his hands till the palms rang again. A lusty handsome man somewhat coarsely built, but a good leg and a swagger, and a roving eye to top it all.

"Why, I swear, Mr. Gay, that there's not its like in the universe. Damme if there is! 'Tis so astonishing new—so surprising fresh! It needs but the embellishing of the actor to make it more than passable."

"I am happy, Sir, in your approval!" says Mr. Gay drily. "But as for embellishment—the closer you stick to my lines and indications the more like you are to take the town. I dare assure you every point is considered."

Rich winked to Walker. He knew as well as Walker that when all's said and done the cast of the die is in the player's hand. But authors (and especially authors so high in favour with her beauteous Grace of Queensbury) must be humoured. Walker settled down with an almost invisible sneer. As for Diana, she hung enraptured on every word. Was ever such dazzling wit in the world before! She forgot herself; she laughed her enchanting laugh aloud when Mrs. Peachum tumbling over is supposed to display more of her person than the mode warrants. 'Twas like silver bells. The company willy-nilly must needs laugh with her, and Mr. Gay stopt, smiling a minute full in her eyes. She remembered scarce at all that she was to shine in it, the thing so carried her away, and after the scene with Lucy Lockit was read, she clapt her hands till she tore her glove. The rest were more pragmatical, comparing it with bygone experiences and appraising it as Diana could not, but all were extreme well satisfied—the only doubt being how the necessary absence of splendid costume and surrounding must affect the piece. The songs being only read naturally lost it much of its attraction.

"For my part," says Mrs. Bishop, levelling her fine eyes, "I vow I like it well enough, but consider the parts should be dressed above the common persons Mr. Gay hath chose to depict. 'Tis my own purpose to wear my wardrobe that I played in for 'The Recruiting Officer.' I have no notion to make myself a fright in any part I play, and 'twon't go down with the public neither. They come as much for glitter as anything else."

"On that point, Madam, I'm adamant!" cries Mr. Gay. "I won't have my play spoilt by the absurdities of fine ladies in satins and brocades when I entend a higwayman's doxies. Indeed I won't, and so I give you notice. 'Tis to reduce the whole to a namby-pamby absurdity. What says Mrs. Fenton?"

'Twas an awkward moment for Diana who desired not to offend either party, though indeed her own good sense took part with Mr. Gay. But all eyes turned to her, Rich laughing a little to hear what Miss Timidity would say.

"Why, Sir,—I am but an inexperienced player and Mrs. Bishop a skilful, but indeed for my own part I think a woman may look as well in chintzes and a cap as in damask and a Brussels head. 'Tis all in the wearing of it and in the face, and sure Mrs. Bishop's face would carry off sacking, and so please Mr. Gay and delight the public."

'Twas so prettily said and with an art so charmingly hid under innocence that Rich laughed behind his hand and Mrs. Bishop gave her a smacking kiss for guerdon. And indeed she stood there so fair an example of her own precept in her flowered chintz and laced handkerchief across the bosom that there was not one but agreed.

"We have however," says Mr. Gay, "the advantage of a gentleman's presence that's an infallible authority both on glitter and the taste of the town. Perhaps my Lord Baltimore will do us the favour of his verdict on the dressing of the piece."

My Lord came forward, his sword at his side, as easy and handsome a gentleman as to be seen in a month's walk. Had he indeed played Macheath—but, Lord! 'twas as well not, considering the poor hearts of the city ladies who moved not on his dangerous orbit.

"Your servant, Mr. Gay, Mr. Rich, ladies and gentlemen!" says he laughing. " 'Tis a distinction to be asked my opinion in such a society. But since you'll have it—why, this fair lady is right a million times over. What! shall such a face as Mrs. Bishop's depend on the price she pays a yard for her stuffs? Does her agreeable humour depend on the feathers in her head and would they make reparation if she were absent? She knows better herself though her modesty won't admit it. No, Mr. Rich. Dress the play in character and I warrant you a success that sets the town ablaze."

"You taste the piece then, my Lord!" says Gay, purring like a cat that has its ears tickled.

"Lord, yes! Why even read 'tis the wittiest thing I've heard in five years. And when 'tis played—— But much is in the players. Which of these charming ladies is your Polly, Mr. Rich? You was in despair no later than yesterday."

Mr. Rich indicated Diana with a flourish:

"Mrs. Fenton, I present my Lord Baltimore."

She sank low in a curtsy while his Lordship proffered his most elegant bow as though 'twere a posy. Rising to the recover, her eyes met his.

Instant, and she knew not why, a wave of colour flowed from her heart to her face and she blushed faintly but divinely—too warm upon so cool an occasion. But 'tis impossible to express the language of his look. A flash only, yet it said the unspeakable in astonishment, admiration, boldness and submission. Be it remembered his Lordship was an old hand at the game, not a move of it unknown to him. His lips said only what any actress might expect.

"Madam, 'tis a felicity to be known to you. Your looks, your voice ensure us a Polly that shall borrow the very car of love and set the world afire."

"That car, my Lord," says Mr. Gay laughing, "was long ago engaged by Mr. Prior to Her Grace of Queensbury. 'Tis not for hire."

He hummed the words relating to "Kitty beautiful and young," and turned off to Rich. Lord Baltimore drew nearer to Diana.

"Madam, your most obedient was interested before in Mr. Gay's venture. I can think of nought else now. Tell me what happy town hath given us so great a wonder, for I have not seen these piercing charms in London."

'Twas overdone, impertinent. He had not so treated a lady. She felt the distinction and levelled her eyes coolly at him but said nothing. He continued:

"Why, Madam, all the Mrs. Fiddlefans in the town will take to chintz, so do you set it off, and jewels will cease to be the mode when you display that posy in your bosom. Confound me if I see not before me the very masterstroke of creation—the ecstasy of nature! I——"

She curtseyed again and turned from him in silence the very line of her haughty neck showing displeasure. He halted on a word, surprised and angry in his turn, then revolved slowly to Mrs. Bishop, his sword clashing as he did so.

Diana made for the door, the business being finished, but not before Mr. Rich said graciously, in an aside:

"You've won Gay's heart, child. That suffices. Win no more hearts until the play is done. You'll have your part tomorrow. Think but of that and of the business in hand and bid the fops flutter about other candles. Yet displease not his Lordship utterly. His word is law to the fine ladies and gentlemen that make or mar us."

She curtseyed again with hot angry cheeks. That night a posy of red roses tied with blue and silver satin ribbons was left for her at Mrs. Scawen's. But no name. She flung it atop of the fire and Mrs. Scawen had much ado to rescue the ribbons for her own wearing to Bartholomew Fair. Knowing the habits of the nobility and gentry she informed Mrs. Di that these colours were the livery of my Lord Baltimore. 'Tis certain that many ladies wore this livery not only on their persons but in their hearts—the more's the pity!

# CHAPTER VI

AFORTNIGHT later, Catherine Duchess of Queensbury—a very imperious and beautiful lady, was seated in her own library, and her companion was his Grace of Bolton. But a few words must needs be said of this celebrated person, Mr. Gay's patroness and (it must needs also be said) instigator in his attacks upon the court. Never was a lady more favoured by fortune. Born of the great Hyde family that had given two Queens to England—their Majesties Mary the Second and Queen Anne, she married as greatly as her birth demanded, becoming Duchess of Queensbury and Dover in her twentieth year, and paling all the beauties of her own rank by her radiant face. A wit, a termagant, with a tongue like a dagger, and the most wilful of her sex, she queened it right royally, and if the majestic Queen Caroline could daunt her Grace 'twas as much as she could, and that by no means always. Certainly no other person made the attempt. For Prior's "Kitty beautiful and young,"—who by the way seemed but to grow in beauty as in years, considered herself the first lady in Europe by right divine, and for those who failed to bow before her sceptre 'twas apt to become a rod, and descend upon their backs with a resounding thwack. But sweet as a summer breeze to those who were fortunate enough to please her Divinity! Of these Mr. Gay had the happiness to be one of the chief, and at the present time his knife and fork was laid daily at her Grace's table and a room kept at his disposal, his Grace the Duke, her husband, approving all that his consort decreed. It came as a consequence that Madam followed every event in the production of "The Beggar's Opera" with as much interest as its author, hoping to launch it with all its sting at her deadly enemy Sir Robert Walpole, the famous minister.

Behold then the fair Kitty—whom her enemies described as a cat—in the full bloom of her charms, more lovely at twenty-eight than when she stole the car of love and set the world afire (to quote again her adorer, Prior) in her teens. A noble looking creature with large lucent eyes and long throat to set off her diamonds, and brown hair shot with gold dressed so as to add to her fine height. She might have been an Empress. Yet, will it be believed that this woman who moved and spoke a goddess confessed, could descend so far as to snatch off her brocaded apron in a fury when those dainty ornaments were forbid at Court, and fling it in the face of the Lord Chamberlain who strove to hinder her Grace's invasion in the contraband garment? Not only did she so, but considered herself the aggrieved party and swept on into the Presence, darting such awful glances at him as must have withered the unfortunate but for the supporting anger of royalty on his side.

Such then was the lady with whom Bolton sat closeted now. They had played together as children and between them subsisted a strong and faithful friendship that admitted of truth on both sides with an unalterable kindness beneath, whatever little whiffs might disturb the surface.

She sat at her tambour frame stitching the flowers of a silken garden, and while she stuck her needle in and out she discoursed of 'The Beggar's Opera.' 'Twas truly in her mind night and day, owing to the malicious pleasure she took in the hope of wounding Sir Robert Walpole with the innuendoes her Grace and Mr. Gay had prepared.

"Gay tells me all goes as well as even he could wish," says she. " 'Twas Heaven's own blessing sent us a Polly he can approve, for like all the tribe of authors he's so thin-skinned that unless all's perfection he expects the sky to fall and crush his hopes. He describes her the prettiest wench he ever set eyes on—a black beauty but with eyes like violets."

"Beauty is not all in a player," says the Duke, caressing her silky lap-dog on his knees. " 'Tis manner—a something seductive, I know not how to word it, but a something that makes the whole world desire to embrace the lady."

The Duchess gave one of her big hearty laughs.

"And doubtless they do so—more or less!" says she. His Grace still stroked the dog's silken ears.

"Why, not in this case, Madam, it appears. 'Tis a case of the chaste Diana, and——"

"What? On the stage? I won't believe it."

"But you must believe it. For one whole fortnight—fourteen days, no less, this damsel hath stood fire and hath not lowered her flag, no, not by an inch. 'Tis reported that her Macheath is so in love with her that he can scarce play the character of the gay libertine that shines on all the ladies alike, and is in public, as in his private character of Mr. Walker, so lovesick that he can't say 'How happy could I be with either,' without conveying by every sign and token that he has no eye at all for the unhappy Lucy Lockit, and that his whole soul is Polly's. Mr. Rich hath scolded, argued, reasoned, and all in vain."

"And Polly?"

"Polly will have none of him, she turns up the most exquisite nose in Christendom, barring your Grace's, and when she must sidle up to him does it with a Don't-touch-me! air that she must certainly amend or incur Mr. Gay's severest reproof."

"Then you've seen her, Sir, I conclude?"

"Certainly, Madam, what would my character for fashion be worth had I not seen the new, the famous, the adorable Polly? I was presented to her in the green-room, but could scarce form a judgment of her face so resolutely did she keep her eyes on the ground and tilt her hat brim over her eyes. There was that in her air that said 'A man's an animal I distrust most liberally. Not a man shall come within the circumference of my hoop but I'll freeze him into awe. Keep your distance, Sir!' Accordingly I kept it. I know not what she is like."

"Then there's a lover behind the scenes," says her Grace, sticking a jonquil and laughing.

"Why be so cruel in your judgment, Madam? Hasn't Mrs. Bracegirdle carried her reputation unspotted through the world and she a famous player? Don't your Grace recall Congreve's verse?"

And in a very mellow and manly tenor the Duke sang *sotta voce*:

"Pious Celinda goes to prayers

Whene'er I ask a favour,

And yet the tender fool's in tears

When she believes I'll leave her.

Would I were free from this constraint,

Or else had power to win her:

Would she could make of me a saint,

Or I of her a sinner."

"But he couldn't—he never did!" concluded his Grace. "Not though he was seven years younger than the lady, and wrote all his plays about her charms! Then why not a chaste—a disdainful Polly also!"

"One swallow doesn't make a summer! But after all, since we expect nothing from these women we're the less disappointed. Has my Lord Baltimore essayed his enchantments?"

"Fie, Madam, fie! Would you have me a traitor? The American Prince revolves on his own princely orbit. I'm but—Benedick, the married man. How should I know what his Brilliance does? I do but look through the window of my prison."

He spoke half melancholy, half bitter. Indeed there were times when his fetters galled him unbearably, and the mystery of his miserable married life was heavy on his spirits. His intimates knew that cloud on his brow and respected it. The Duchess stretched a fair hand weighted with great emeralds and laid it on his, but said nothing save with her eyes, softened and kind, for the nonce. A moment past and she spoke under her breath;

"A long punishment for a moment's madness, my friend!"

"And not even my own madness! I have not so much as that poor consolation to aid me in bearing my punishment. A boy of eighteen and—But I have sworn no word shall pass my lips. What use hath the world for us if we growl and whine? No, Madam, help me to laugh. What were we discussing?"

"Polly," says she, with a sadness in her eyes that became her very well. "But, Bolton, before we quit the subject, tell me this—that am your friend. Is there never a woman in London that you could make your mistress?"

"Thousands!" says he with a harsh laugh.

"No—no. I meant not so. But a good woman, beautiful and kind, who might mend the sore place in your heart and give you at least some sort of a home? You're thirty-two now—Four years older than me,—and even I don't always feel young whatever way my looks may lie. You need a home. 'Tis a thing often done, Bolton. Yourself knows that I could run off a list this minute of half a hundred men that have done this and who thinks the worse?"

"I'll ruin no woman's life!" says he, with his dark sad eyes upon the ground.

"There's many would think it promotion, not ruin."

"What! To live with a soured disappointed man, fettered hand and foot, sick of life at times, distrustful of all women except his friend—the lovely Kitty? Unable to love any woman however he may amuse himself in passing. No Madam! What has any poor fool done that I should expose her to a life like this? I can be cheated with good humour, but I will not cheat. Say no more. I have my amusements like other men and I value them as little as the cards and horses and other follies that make our days and nights. You have a soul above them—I also. See, I'll tell you a secret, I have a dream—a vision——"

"Of the inexpressible She?" cries Kitty, suspending her needle in air.

"Yes and no, Madam. An inexpressible She indeed—but one of the Muses. I think to write a book. I have a story in my head, and as yet no words to tell it, but some day——"

He paused, and again said bitterly:

"But what use? The town would laugh itself sick over the foolish nobleman who aspired to author. Rank, Madam, is a fetter as well as marriage. It galls me sometimes. What if I run off one day to Baltimore's American colony, and renounce all this glitter for my cousin the heir? 'Twill be his indeed, for heir of my own I shall never have."

"Never is a long day!" says her Grace, re-threading her needle. " 'Tis my eternal aversion to hear you despond. 'Tis true your wife pinches you execrably. But 'tis true also that she may run off with her physician as Lady Selby did but last week."

"We won't jest about my wife, Madam, if it please you. After all, she's my wife and I respect the position if I don't respect her. Hallo—who comes here? Mr. Gay, your servant!"

For the door opened and Mr. Gay the ever-welcome, appeared unannounced, bowing low to her Grace and her companion. She flung her tambour frame aside and sprang lightly to her feet.

"Hallo also! How goes it Gay? Gayly? Do they speak the lines with point, with malice? Are the pretty chickabiddies all learning to flutter about their Macheath? Why this anxious brow, man?"

"Because, Madam, I'm harassed about Polly."

"Not bolted—not flown? Trust a prude!" cries the Duchess.

"Nothing less, your Grace. But she was lodging with Scawen, Rich's old factotum that does all his odd jobs and's a kind of remembrancer to him. Well—the poor old trot has catcht the small-pox, God knows how, and poor Polly is homeless and Rich distraught. She can't go home, for her mother's husband would fain use her for a pretty decoy-duck in his coffee house (which between ourselves deserves a worse name), and Rich knows of no decent lodging for her high or low. You are aware, Madam, that his acquaintance is not the most straight-laced. 'Tis a droll quandary, but troublesome. The girl is so pretty she needs a guardian."

"Lord save us!" says the Duke. "Won't your own character constitute you a duenna, Mr. Gay? I don't imagine either a tongue or a sword would wag if you safeguarded the lady's morals. But is she in truth such a Dian?"

"I beg you won't jest, your Grace!" cries Mr. Gay, pushing his peruke off his brow in his perplexity. "I am aware that a young woman's virtue is a subject for mockery to all the fops in town, but, notwithstanding, this untoward circumstance may put an end to our hopes. The girl knows not where to go nor what to do. She sits in tears, and her mother declares she shall go to an aunt in Sussex tomorrow, for she don't give a fig for the play. Would sooner the girl didn't play at all!"

"Lord save us!" says the Duchess. "But isn't there any among the player-women can give her house-room?"

"Why, Madam, Mrs. Bishop—Well, not to be indelicate, we all know Mrs. Bishop is not the duenna one should choose for a virgin, and the rest—well, there's objections to them all."

"Lord bless me!" repeats the Duchess. "Little did I think our Polly to be so fragile a porcelain;—who in the world is this icicle, Mr. Gay?"

Mr. Gay looked about him cautiously:

"Why, I'm under bond to Rich not to reveal the particulars, but with your Grace I know 'twill go no further. The young lady's name's not Fenton, as will appear in the bills, but Beswick. Diana Beswick. But her mother and she insist it be not known, she being a gentlewoman."

"Diana!" says the Duke, laughing, " 'Tis certainly appropriate."

"Beswick!" cries the Duchess, "Why there was a Mr. Beswick in the King's naval service. 'Twas in command of the Diana sloop that he saved Mr. Francis Hyde, my cousin from a watery grave. Ask Lady Louisa else! They presented the gentleman with a gold watch and a hundred guineas, and later he went off to the American colonies and they heard no more."

"Damme, if it isn't the very man! Why, Rich told me of the American business no later than last night. Depend on't, he called his girl after his ship," says Mr. Gay.

The three stood looking upon one another like persons amazed. The Duchess collected herself first.

"Why, then, Mr. Gay, the girl's a gentlewoman. Mrs. Boscawen asserts Mr. Beswick was the son of persons of condition in Sussex. The poor unfortunate!— And is she sunk to this! Then I'll tell you what—if you can assure me she'll not corrupt my woman's morals, (and God knows I think 'tis more like to be the other way about,) I'll give her bed and board here. 'Tis a thing I would not have chose, for I am spoke about enough already in connection with your play; but I won't have it hindered, so I won't! And if the girl's honest it shan't be my doing if she don't remain so. Fetch her hither, Mr. Gay, and instruct her to keep a quiet tongue in her head about the playhouse, and if the world talks why here's one can stand it!"

Both gentlemen stared at her Grace amazed. To take a poor player into her ducal house.— Lord, what a freak! But 'tis to be remembered her Grace of Queensbury was all freaks and snapt her fingers in the Devil's face as soon as look at him. What gave Mr. Gay pause was not so much this as that his play was assuming a political complexion in public minds from the allusions and double meanings it contained, and he might doubt how far 'twas politic to pin it to the Duchess's petticoat tail. Nevertheless he was in a sad quandary and here was his way out. He dropt on one knee like a courtier and kissed the fair hand, so loaded with jewels.

"*O Dea certe!*" he cried. "You come indeed a divine being to the rescue. I'll away this moment and bring the chaste Diana to your feet. Indeed 'tis a modest girl, Madam, and I think you'll not regret your kindness. Moreover, so many flies are after the honey pot that 'twill be an ease to my mind lest we have an affair like Bracegirdle's with my Lord Mohun, of which there have been examples both before and since."

He alluded to the infamous Lord Mohun's attempt to abduct the beauteous Mrs. Bracegirdle. A circumstance very notorious in its day and known to both their Graces.

"Lord! You make me shudder, man!" says the Duchess, "No, but we won't lose our Polly! I suppose you fear my Lord Baltimore. I heard from a sure hand he was buzzing about her. So, off, Mr. Gay, off! Lose not a moment. Sound my whistle, Bolton. I'll give directions."

Mr. Gay was off in a trice, and the Duke caught up the little gold whistle on the Buhl table and whistled softly till a small black page ran in,—the latest fancy of modish ladies, a droll little figure in turban and gold coat and girdle, grinning and saluting with head and hands.

"Call Mrs. Francis, Pompey," says her Grace, and the imp bows to the ground and runs off helter-skelter.

Directions given, the lady turns to his Grace.

"Wait and see the arrival! I protest I'm vastly curious to see the fair cause of so much pother. 'Twas a prodigious strange circumstance I should hear of her father. And stranger still I should commence duenna—I that never heeded a prude in my life nor ever will! What say you to me in my new *rôle*, Sir?"

She pulled down the corners of her lovely mouth and rolled up her eyes sanctimoniously and made a face so droll, that he must laugh whether he would or no, and until Mr. Gay returned with his prize her Grace amused herself by preaching over the back of her chair an extreme outspoken sermon on the perils of the town and the best means to avoid them. 'Twas in the manner of the Right Reverend the Bishop of London and none the less droll for that. She was but at her Amen when the door opened and Mr. Gay re-entered followed by a shy figure in cloak and hood, the groom of the chambers preceding them scornful-eyed.

"Mr. Gay, your Grace, and Mrs. Lavinia Fenton."

The Duchess curtseyed imperceptibly, 'tis so difficult to divest the mind of the prejudices of rank, and then came forward smiling to the shrinking girl—too terrified almost to remember her manners.

"You'll pardon me Mrs. Beswick (Diana started back), and the liberty I take when I say I have the good fortune to know some matters relating to your respectable father and his gallantry that saved Mr. Francis Hyde's life. His daughter hath not forgot that circumstance, I dare swear!"

'Twas kindly and graciously said, and Diana lifted an April face and curtseyed lower.

"Indeed, your Grace, I have not. I have the watch now. Is the gentleman of your Grace's family?"

"So much so that I take it as a debt to be repaid to your father's daughter, Madam. And I am now to request that in this unforeseen difficulty just arisen you'll favour me with your company here for as long as is convenient to yourself."

"But, Madam—Your Grace—The playhouse hours, the rehearsals! I'm overwhelmed with your goodness but know myself a very inconvenient guest."

"That shall be my care, not yours, Mrs. Diana," says the Duchess, laughing her charmingest. She laughed with a gusto, this lady, that carried all with her, and Diana looked at her, amazed and comforted by the condescension and obligingness of so great a person. She was bewildered indeed. To be rescued from all her perplexities and griefs, and carried off thus suddenly into what appeared to be a heaven of gentle voices and kind looks and beauty, was more like a dream than any waking occurrence in her short and somewhat sad life.

"I have no words—no none—with which to thank you, Madam, but indeed I vow that my conduct shall be answerable to my gratitude and that your Grace shall have no cause to regret your condescension."

"Child, I look in your fair eyes and have no fear. I see in them the mirror of a candid soul!" cries the Duchess, too beautiful herself to disparage the beauty of others. This lady had the frankness of a man rather than the finesse of a woman and spoke her thoughts with a candour sometimes charming, sometimes embarrassing in a high degree, but always her own. She added now:

"And indeed your looks are such that you need a shepherdess to keep so pretty a lamb in the right pasture. There are wolves about, child, and some of them in sheep's clothing. Doubtless you know this already?"

"Unfortunately, too well, Madam!" She said no more but there was a trouble in her face that spoke volumes as she stood patient by the table, waiting the Duchess's pleasure. It was then for the first time that she became aware of a tall gentleman standing silent by the fireplace. A very splendid gentleman in brown and gold, and with a dark and melancholy face like the Stuart portraits at Hampton Court. It was not without the hidden sanction of the blood that his Grace resembled a fine Vandyke of that unfortunate family. Clothe him in armour and a falling lace collar, and his connection needed not trumpeting, but spoke for itself in long dark eyes and lips full of sensibility and tenderness. But that's an old scandal.

Diana knew nothing of this, but as she looked upon him a strange romantic interest that surrounded him like a vapour, not to be expressed but visible, was perceptible to even her young untutored mind. Worded, it was nothing but this:

"Who may be this great gentleman who looks so proud and sad?"

Thought, it was a hundred things more and all inexpressible. He moved slightly forward, and the Duchess revolved majestic in her hoop.

"This is his Grace the Duke of Bolton, Mrs. Beswick. A great devotee to your charming profession. Rely on't the secret of your name shall go no further than his Grace. He and I are sworn friends, and wherever 'tis possible to advance your interests he'll second me."

"I had the happiness to be presented to Mrs. Fenton in the green-room at Portugal Street, but sure she can't remember one stranger among so many."

She looked full at him. Certainly he could not complain that he saw not her face now. He thought it one of incomparable sweetness, lovely in feature and colour, but how should any man think otherwise? He drew a little nearer as if he would have willingly had her speak with him.

And at that moment two footmen flung the wings of the great door wide open, and the groom of the chambers announced:

"My Lady Fanny Armine. My Lord Baltimore."

# CHAPTER VII

THEY entered, his Lordship with an excess of gallantry, if such can be where a fine woman and a Duchess is concerned, and her Ladyship in a prodigious hoop and scarf all ruffles and frills, the latest adornment from Paris, a hat with noble plumes curved high over one pretty ear and drooping above the other. A perfect Madam Flippanta so far as looks and dress went, but more, much more in her than this for those who knew how to comprehend. She ran to her Grace with a pretty little cry and a butterfly kiss on the cheek, and swept a careless curtsey to Diana, seeing merely a young lady, supposedly some country cousin of the Duchess.

"I'm come, my dear Duchess, on a charming errand. 'Tis to bid you come see my new Chinese monsters, the dearest, most enchanting porcelain lions, and you do but put a stick of scented something—I think 'tis incense—in their jaws, and their eyes glow and the whole room is perfumed."

"Enchanting indeed!" says the lovely Kitty, cursing their presence at this inopportune moment. "But sure you didn't want them, dear Lady Fanny—you that has a whole museum of such exquisite monstrosities."

"A fashionable woman don't buy things because she wants 'em. Why, what a fiddle-come ill-bred reason is that! However, as I met my Lord Baltimore at your Grace's door, and find the Duke of Bolton here, I can't do less than include them in my invitation. If this young lady——"

She paused and curtseyed slightly towards Diana. She was curious as to who the lovely stranger might be, not as yet catching more than her profile and drooped head. Indeed the three finest women in London, each in her own sort, were met in that happy library that day! It certainly so appeared to the three gentlemen, but one at least of them was so discomposed by the meeting that it took all his worldly wit to hide it, and as it was he let his hat drop, and got his sword between his legs stooping to recover it, ere he could dissemble his face and plot a careless eye. For my Lord Baltimore knew very well the history of the past fortnight and why Diana's lashes lay so still upon her cheek that she might not look his way.

But imagine his consternation and wild surprise to see her in such a place and company! It added new value and new terror to his pursuit all of a moment. And Lady Fanny for spectatress! Was ever a man in such a medley of perplexities? Having saluted the ladies he drew near to Bolton and talked with him. But my Lady Fanny's curiosity could not be stayed. She caught the girl's face full of a sudden. She started. She whispered aside to the Duchess:

"Who's the new beauty, Kitty? A charming figure of a woman indeed. Her dress is trifling, but what matter with such eyes. Pray present me."

Her Grace kept even her intimates in order, and here her Fanny presumed too far.

"Your Ladyship will excuse me," says the towering Duchess, very near to one of her towering rages;—the visitors came so inconvenient! " 'Tis a young person come to visit me, and with your permission I'll put her in my woman's hands and be the more free to enjoy your company. Bolton, sound my whistle."

He sounded it obedient and the little black boy ran in grinning and bowing.

"Conduct this lady to the ante-room and send for Mrs. Francis. Adieu for the moment, Madam. I'll see you again presently."

And Diana thankfully followed the little black sprite attended by Mr. Gay, and leaving my Lady Fanny in a bewilderment not to be described, and this for a reason presently to be mentioned. She scented a secret but for the life of her could not tell its cause. The Duchess still standing she rose also, her pride taking the alarm.

"Your Grace is engaged, and as I hope to see you no later than Tuesday I'll bid you adieu now. I need not ask if you are pure well, I never saw you look so charmingly!"

They kissed again, and curtseyed, and 'tis very possible her Ladyship hastened her departure in hopes to catch the fair mystery still in the ante-room, but if so she was disappointed. She threw a look over her shoulder at the American Prince, but he was engrossed with his friend and only performed a bow of prodigious grace and suavity.

That night again did my Lady Fanny take pen in hand, and writ a portion of her heart—for what woman can write all?—to her cousin in Ireland.

> "*My kind Kitty*, whose sensibility and feeling heart are always my consolation, here come I again with my pack of news. With my own I'll begin, for indeed I have perplexities that need counsel, and your latest letter is so kind, so sisterly in its terms as draws out all my confidence. But are you well, Kitty, and how does Sir Richard and the sweet boy?
>
> "I writ you of Bas in my last and I thought in this to tell you he was at my feet openly, as indeed he hath been almost publicly this two years. And now—I can't say it as I would—'tis so perplexing!—but we seem no nearer than a fortnight since. O Kitty, let your calmer mind consider what I shall tell and reply as frank as if you were my father-confessor, for in this gay glittering

world I live in, honesty's much rarer than diamonds, and more to be valued.

"After I sealed my last letter I had a billet from Bas, and certainly any woman had called it a declaration though 'twas but to bid me to a water-party. 'More, much more I will say when we meet,' it ended, and I may say that when we took boat I thought I saw in him my pledged lover. 'Twas a small party, but merry, and as we rowed up the river, Mrs. Sandford sang so charmingly that several other boats rowed up pretty near as to share in the concert.

"I saw in one as pretty a young woman as ever I beheld in my life, dark hair and what your Sir Richard calls violet eyes, an uncommon combination, her dress merely so-so, and the persons with her of no condition. What's all this preamble then? says Kitty. Who cares for the rascality that takes the air in skiffs on the Thames? Well, but wait, Kitty! I saw her glance at Bas, and as plain as possible she blushed up to her eyes and turned her head away. I can't be sure if he saluted her or no for my eye was fixed on her at the moment, but I saw her speak to the watermen and they rowed ahead of us. She had an old woman with her for duenna, and an elderly man for cargo. Nothing, you'll say, but listen. Later in the day we moored by one of the aits in the river, and ate our refreshments under the willows. And sudden, from t'other side of the island arose the most delicious warbling. Larks my dear Kitty, nightingales, 'twas like a whole choir of them singing clear as dew drops. We all hushed our breath to listen, poor Mrs. Sandford entirely out-piped, and the sound ringing over the water as if the sirens was singing. I turned that Bas might join in my delight, and, O Kitty, 'twas more than music that caused his disorder. I noted a kind of—How to describe it?—consciousness. Not a blush nor a tremor (men don't do the like!) but, in a word, I knew 'twas not merely the singing—'I attempt from Love's sickness to fly,' but something deeper. She sang again with ravishing sweetness the chief soprano air from Mr. Handel's opera, 'King Richard the First,' and I protest the very leaves hung silent till she ended. Her boat then put out and crost ours and behold! the same pretty young woman I saw before, singing as if to delight herself, for certainly neither of her companions, had souls for music. She stopt instantly on seeing us and looked away, and so it past off, but, Kitty, we landed on the island and wandered hither and thither, and though 'tis small there was opportunity for any lover. But Bas was always concerned with

Mrs. Sandford or Lady Mary unless I had another of the company and then was assiduous in his gallantries at once. Kitty, couldn't I read him like a book?

"I needed no telling that what he wished so passionately to say a few days since he did not now desire. Nor need I tell my Kitty neither that this being so I flirted and laughed and jested with Colonel Mainwaring until my throat was sore and my lips like to crack from smiling. A hateful—a horrid day! It should have rained waterspouts and blown hurricanes to please my humour and instead the birds sang in a fair sunshine and the river smiled back at a sky as blue.

"Unfeeling capricious nature!

"So it ended. I could not complain of any luck of attention. Bas's good breeding and gallantry will never fail him, but the soul of it was gone. 'Twas like the picture of a rose instead of the rose itself all dewy and perfumed. He was on his guard—I on mine.

"Kitty, do I love the man? For God's sake resolve me, you who love your Sir Richard. At the very least he disturbs me greatly, affects my sleep, holds me in a horrid suspense. Do I love him?

"But my story is not yet ended.

"Today I went to the Duchess of Queensbury's, meeting Bas at the doorstep. Conceive my astonishment when who should I find with her but Bolton (he's always there however) Mr. Gay, *and* the fair stranger! God help us, Kitty, such was my astonishment that 'tis a marvel I didn't swoon into the great sopha. 'Tis true that your namesake, the fair Kitty, is surely a little brainsick, so amazing are her whimsies, but this past all the mysteries of all the French romances. I took a sharp quick look at Bas under my hat and again saw the same smothered perturbation. Bolton stood grave and quiet by the mantelpiece and in his handsome face none can read but what he wishes. And Mr. Gay was the same busy-body as ever. So I took nothing by my inquisition.

"I tried the Kitty of Kittys then (but not so charming as my own Kitty) and asked an introduction. Her Grace rose, looking at least seven feet high and bundled the lady out of the room at the heels of Pompey and Mr. Gay. So I saw 'twas my room preferred to my company and, came off as handsomely as I could, and Bas stayed behind.

"Now, what should this mean? Sure the young person is a woman of condition, for we all know the Queensbury pride. I'm tost about and know not what to think. But this I can tell them one and all. I'll be at the bottom of their secret before the week's out. What! Three men and a woman know a secret and hope to keep me out! The Lord forbid. I must be in my dotage before such infamy befall me.

"—As for news, the play at Court is frightful high and I have just lost two hundred guineas at hazard. And at the same table the Princess Emily lost seven hundred—and Lord Godolphin thirty, so he got off the cheapest. The Princess's spirits was beyond anything I ever saw. She laughed so as she sat in her chair as I thought she would burst her staylace. But for my part I think play a folly, and find no recreation in it. 'Tis the mode— That's all there's to say.

"The Prince of Wales and Miss Vane on horrid bad terms with Papa and Mamma. Such calling of names on both sides! But I won't make this letter contraband with Court scandals.

"Write soon, my Kitty, my more than cousin—indeed my heart's sister.

"Your loving cousin and servant to command,

"FANNY ARMINE."

She pushed the paper away and sat long considering. Then catching up her pen again she writ a billet to the Duke of Bolton commanding his attendance at her chocolate next day. That done she summoned her maid and prepared for the sleep that did not come, though a very bevy of cupids must need hover over a couch so charming that they might nest in the curling locks which outrivalled those of Mr. Pope's fair Belinda.

Meanwhile Diana slept no better that night. The Duchess's majordomo knowing that his mistress did nothing by halves, gave orders she was to be received as one whom her Grace delighted to honour. Consequently the poor girl was installed in a room with mirrors and carpets from Eastern looms, and a great red velvet bed like a catafalque, and felt as much at home as a woodland wild rabbit might do, deposited in the like surroundings. She had the same temptation to bolt for her life and 'twas only the impossibility of so doing that kept her head on the great down pillows. True the Duchess was kind, but 'twas an awful and condescending kindness as of a being from some higher sphere. And moreover it had been a horrible surprise to find my Lord Baltimore follow her into that sanctuary as a friend of its haughty mistress, for during the past fortnight he had besieged and besought the girl until she would run like Daphne from Apollo when she sighted his Lordship coming down the street.

He wrote her billets, posies of flowers appeared at Scawen's lodging, little accustomed to such rarities, and on one alarming night was left a casket of inlaid mother-o-pearl containing a jeweled chain. It had no name attached and Diana, who loved the pretty sparklers as well as any girl, stared at them in terror, not knowing how to return them lest she mistake, and be perhaps took up for theft—all sorts of wild notions let loose in her inexperienced head. For his Lordship was by no means the only suitor. There was Sir Harry Villars, and more, and no woman could mistake the look in Mr. Walker's eye when as Macheath she must permit him the stage liberties of a favoured lover.

She had sat long with the jewels in her hand and after deep consideration besought a private audience of Mr. Rich, to be granted somewhat unwillingly so immersed was he in preparations for the Beggar's Opera, and Mr. Gay like his shadow. This secured however she placed the jewels in his hand.

"I entreat you, Sir," says she, looking at him with those moving eyes, "to be so good as take charge of this chain which is not mine nor never shall be. 'Tis hard a poor girl may not appear in public without these insults."

Mr. Rich weighed it thoughtfully in his hand.

"My dear, 'tis hard, but 'tis a necessary disadvantage of a profession that hath many advantages. Is it known to you whence these jewels come?"

"I don't know, Sir, but may suspect. I think it to be my Lord Baltimore. May I ask so much as that you would return them and entreat his Lordship to trouble me no more?"

"Child, I can't do this. I will take charge of the chain and you'll then be clear of accepting it and I'll hold it at your pleasure. But offend his Lordship I dare not. 'Tis as much as the play is worth. You little know his influence nor how the town follows him. But be at your ease. You are a good girl and all shall go well. Do but wait until the play is produced and the run over and then, if you must, affront his Lordship. Endeavour meanwhile to take it lightly, and but as a tribute to the beauty of my and Mr. Gay's charming Polly. Bethink you, it may not come from him."

What more could she say? She dared not ruin the play and her own career also at stake. But it must be owned 'twas hard. A singular thing also that my Lord Baltimore, the irresistible, the adored of half the London ladies, inspired her with nothing but fear. She blushed and trembled when he looked at her, but however he might interpret these signs they were not love. The smooth fairness of his face, the cold sweetness of his eyes with the dangerous sparkle behind it, his easy carriage, his splendid dress, the impossibility to make him believe his attentions unwelcome to any woman, all these caged the freedom of her spirit until she raged against her bars and bruised her poor breast more than enough.

It had this harm also, that Mrs. Bishop had been a former recipient of his Lordship's flowers and jewels, and now, seeing herself deposed for a younger and lovelier rival, took her revenge in a thousand ingenious ways on the unhappy Polly. 'Twas more than mere stage looks of hatred and vengeance that Lucy Lockit darted at Polly Peachum, 'twas her joy to trip her in her part, to confuse her, to spread stories to her disadvantage. Indeed the girl found that success has its sting as well as its honey, and though Mr. Walker did his clumsy best to protect her on the stage, what is a man against a woman's petty malice?

Diana therefore had much between her and sleep as she lay in the great red velvet bed. 'Twas a difficult case to mingle the two parts of Polly and Diana. For Polly must be all bewitching arts and graces, every movement of her arms an embrace to the public, every glance a ravishment and a veiled invitation. And indeed she was perfect in her part. Mr. Gay and Mr. Rich owned it daily. But poor Diana must combat the amatory attacks that the fair Polly invited from all the world, and how to do it she scarce knew. She must languish at the gallants who crowded the stage as near as they could, she must droop her long lashes at them to hide the soft fire, with a smile to drive them frantic on the roses of her lips, and then, behind the scenes, repel the most audacious advances, for nothing could be supposed freer than the manners of the fops who buzzed about the theatre.

Lord save us! what a task to be Polly-Diana in one fair person, and this without offending Mr. Rich, who looked to her as the best house-filling actress of her time—as indeed she was to prove. His own humour saw the difficulty, and he would say laughing, "Let not Polly run off with Diana, my dear. Diana is the elder sister. She was born long ago in grace and hath a reputation to lose, whereas Miss Polly's but a pert slut though a charming, and a thing here today and gone tomorrow. Allow me to assure you that Macheath is true to the life in his ardours with so many. Listen then to the counsels of Diana, rather than the songs of Polly, which indeed are so adorable, especially coupled with that dimple in her chin, that I can't wonder at nor hardly blame the men."

And this was all her consolation. No wonder she slept as ill as my Lady Fanny.

The Duchess sent for her next morning ere she left for rehearsal, alarmingly handsome in her flowing *negligée* without a hoop beneath it. A goddess indeed for height and pose.

"A chair is ordered for you, Mrs. Beswick," says she "and two footmen to attend it, for Mr. Gay tells me you've been much pestered with attentions you could dispense with. This chair is at your disposal whenever you need it."

"I thank your Grace most sincerely. It is true I have suffered much annoyance. Perhaps when 'tis known I have the honour to be under your Grace's protection it may cease."

"I think there are so many who desire to extend their protection to Mrs. Polly that even my Grace's won't secure her from their offers," says the Duchess, with her hearty laugh. " 'Tis Mrs. Diana and none other who must guard Miss Polly's virtue and I'm certain 'tis no sinecure. But be seated a moment. I have a thing to say."

Diana sat herself instantly, too well-bred to dispute her superior's command with any false politeness. Her Grace looked her steadily in the face while she spoke.

"I am resolved to say a word of warning to you, child, about my Lord Baltimore. He's a gentleman of most alluring address, and your own eyes can appraise his good looks. I know him as well as another,—better since my eye is keener. Mistrust him, Diana (for I will take that liberty with your papa's daughter), he is a man of honour as men count honour, but I think he has no heart, and was you to suppose that your beauty (which I fully admit) could win you a wedding ring from the gentleman, or even so much as a continuity of passion, let me tell you you would be hugely mistook. For when nature assembled so many graces at his birth she left no room for a heart. Such at least is the conviction of myself, and the gentleman who best knows him—the Duke of Bolton. Consequently, you have here the testimony of a man and of a woman, and rest assured 'tis true. His Lordship also is bound in honour to a woman of quality."

The Duchess concluded her sermon and looked half sadly, half humorously at the glowing face before her. Woman though she was, she could estimate the charm that thousands would presently admit.

She pitied the girl.

Diana clasped her hands—a favourite gesture with her when eager.

"Madam, from my heart I thank your Grace, 'tis true. I know it. And I beg you to believe that I have no interest in his Lordship and I am certain that he hath no heart for me or any. I dread him more than any other, and even his good looks alarm me—so cold, so smooth, and Lord knows what beneath the surface. I think he sent me a chain of jewels which I have committed to Mr. Rich since I knew not for certain. O, Madam, could your

Grace, whom all the world must obey, not command him to desist from this pursuit of an unhappy girl?"

"Child, in our world things are not done thus. But I will speak with his Grace of Bolton. One man may say to another what a woman cannot. It shall not slip my memory."

"Was that the tall gentleman with a grave countenance whom I saw last evening?"

"The same. Now depart to your work, for much hangs on Polly. Be a good girl and rest assured of my protection. 'Tis safer than others more gaudy."

'Twas the signal for dismissal, and Diana rose and ventured to kiss the hand which lay like a snowflake on the damask *negligée.* It did not displease her Grace, who was used to almost more than royal homage, and she looked kindly enough at the retreating beauty. Then, dismissing her from her mind, she whistled for Pompey and her woman, her friseur, her jeweller and what not—the trifling persons and doings that made up her Grace's morning. The Duke was in Yorkshire and had he even been there had counted somewhat less than the lap-dog Zaide who lay on the satin cushion at her mistress's feet.

# CHAPTER VIII

THE playhouse in Portugal Street was rocking to an applause so frantic that it seemed as though the walls would fall like those of Jericho. Miss Polly, Miss Lucy and all the company stood on the stage to receive the plaudits—Diana like to faint with her emotion. The lights, the faces swam about her in a glittering whirl, and she saw all, yet not one distinctly. The crowd shouted for "Polly! Polly!" and, Walker relinquishing her hand, she stood alone a moment, the lovely mark for all the cries and cheering. What does a woman feel when she knows herself a queen enthroned and crowned by an adoring people? Surely something of this triumph must a player taste that has topped her part and outshone the stars, and knows her every smile, her every look a conquest.

The crowd cried for the author, coupling his name with Polly's, and Mr. Gay, exquisitely fine in a purple coat laced with gold, came forward and taking her finger tips led her forward to the footlights and bowed first to her, then to the audience. Such a scene was scarce known as the two fronted the London public and the gallery screamed till 'twas hoarse for one song more—They would, they must hear that silver voice again. Mr. Gay turned to her, bowing:

"Will you oblige our patrons, Madam?" and instantly the orchestra broke forth and her clear voice out-soared it all, and she trilled and laughed, and threw her sweet glances with a kind of surprise and joy about the house, seeming to receive as well as give a heartfelt pleasure. And since they still would not be quieted she stretched her arms as if to embrace the charming persons that were so kind to her, and then slowly and reluctant passed up the stage and disappeared from their eyes.

Twice they recalled her, and at last when the curtain was forced to be dropt 'twas extreme difficult to clear the house of the enthusiasts. Behind the scenes Mr. Gay claspt the girl by both hands and in his joy and excitement saluted her on the blushing cheek, nor did she draw back.

"My dear, I thank you cordially," says he, "You bettered my creation. You added graces of your own that I dreamed but could not embody in pen and ink. You assured my success with your own."

"And mine!" cries Mr. Rich, joining them. "Never was such a bumper house. I saw her Grace of Queensbury break her fan applauding. And as for the gallery—six women were dragged out fainting with the press. And yet so far as the audience was concerned you might hear a pin drop at any moment. Your Benefit's ensured, Mrs. Fenton."

They were so occupied with the young beauty that neither observed Mrs. Bishop hovering near with a sullen air as of one neglected.

“Since Mrs. Fenton did not perform the whole opera herself, I trust, gentlemen, to hear that the other performers did not wholly displease you.”

They turned somewhat shamed, and Diana with them.

“Indeed, Mrs. Bishop, your voice was divine,” she cried;— “Little could I have done but that your presence gave me confidence and the beauty of your singing was a lesson in every note. I thank you sincerely.”

’Twas generous, for the petty malice of the woman had impeded her more than once had she not been rather Polly than Diana all that night. The two gentlemen expressed their acknowledgments to Mrs. Bishop and all the company in terms so handsome as almost to satiate even the vanity of the player—the most avid vanity of the world.

But when Diana turned away to her dressing-room she saw before her a gallant figure with his sword by his side. At first in the flickering candlelight she knew not the gentleman and ’twas Miss Polly greeted him all sparkling smiles and delight, the glow of the applauding house still upon her. My Lord Baltimore stepped forward, bowing low, and instantly Polly vanished and Diana, cold and haughty as when the huntsman surprised her in her forest pool, stood before him. She said not a word and made as though to pass to her dressing-room.

“Madam, I am come for the answer to all my words writ and spoken. Give me but a tithe of the courtesy you bestow on the public and at least deign a reply. If I am not odious in your eyes, pity the madness that has reduced me to this plea. I love you. Does this avowal excite no generous emotion?”

They stood in the angle of the wall, and the players were still engaged behind the dropt curtain with their friends who swarmed upon the stage to rejoice with them.

How far was his Lordship sincere? Diana might ask herself this, but ’twas more than he himself could answer! He writhed in a flame of desire but the mask of his composure hid it, and ’tis well known that desire and the heart need have little in common unless it be rooted in a love native to all the higher and nobler sensibilities. No woman had ever yet flouted him. A passion of anger and incredulity that it now could be, fanned the flame of desire and made it dangerous. Reason was routed, honour—for he knew himself bound in honour to another—vanquished.

My Lady Fanny had been within his sight all that evening, beautiful and glittering. He had seen her blue eyes turn his way and hastily averted—those bright audacious eyes that never dropt before another. But the magic of her presence was evaporated. He saw her and marvelled that she had swept him away into an emotion he was now incapable of feeling. Diana stood before him, and to hold that proud but shy beauty in his arms, to know it his and his only, to have those lips against his own, that velvet cheek pressed to his, and more than all this, to know himself the conqueror where he had been disdained,—there was nothing in heaven nor earth that he would not have given at that moment to bend her to his will, and none the less because her bright graces had made her this night the idol of the only world he valued. Her possession would exalt him beyond all former successes. Not a man but would envy him,—not a tongue but would tell his triumph.

He prest nearer to her.

"I loved you before your success, Madam, therefore you know my love honest, and your success I value not because it does but give you hundreds of lovers more to plunge me in jealousy and despair. Yet tonight—though I had rehearsed all your charms and each a dagger in my heart, I discovered something—O how can I name the unspeakable!—even more bewitching. Indeed you are a jewel a King might wear in his crown. Beloved, worshipt, O hear your adorer. My dearest life, I entreat!"

She drew herself back against the wainscot and stood there quivering, but with a courage that surprised herself after to recall it. 'Twas the courage of the deer at bay.

"My Lord, I have returned you no answer and you had done better to take that as it was meant. But since it is not so I will ask you this. What do you offer me?"

The clear candour of her tone together with her direct gaze for a moment nonplussed him, but he recovered his coolness quickly. Aha! so the sweet frost-piece could traffic against her virtue! Then the bargain was all but sealed.

"Madam, my whole heart. My adoration. My entire and eternal devotion. And more."

"What more, Sir?"

"Madam, yourself shall write what conditions you will and this hand subscribe them unread—even to the half of my kingdom, as another lover said long since."

"That lover addrest his offer to his wife, my Lord, if I remember the Scripture rightly. Do you?"

There was a moment's silence. It came so unexpected. His outstretched hand fell by his side—his eye wavered. What? But no, 'twas impossible. She was but setting her merit high that there might be margin for a descent when the terms were fixed. To parley was the beginning of surrender.

"My charmer knows there is nothing I can refuse her. I am acquiescent to her lightest command. And if a mere ceremony which is nothing in the eye of true affection can solace her timid scruples I own 'tis a matter to be considered——"

"Your Lordship had not already considered it?"

"Why no—I own it. 'Tis love that's all to my mind,—the true union of two minds and bodies formed to harmonize for eternity. What should a currish parson have to do between my charmer and me? And how could he still further strengthen a bond that only death can end? My restless days and miserable nights teach me that my darling is all to me. Can any foolish ceremony bind me to more? All I have and am is yours. Take and use me as you will."

"In short, your Lordship offers me the position of your mistress. Setting aside all protestations it comes to this."

"Why that harsh name that the world misuses, my beloved? It is true you shall be my mistress for I will be the humblest and faithfullest of all your servants. But what I offer you is to be my heart's empress, and these blushing hesitating questions of yours assure me that I am not odious to my angel."

He prest nearer and took her hand. She twitcht it sharply away. Certainly there was neither blushing nor hesitating on the lady's part whatever he might choose to call it.

"I put these questions that they might strip your protestations of glitter and show them as they are. What you offer me is contempt and shame and the laughter of men and the mocking of women, and to be flung to another or to the gutter when you weary of me. I am a simple girl, my Lord, but honest, and I refuse your offers now and hereafter. And if you answered to my test and offered me your name as well as what you are pleased to call your heart, I would refuse and despise it as I do yourself."

She flung from him magnificent, and he heard the door shut and the key turn behind her.

Deadly pale and dangerous my Lord stood there. That he did not believe her assertion was nothing, for he was convinced that the ring was all she asked. For an instant he hated her, who had thus humbled him, and then again the tide of longing rolled back upon his seared heart, with the passion for revenge, the longing that in turn he might humble her and see her yet entirely at his feet and in vain. 'Twas so mingled with the sensual passion that he could not as yet tear them apart in his distracted mind. And as he stood there, outwardly calm and composed in appearance, a very great nobleman, Mrs. Bishop came tripping up, her vast hoop swinging, on her way to her dressing-room.

"What, my Lord, waiting for Polly? Has she not past this way?"

There was a sneer under the lightness. The woman could recall when he had waited there for her and not in vain.

"I have not seen her, Miss Lucy!" says he, calling her familiarly by her stage name. "Nor did I so desire. I waited here to tell the seductive Lucy Lockit that I have not seen nor could imagine a part better played than that of the forlorn mistress of Macheath."

Even such as my Lord Baltimore may fail in tact sometimes. A sullen fire lit in the lady's fine eyes.

"Why, my Lord, I have had such practice in the past of the deserted one—'twas yourself taught me you know, that 'tis no wonder I should succeed. There are Macheaths at Court as well as in Newgate though their booty is hearts not purses."

"Amoret—Amoret!" says he shaking his finger at her and laughing—"When the summer is past 'tis past and the flowers drop. But you'll own you were happy while it lasted, and is that nothing to be grateful for? I made you happy—you owned it a thousand times. Would you now repay me with anger?"

"Not you—not you!" she cried with a sudden fierce tenderness— " 'Tis that partial little devil I loathe, that wins all hearts, that has stole yours from me."

"My dear, it left you long since. Don't the swallows fly away with the summer? My heart has wings. I never pretended otherwise to my Amoret."

"You did. You swore—but why waste breath? You have no heart. You never had. But let me tell you this, my Lord—this smooth-faced little devil is my abhorrence. She hath pushed me down on the stage. Do you think I didn't see that all the world looked at her tonight and I was but her foil? She has made a fool of Rich, of Gay, of Walker—of all the persons who could advance or help me. If I could ruin her this minute and drag her in the dirt with a wish, I would do it. Some day I *will* do it, though she be a duchess's favourite, and a nobleman's——"

She spit out the hateful word and made to thrust by him. He caught her hand as she past and stared in her face.

"And some day you *may* do it, my girl!" said he. Then released her and walked back with his easy languid step to the stage.

When Diana's chair set her down at Queensbury House, the Duchess, the Duke, and Bolton were assembled in the library, and Pompey summoned her to an audience. The excitement of the night had passed off and her lovely brow was sweetly serene as she entered. She was much more at her ease with the imperious Kitty now, having received much kindness from her and understanding her moods perhaps better than did any other creature. For others made her Grace a goddess and when that is done a goddess the lady will be. But Diana met her with a cheerful and grateful simplicity and a warm sunshine of affection tempered with the awe due to such commanding rank and power. 'Twas human—that sums it up, and the proud Duchess sought the poor player's company in odd hours, would have her sing for her, read to her while she worked her jonquils, and let some crumbs of sincere liking fall from her high table to this humble dependent. For so she considered her as yet.

"Come hither, my Polly, my charming Polly, that has made Gay Rich and Rich Gay," she cried, with her loud hearty laugh. "Why, what don't I and all the world owe to you for this success? The town is run mad over you—'Tis Polly, Polly on every tongue, and Mr. Gay is gone to bed perfectly exhausted with plaudits and triumph. Not but what the piece is supreme. There is not its like in the English language. It hath a French sparkle and—but I rave, and what I would say is that with another Polly it could not so have smote the heart however it dazzled the brain. What say you, Queensbury?"

The Duke, good easy man, would say nothing but what his wife said.

"My dear, you are ever in the right. A more bewitching Polly couldn't be imagined. In every scene Mrs. Diana triumphed. My felicitations attend you, Madam. But won't you come with me one moment, my dear, to the next room, for sure you forget you desired Mr. Rich's company to drink a bumper to our success, and the little gift is prepared there that you would honour him with."

The Duchess ran off like a girl.

"Wait till I come back, Mrs. Di. 'Twon't be long first."

She was alone with his Grace of Bolton. He rolled a chair forward for her and she untied her satin hood and it fell back on her shoulders. Her face was pale now as if with fatigue and the coral of her lips showed lovely against the ivory. A shadow under her eyes enhanced their soft fire, and the delicatest little tendrils of hair imaginable made her white brows whiter. Most lovely the feathering of each fine-pencilled eyebrow that gave an air of nobility and distinction to the whole face.

The changeable girl—the infinite variety of her! Miss Polly was left in Portugal Street and the charming creature sat there in soft remote beauty—the chaste and gentle Diana.

The Duke approached his own chair to hers and leaned forward.

"Madam, though I be the last to express it, I am one of the most ardent of your admirers. Tonight was a delight so high that I venture to predict you have conferred immortality on Mr. Gay's fine piece, and that it will be performed and delighted in when all we who applauded tonight are dust."

There was always a background of sadness to my Lord Duke's thoughts. He could not escape the shadow of his darkened life.

Her own face saddened.

" 'Tis indeed a very brief triumph," she said, "I tasted it for a moment, but your Grace is right. The triumph is Mr. Gay's, for he may well be immortal, but we players are the sparks from a dying fire. Others will sing the songs and hear the laughter, and we in the dust."

"O Madam, forgive me," he cried, his dark face softening instantly.—"Why, what a wretch am I to poison your young rejoicing with my melancholy. Life is sweet, and sure few ever had a sweeter cup poured than this of yours—all beauty and genius and a harvest of enchanted hearts. Rejoice in it and forget everything but the happiness you deserve and give."

She looked at him with an expression that pitied him and herself though for very different reasons. She could not be so long in the Duchess's house without knowing somewhat of his story, and when they had met, as they did sometimes in her Grace's presence, he paid her a distant but deep courtesy that was like cold water applied to a burning wound after the blows her self-respect must daily sustain elsewhere.

"He does not treat me as a player," was her thought, "but as a woman that may deserve courtesy as much as another."

This was a foundation easy to build on. One so considerate and obliging must be a great gentleman so to condescend to one in the position of an actress—whose only road to the companionship of gentlemen lay through dishonour. This man put forward no pretension to gallantry in her favour, and she must be quick to recognize the distinction between his Grace and the other men who buzzed about her. It is true, and she knew it, that he had the reputation that most men of his rank have with women, but he did not sharpen his weapons on the Duchess's dependent. He would have despised himself otherwise since her Grace made him welcome to her rooms where she sat with Diana in private and 'tis strange how natural, simple and easy the talk of these three persons, so unlike each other, became as the days past by. Therefore his way of thinking was not unfamiliar to her. She knew that cloud on his brow, and would have given much to charm it away by some innocent kindness such as a sister might bestow, were it not for the vast distance between them of rank and sex. Still, she ventured a little, timidly.

"Your Grace, I was happy tonight, it is true, but I had scarce left the stage when fear and trouble awaited me. And so I think it will be always—brief sunshine and a cloud to swallow it up. I expect no better.

"Fear and trouble!" says the Duke earnestly, "but how and why? Sure there could be none so base as spoil your hard-earned triumph. Tell me what caused it? Now I look closer at you I see tear-marks about your eyes. Indeed this night should have been joy unmixt and perfect."

"When is it so?" she asked, avoiding his question— "Do I not see your Grace that hath youth, health, riches, splendour—everything, sad enough sometimes? Who then shall be happy?"

"Youth, health, riches, splendour!" he repeated— "Yes, but set against them, Mrs. Fenton,—loneliness, sorrow, shame, hatred.— Do that sum in subtraction and what is left? Nothing."

"Yet your Grace is gay often?"

"How could a man live otherwise? But my life is desolation. O fool that I am to talk thus and to a young and beautiful and happy woman. What should you know, child, of care—you that have life in radiant sunshine before you? I ask your pardon for being so selfish as to remind you that there are clouds even in a summer sky."

"I did not need reminding. My life is a struggle too, your Grace."

Her eyes dropt, and her cheek flushed.

"I know your reason," he said, looking earnestly at her. " 'Tis a hard case that men do not nor cannot distinguish a legitimate prey from one that 'tis cruelty to attempt. There have been moments when I despised my whole sex—not sparing myself—for our blindness and selfishness in this respect."

"Not you—not yourself," she cried eagerly. "I have never heard a word from your Grace nor seen a look that did not honour the woman you spoke with as well as yourself. I have learnt from you what a gentleman may be, whereas before I had only dreamt it. And I have thanked God for it for I am very sore beset."

She spoke with such warmth of gratitude that the water stood in her eyes, and the Duke looked at her astonished and humbled.

"Madam, I take shame to think how little I have deserved your esteem and it gives me a pang to know you grateful for the mere absence of brutality. You must indeed have suffered if such is the case. You have no brother, no father to protect you, and no man knows better than I that your profession exposes you to insult. I beseech you to honour me by remembering that if any man insults you my sword is at your service. 'Tis no empty proffer. I mean it."

She looked up at him with the tears dewing her long lashes.—

"Your Grace, I thank you with all my heart. It does not surprise me. From you I expect nothing but what is noble and generous. But 'tis useless. What would be thought of the poor Polly if a great Duke took sword in hand to defend her honour? What would the town say? No, I must fight my own battle. Why, the very man against whom I most needed protection might by chance be some intimate of your Grace's."

He caught her meaning instantly though 'twas not intended he should.

"And if it were so, Madam, I set right before even friendship. Call upon me and you shall never call in vain. I have not seen you of late without knowing that I had the honour to converse with a woman whose nature matcht her fair face, and both incomparable."

This suddenness startled himself and her.— 'Twas not said with the idle floridness of gallantry and the composure that cares a fig for nobody, but in earnest, he leaning forward and speaking with his soul behind it. Instantly however, realizing his own manner of speaking, the Duke drew back formally, and endeavoured with a bow and a smile to make it lighter. But though Diana past on hurriedly to another subject the thing was said and to be remembered. Her heart beat a quicker measure, her spirits were hurried and uneven. She rose and but for the Duchess's command would have retreated.

He spoke of indifferent things for a moment and then saluted her and departed, leaving his excuses for her Grace who received them carelessly when she returned to dismiss Diana to her rest. She did her the honour to kiss her on the cheek with the most obliging patronage and yet further to clasp about her neck a beautiful miniature of herself by Zincke set in pearl and enamel. Almost overwhelmed with such goodness, the girl kissed the lovely hand that bestowed such favours, and then glided away to the red velvet temple where she slept but brokenly for a voice that dumbed all the music of the night, repeating: "A woman whose nature matches her fair face and both incomparable,"—and dark eyes glowing through their sadness that winged the words. How should she rest?

# CHAPTER IX

TIS known to all the world that the success of "The Beggar's Opera" was prodigious. Never had such been known. As my Lady Fanny observed in a full conclave of ladies at her pool of commerce 'twas more like a general infection than a reasonable admiration.

"I went for the fourth time on Thursday," says she, "and could compare it only to a battle to get in at the doors, ladies squawling, shrieking and their lappets tore off in the press, and Mrs. Maynard's foot so trod upon as she is in bed since. 'Tis true her foot is of that size that a grenadier might make it his pedestal, but as no doubt she wore the shoes borrowed from the Hungarian Giant at Bartholomew Fair their spoiling is to be pitied."

Her Ladyship's own foot defying criticism this sally created laughter, though Lady Weston and a few more re-arranged their hoops to discretion.

"But, what think you of Polly?" cries Lady Carteret. —"All the men rave of her, and 'tis declared by those who should know that she is such an icicle as makes some suppose Mr. Rich has reverted to the ancient fashion and drest a pretty boy to play the siren's part. Indeed 'tis reported she kicked a forward admirer out of the playhouse last week.

"If so," says another with mock gravity, "it speaks very ill for her Grace of Queensbury's modesty that has Miss Polly constantly about her person. No, no boy had ever those languishments, those airs and graces. She becomes all she does as only a woman can."

There was a moment's pause while the pretty ladies sipped their chocolate served to them by my Lady Fanny's Mesrour and Selim. Because others had one small blackamoor to serve them she must needs have two, and very well they became her boudoir and her Ladyship's own immaculate fair complexion, in their Eastern dress of gold and bloom-colour. 'Twas my Lady Mary Wortley Montagu next took up the strain:

"All the same, ladies, I would give more than a pennyworth to know why her Grace is so tender of a mere player. Look at it how you will 'tis an astonishing circumstance. 'Tis whispered that Mrs. Fenton is in truth the daughter of Mr. Francis Hyde and her mother too great to be mentioned."

"Lord, Lady Mary. Sure you must be choked with scandal to cough it up thus!" cries Mrs. Fentrevor. "Do but consider what you say! This girl's eighteen if a day, and Mr. Francis Hyde but thirty-two. 'Tis attributing a precocity that——"

The remainder of her sentence was drowned in a general laughter, in which my Lady Fanny pretended to join though in truth watching every word. 'Tis needless to express the amazement with which she had beheld the lady of the boat and of the Duchess's library trip on to the stage as Polly. It sent her heart to her throat in a fluttering fit that had near burst her staylace. What in the world might it mean? She sought and strove, and rummaged her poor brain, and nothing at all could she decipher. She watched my Lord Baltimore during that performance as a cat does a mousehole, and yet today was no nearer the solving of the mystery than before. What wonder then she should listen breathless to each and all of the pretty gossips lest one or other should hit it. Trembling now lest the talk should turn elsewhere she led it back, unfurling her fan with an air.

"Look here, ladies! Is not this to be in the forefront of the fashion? Look at my fan that Sir Harry Vane hath sent me. Pictures of Polly and Lucy on either side of Macheath,—of Polly with her papa and mamma, of Polly with the bevy of beauties and their babies. Is it not a gem—painted as you'll see on satin? Indeed the girl has an agreeable air."

'Twas past from one hand to another with much jealousy that none but Lady Fanny should catch up the mode. But indeed 'twas always she to trip the flying feet of Fashion, the rest were mostly a day after her nimble Ladyship. My Lady Mary Wortley Montagu looked longest at it.

"Say what you will, there's a resemblance in the features to Kitty Queensbury," she said, "and 'tis known that family is none too straitlaced. Herself can't be guilty, for her age is known to us all, but let us run over her sisters, brothers and cousins and consider of the possibilities."

"Then we shall sit here till tomorrow," cries Lady Fanny, "for the Hyde family tree is as fruitful as the Jewish Kings'. Lord, no, Madam, you are on a false scent. 'Tis perfectly simple. Her Grace set her whole heart on the success of Gay's piece and any one contributing to that is an angel in her eyes. Sure we all know her oddities. But behind them a heart of pure gold. I'm her friend and know and love her well, and the better for her whims and fancies, and will answer for it."

"The greatest oddity of all," retorts Lady Mary, "is that she will have so promising an affair going on beneath her roof as Mrs. Fenton's intrigue with my Lord Baltimore. I have as strong a stomach as most, but I confess it makes me qualmish."

"Lord Baltimore?" cries Lady Fanny, repelling with her gay laughter the piercing glance of her elder. "Why that's nothing to the purpose. He goes there because Bolton goes, and Bolton goes to tell his woes to the Duchess, and 'tis incredible that a mere player is admitted to sit with her Grace. My woman has it from the Duchess's woman that the girl is but given bed and board and sees no company whatever. You may trust her Grace's dignity.

No, no—my Lady Mary. He may pursue her at the playhouse, but she has a potent rival. His own self-love."

"Why 'tis that sends him after her. Polly is so much the mode that to win her would be the last finish and polish to his Lordship's success. He disdains all his former charmers."

Lady Fanny resolved on bold action—so piercing, so malicious was the eye that held her.

"Indeed that's very true, Madam, and who should know it better than your most obedient. I think 'twas for two months or more the Basilisk favoured me with such attention that had I been an ounce vainer I had thought myself the chosen American Princess. But, Lord! I knew him too well. I did but wait my retirement in favour of a more beauteous pretender, and here she comes in the adorable Polly! She's welcome, for me!"

It baffled the lady, who drew back to wait for the next opportunity to sting. The rest laughed good-humouredly.

"Depend on't we hear of a great scandal one of these days!" says the pretty bouncing Mrs. Tate.— "The Basilisk never wanted anything that he did not take sooner or later. For my part, I pity the girl unless she favours his suit. Not even the Duchess can protect her. As to the friendship between him and the Duke of Bolton 'tis well known it's wearing as thin as gossamer. They are little together now. But shall we to our commerce again, Lady Fanny?"

A part of the company took to their cards while those fair Philomels, Mrs. Donnellan together with Mrs. Fane, favoured the rest with a song to my Lady Fanny's harpsichord from "The Beggar's Opera" that indeed was not inappropriate to this charming talkative society.

'Twas the dialogue song between Lucy and Polly they sung.

Why, how now, Madam Flirt?
  If you thus must chatter
And are for flinging dirt,
  Let's see who best can spatter,
    Madam Flirt!
Why, how now, saucy jade?
  Sure the wench is tipsy!
How can you see me made
  The scoff of such a gipsy?

Saucy jade!

Mrs. Slammikin, Mrs. Coaxer and their friends could not have applauded louder than that merry party.

'Twas impossible to get away from the thing. 'Twas sung and hummed and bawled and shouted wherever you went from St. James's to St. Giles's. The town seethed with stories of how Sir Robert Walpole, attending it and hearing an allusion that pinched him, cried out jovially (seeing all the house watching him), "Again, again! A roaring good song. I insist it be repeated"—and so spoilt the malice intended. But indeed the town talked of nothing else in one form or another, and poor Mr. Handel and his stately and harmonious operas languished on the shelf with the dust gathering upon 'em. The sprightly *olla podrida* of songs in the other swept all before it.

But when her company was gone, my Lady Fanny sat staring into the fire thinking thoughts she would not have known for the world. She had learnt one particular that might furnish a clue in the maze—namely that my Lord and the Duke of Bolton were now seldom together. The Duchess she dared not approach. A slap in the face from that white but powerful hand was as likely a finish to what her Grace might consider impertinence as any other. But Bolton——! A lady may count on a courteous answer from a gentleman she knows and honours, whether he reveal the truth or no. She had therefore writ him the sweetest little perfumed billet requesting his company next day. As an old friend. He came. He had a sincere liking for her—and likings with the Duke were a kind of fidelity.

So behold the pair seated—the lady graver than she dared or cared to be with her own sex, but keenly on the alert. No need to record the beginning of the talk while she manœuvred him steadily nearer and nearer to the point. She had herself never seen the Inconstant since the day of the water-party save in the distance—a circumstance so singular and cruel that it might well excuse her anxiety. Indeed she was unfairly used! It came at last to the point. She knew her man. She was candid with him.

"Your Grace, I have a question to ask you, and I ask the favour that it may lie between you and me only. For 'tis an uncommon question, I know."

"Madam, your Ladyship's command honours me and shall be faithfully obeyed. 'Tis a distinction to share a secret with you."

He observed her face to be anxious—a very unaccustomed expression with one so gay, and looked kindly upon her.

"I would I knew this, your Grace. Why is the friendship between you and my Lord Baltimore lessened?"

The attack was so sudden that he flinched.

"Surely, Madam——"

"I know, I know 'tis a most unconscionable question. I am ashamed as I ask it. But I am no stranger to your kind heart, and when I remind your Grace that I have no father, husband or brother to protect me and that my marriage was miserable, I trust you will see I am driven to a self-protection that happier women have unasked from the gentlemen of their family."

'Twas beautifully said however felt, and the little break in the sweet voice perfection. It moved the Duke.

"My dear lady," says he, "There's not a man in London would refuse any request of yours especially so movingly prest. Ask anything you will, and if I don't reply know 'tis only because honour forbids. You would know why the friendship is lessened between Baltimore and me. Who tells you that it is?"

He was not to escape that way however.

"The whole world!" says Lady Fanny, thus amplifying Mrs. Tate, and sat, her cheek leaned on her hand, looking beseechingly at him.

"You force a very unwilling man to speak, Madam. I own then that the friendship is lessened, but the reason I can't give. Suffice it to say his Lordship is taking a course I can't approve of. Pray be so good as ask no more."

"I need not. I am aware 'tis the pursuit of one in whom your Grace is interested that hath come between you and your friend. I hear on all hands that he pursues her with a fire unknown to him hitherto, and that the lady does not repel his flame."

" 'Tis false as hell!" The Duke entrapt, started to his feet, his hand seeking his sword-hilt. "She loathes, she trembles at his pursuit. She's pure as her name——"

"Polly?" suggests my lady. It brought him to a full stop, and to a stern gravity. Once more he seated himself.

"Her name is Diana, Madam, and she does not belie it. You have led me into an admission that I intended not to make. I desire to know nothing of my Lord Baltimore's concerns."

Again she changed to a woman beset with fear, tender, pleading.

"Your Grace, I would I could say the same. But I do desire most honestly to know his concerns, and I have none to counsel me—none! If I say I had reason to think—to imagine——"

He helped her out, with pity.

"The world knows, Madam, that he was at your feet. It seems he is so no longer. What counsellor do you need but the pride that beseems you?"

"O more, much more!" she cried, her beautiful eyes drowned in tears—"You know nothing if you imagine that pride will heal my sore, sore wound. The world mocks me as deserted and humbled. Me! But that's the least. My own heart——" Her voice was strangled in a sob. He looked upon her bowed head with pity.

"The lady whose heart is engaged there deserves much sympathy. Madam, you are not only beauty's self, but you have wit and intelligence far beyond your sex. Can these, and a wholesome pride, not aid you to cast aside regrets and go on your way as the stars you resemble emerge the brighter from a cloud? Were he at your feet once more, what have you to build on securely? And after marriage—what? Marriage—"

He paused and the dark shadow descended on his face. That word had terrors for him, and my Lady Fanny knew it.

"Your Grace," she said gently—"your sympathy is more precious than another's, for you have suffered. To whom else than to such a gentleman could I have opened myself. I know not how it is, but you are one that women naturally turn to in trouble—full of kind and noble thoughts and a grave sympathy. If I had a brother I could wish him so. Indeed I am in trouble. Tell me, I beseech you, the truth that it may help me like a bitter potion. Is this woman his mistress? But if even she is not, a pursuit so base must for ever dishonour him in my eyes."

His own flashed, but he subdued the rising anger, and confronted her calmly.

"Consider me your brother, Madam, and hear a plain truth. She is not his mistress nor any man's. She is pure as yourself.— Can I say more? for 'tis known what temptation you resisted during a hateful marriage. And his pursuit in one sense is not base in that to love such a woman should ennoble any man. 'Tis base only because he would drag the chaste moon from the heavens into the mud of a vile passion. Were he to share his name with her I could honour him, but as it is——"

"Share his great name with a player-woman!" she cried, in horror. "Madness! Impossible! Why—(she made a long pause—then said very low) your Grace yourself loves her. Else you had not said this."

They stared at each other a second—almost in a kind of terror, his dark face paling. There was a dead silence. She then spoke hurriedly.

"Forgive me. I have pried too far. I did not know—I could not guess. The world seems reeling about me. We will keep each other's secret—my brother!"

For the Duke—he sat almost stunned. Her words had tore apart a veil in his own heart that covered things strange and undreamt of. Friendship, homage, charm—the pleasure to talk with a creature so simple, so delicate of thought, so ardent in her youth, with a gallant courage to carry her over hindrances, and a pleasant humour to laugh at them. A true and sweet companion for a man. All these things he knew and acknowledged gladly—his sword was at her service. What man could stand by and leave unprotected one so friendless with all her renown? But that there should be more beneath it—Love the conqueror, had not as yet crossed his thoughts. He knew much of women, nothing of love. 'Tis to be remembered that the first knowledge often obscures the last. Its dazzle is as the sun flashed in a mirror that hides the sun itself. But this keen-eyed lady in a swift-darted word revealed him to himself.

Love? Should he be my Lord's competitor? She trusted him, indeed he knew himself agreeable to her. Love? His heart repeated the word in a kind of passion and could grasp nought else for the moment. He rose to his feet.

"My Lady Fanny, I ask your permission to leave you. I know our interview will be as secret with you as with me. For what you have said of me;—I am a man bound hand and foot, and I will offer dishonour to no good woman. For yourself—indeed I counsel you to put from your heart any man who deserves not the happiness of your esteem."

He paused, and she sat looking up at him in silence. He then continued.

"I know your esteem to be valuable despite the gay mask you wear. I bespeak it, Madam, for a woman, young and beautiful, sore beset and with a soul as transparent as her eyes. I know not if your path will ever cross hers—so different,—but if it should, remember my entreaty."

She rose also, and stretching her hand clasped his, like a sister.

"I promise. I know well that life is not all a comedy of Congreve's—witty, wicked, and with no truth anywhere. Your Grace is all honour. I will shape my steps by yours."

He bowed low, and kissed the hand that held his,—then departed in silence.

My Lady Fanny sat alone weeping.

# CHAPTER X

TWAS at this point that life became very difficult for both Miss Polly and Madam Diana. Her company at the playhouse was not what she would have chose, to say no more, and Mrs. Slammikin, Dolly Trull, Mrs. Vixen, Betty Doxy and others might possibly play their parts so finely as to charm the town because they were almost a second nature with them. She certainly believed it so, and it stood in the way of the comradeship of players which, however mixt with jealousies, subsists behind the scenes. Affront her openly they dared not, for Mr. Rich's piercing eye was about, and his consideration for a Polly who had lined his pockets with gold until they jingled again, prevented any open persecution. He knew well how much he owed her, and even were gratitude lacking as it was not, he knew that Mr. Gay had it in hand to write a sequel to this shining success, and was in mind to call the new piece "Polly." Where then in all the world could it be possible to replace the lovely Polly who had crowned the first venture, should she go off in a tiff?

Beside, the girl was the rage. Verses were made on her, and not one but lauded her grace, her starry eyes, her voice angelic, and the Lord knows what! Pamphlets were writ of her life with scarce a grain of truth to the bushel. Fine ladies wore a head-dress surnamed the Polly head,—a little cap of Quakerish demureness with a straw hat atop,—but they loaded it with flowers and ribbons and so spoilt its simplicity. Her figure, appealing, gentle, with claspt hands praying to her Macheath, the violent Lucy t'other side of him, took the town with a kind of emotion as yet untasted, the women as well as the men. They too would pet the pretty creature and give her her heart's desire for the sake of those sweet virginal looks blooming like a flower in the Newgate filth and obscenity. They laughed with her but never at her. The music was sung everywhere and the trills and quirks of the Italian Opera utterly forgot in favour of the fine old English tunes, "Lumps of Pudding,"—"What gudgeons are we men,"—"London Ladies," and so forth, which bespangle "The Beggar's Opera," to Mr. Gay's fine new words.

'Tis a strange truth but the piece made a kind of artlessness the fashion, doubtless aided by Polly's kind simple looks, and for awhile—awhile only, ladies tried to drop the modish jargon that Mr. Congreve and Captain Farquhar had made fashionable in their wicked comedies and to look up innocently and protest a taste in primroses, syllabubs and other country delights. 'Tis hard to unravel, but so 'twas. Indeed Mr. Pope himself composed a madrigal—

"My Polly as a primrose fair,"

set to the air of "Haycock of June," and had Dr. Swift not laughed him out of countenance it had been gave to the town.

The playhouse was beset by fine gentlemen shouldering for a word with the beauty, and Mr. Rich, divided between fear of offending them and terror of losing his Polly, became a perfect Cerberus, and would bark furiously when so much as a harmless haberdasher left a posy for the goddess. 'Twas remarkable how this gentleman, known for his own easy living and morals, might, so far as Diana knew, have been a bishop for the austere regard in which he held her personally and the manner in which from the first he softened his somewhat gross tongue to her ear. She had a grateful regard for him in return, and 'twas not a negligible element in her triumph that she knew it so valuable to him.

It chanced that, standing at the wings during a performance, he noted the scene where Lucy Lockit in her jealous rage (which Mrs. Bishop played to the life, he thought) presses upon Polly a glass of poisoned wine. Polly, on the alert, drinks not from it but drops it as hastily as she may. Revolving the by-play, Rich, when the house was cleared and he chatting with the ladies, recalled it.

"I know not, Mrs. Fenton and Mrs. Bishop, that ever I saw a scene better played, if so well. It does the two of you infinite credit—I know not which is more true to the passions. But one amendment occurs to me, and if I name it 'tis with diffidence, so well is all now."

Mrs. Bishop immediately besought his correction and Diana followed suit. She knew, none better, how much she owed to his tutoring.

"How would you have it, Sir?"

"Why thus. At present the audience is held in no suspense. There is no anxiety for Polly. She suspects too soon—she drops the glass, and the attempt might as well not be made for all the effect got from it. Now I hold that no effect but must have its full value on the stage. I would have Polly's face innocent as a daisy for the moment. She knows—suspects nothing. The audience, knowing, trembles for her."

"I see your drift. Thus!" says Polly, and instantly her expression changed to what he desired.

"Right. That speaks to the heart. Myself who has played Harlequin knows that gesture and expression go as far or further than words. So! Well then, I would have Polly take the glass, hold it a moment and lift it to her lips absently. She sips—the house watches. No—'tis bitter! She drops it as Macheath is led in. You follow?"

"Entirely. What thinks Mrs. Bishop?"

"Mr. Rich can't judge amiss, and Mrs. Fenton will add a new charm to the part."

She bowed to him sombre-eyed, and went out with a sliding curtsey to Polly as she past.

"My dear," says Mr. Rich, "I would not have you too familiar with Mrs. Bishop. She is a fine forthcoming actress and in some respects a worthy woman, but too free with gentlemen to be your companion. Is she kind with you?"

"Sir, she has never shown a desire for my companionship, nor have I intruded it. But I have no unkindness to complain of. If you ask for complaints—I wish 'twere possible to keep the dressing-rooms and the passages leading to them more private from young men of the town. I hate——"

"Why, so do I wish!— But what's to be done? It might provoke a riot and ruin the play was I to interfere, and remember also, Mrs. Fenton, 'tis only yourself that objects. Could you find even one of the women to second you?"

"I think not, to be honest, Sir."

"Well, then, be your own judge! What can I do?"

"I see, Sir," she answered and turned patiently away. Indeed she did not complain without reason, but might have borne the rest but for my Lord Baltimore, of whom she now almost dreamed, though not as he desired. Night after night she would see his face in the shadows of the way to her dressing-room, pale, handsome, with thin lips compressed and a look indescribable in his eyes—something that threatened yet implored and bided its time. He would speak occasionally as she past, though but of the play, or some gossip of the town—never of love. More often, he spoke not at all, merely bowed and waited outside till she was ready for her chair, and when she came out cloaked and hooded, she would see him still, standing in the shadows and watching her with white fixt face, and burning eyes.

The chair, lined with red velvet and bearing the Duchess's cypher, was ever in waiting at the stage entrance, and two footmen in her liveries handed the young lady in, and went on either side as the chairmen proceeded. There were times when she rejoiced to know herself guarded, remembering the fixt face that watched her.

Once she looked back in the moonlight and amidst the careless people in the street, still discerned him, standing with folded arms and staring after her. She drew her head in with a shudder and never lookt back again. It made the playhouse dreadful to her for all her triumph.

The next night, before her scene with Lucy Lockit she recalled Mr. Rich's request to the dark sullen creature waiting to go on.

"I thought him in the right, Mrs. Bishop, did not you?"

" 'Tis nothing to me either way. 'Tis your effect, not mine. But I can have no objections."

She said no more and moved off.

Diana ailed somewhat that evening. All day had her head ached and her pulses throbbed. Could she have been excused from the play she would gladly, but knowing Mr. Rich leaned on her, and her understudy, though a pretty girl and letter-perfect, by no means the true Polly, she forced herself to her part.

The play proceeded. At the due point Lucy tendered her the glass of wine—good claret, for Mr. Rich would have it so, and innocent as a child she put it to her lips and more than sipped, for she found herself faint and wearied. She swallowed a mouthful and then dropt the glass. It shattered on the ground and, putting her hand to her head, she sank sideways and fainted dead away. In an instant a gentleman seated on the stage flew to the rescue with Mr. Rich and they carried her between them behind the scenes—my Lord Baltimore! Indeed he almost lived at the play at this time and was as well known as Macheath himself to the audience. It gave rise to much gossip.

The understudy was immediately ready and the play proceeded amid the whispers and confusion of the audience,—while Diana was carried to Mr. Rich's parlour and there reclined in a chair. My Lord Baltimore stood beside her with Rich on the other side, her dresser hurrying for the apothecary.

"My Lord," says Rich while they waited assistance, "you were near Mrs. Fenton when she fell. Was there any accident, or how?"

"She drank but a mouthful of the wine and fell instantly—almost as though it had been poison. But that's impossible. And yet——"

Suddenly he ceased, with a look of horror.— Rich who knew the circumstances of the former amour as well as he, caught it and reflected it in his own face.

"Impossible," he repeated. "And yet—O, my Lord, a jealous woman,—Doubly jealous, of yourself and of Mrs. Fenton's triumph; is anything impossible? You play with fire—I dare assure you. I had not considered it fully before, but Mrs. Bishop is not one to trifle with. She has carried it all so quietly that my fears were never roused."

"If I thought this," my Lord said under his breath, "she should repent it the longest day she lived. But say nothing—nothing, Rich, as yet. We don't know. The wine was all spilt on the ground, the glass broke and no proof left. Mrs. Fenton appeared pale and languid at the opening. Say nothing yet, I warn you!"

They stood mute for a minute or two, she lying unconscious between them—Baltimore unable to consider the thing for the deadly fear that filled him, Rich in a tormenting anxiety on more counts than one. Presently the woman returning with the hurrying apothecary, the gentlemen were bid stand back and restoratives applied. They watched until her eyelids fluttered and then Rich approached his mouth to his companion's ear.

"My Lord, resent not my entreaty that you would withdraw before she has her senses. If she fears you——"

"Fear?" repeats my Lord haughtily. "Surely, Rich, you don't need to be told that a woman fears most where she loves most, especially in such a case as hers and mine. There's a perfect understanding between Mrs. Fenton and myself though she conceals it. I have the right to be here."

"If that's so——" says Rich hesitating. He knew not enough to disbelieve, and Polly might be as deep as others for aught he could tell.

"*If?*" says the other, and laid his hand on his sword. Rich stared, and at that moment the apothecary called him softly, and he went to him, Lord Baltimore drawing back into the darkest corner of the room.

"Sir, Mrs. Fenton recovers. Oblige me with particulars that the treatment may be answerable. I should judge she had partaken of something unwholesome."

From the shadow Lord Baltimore put his finger on his lip and Rich observed the gesture.

"Why as to that," says he, "I can't throw much light, Mr. Meynell. The lady was unwell when she came to play and she fainted dead away in the prison scene. I hope 'tis a trifle."

"Tomorrow will declare more, Sir. She has youth and a fine constitution. If agreeable to you, Mrs. Jones and myself will convey her to the care of her friends. 'Tis certain she can't play tomorrow or possibly the day after."

She lay, conscious at last, but with closed eyes and as if too heavy for speech while the arrangements were making. Rich stooped over her and took her hand and she returned the kindness with a faint pressure.

"I'll play tomorrow, fear not!" she said in a little breath, and he with cordial warmth:

"My dear, am I a brute? Rest all you will and need. I'd sooner bilk the play than hurt my good Polly."

He supported her out with the apothecary, the woman following and she had never glanced my Lord Baltimore's way. Indeed 'twas as much as she could do to reach the coach. Presently Rich returned, the other standing moodily with a downcast eye where he left him.

"My Lord," says he, "I know not the rights of this matter. 'Tis beyond my sounding, but this I say candidly. I shall never know ease of mind while Mrs. Bishop is in the cast with Mrs. Fenton. If what you say is true of the relations between you and Mrs. Fenton I am the more uneasy. 'Tis very possible we have escaped a frightful calamity, and 'twould not be the first of the kind. 'Tis not so very long since in "The Rival Queens" that Mrs. Barry stabbed Mrs. Boutel on the stage, and had all but done for her—the audience suspecting nothing. I'll have no Rival Queens here. This is the last night Bishop plays for me."

My Lord avoided his eye.

"I can't say but you are right, though it be painful for me to injure a woman specially one where I'm not entirely conscience-clear. At the same time we may suspect far too much—'tis probable we do. And I am to request, Mr. Rich, that you will be generous in your terms with Mrs. Bishop, for which I will be at the cost. We may be unjust in the one matter. Let us not in the other."

Mr. Rich agreed, then in a hesitating manner he added—

"My Lord, you have condescended to honour me with your company at the playhouse for many a day. May I in return ask a favour?"

"Ask, man, and have, if it be possible."

"Well—'tis this. Your presence here so often disturbs the women. I am the last to meddle with a gentleman's amours, but there are times and places to be observed, and this has made much talk. Need I say more?"

Baltimore frowned on the hint, then cleared his brow.

"I take you, Sir. I think your application reasonable. I will attend once weekly or less. Fear not that any affair between me and Mrs. Fenton shall disturb your arrangements. She is loyal to you, and her wish is my command. May I in return request to be present unseen when you dismiss Mrs. Bishop. I desire to know the truth as a safeguard."

Mr. Rich agreed, motioning to the deep closet behind his scrutoire, and went off, his Lordship remaining behind him in deep thought.

So he remained until the noise of plaudits and then the departing audience could be heard, and presently the players began to stream past the door on their way to becoming sober citizens once more. Lord Baltimore stepped within the closet and drew the door to a crack as Rich's voice approached together with the swish of a hoop.

"Be seated, Madam," says Rich, pushing a chair to her when the door was shut behind them. "I have a matter of business to settle with you."

"Sir, your most obedient."

My Lord could see her from where he stood. She sat pale, heavy-jawed, handsome, her eye on Mr. Rich with a furtive watchfulness, her hands strongly claspt in one another.

"I regret to say, Madam, that we must part. Henceforth Lucy Lockit will be played by Mrs. Parker."

She sprang to her feet.

"Sir, my contract——"

"Madam, you'll find your contract does not cover such extras as your attack upon Mrs. Fenton. Beware lest you lay yourself open to such a charge as may make Newgate a reality to you instead of a play. I desire not to be more particular in an affair that may ruin you, especially as I judge it may have no serious effect. But I will risk nothing more."

Mr. Rich's manner was perfect, calm, judicial, severe. Mrs. Bishop's was equally so in its way. She was all injured innocence in a moment.

"Sir, I am entitled to ask for the charge. Hath Mrs. Fenton declared me culpable in any matter? Am I liable because she swoons? Mrs. Allen did it a week since and no to-do made!"

"Madam, I charge you with tampering with the wine Mrs. Fenton drunk on the stage tonight. I charge you with a dangerous jealousy of that lady which may lead to trouble. And because I will avert such trouble I bid you begone. Your money affairs shall be handsomely treated with. I counsel you to avoid such talk and noise as may damage you beyond repair and to go quietly."

"It would ill beseem me to risk my character in a place where such odious accusations can be made against an innocent woman," she cried furiously, clutching the arm of her chair as though 'twere Mr. Rich's throat. Baltimore could see the knuckles stand out white as chalk. "So I'll go. I have no protector. But I know who's at the back of this business. My Lord Baltimore helped to carry off the fainting angel. He's her lover, Mr. Rich, her lover (a slow smile parted my Lord's lips), and I leave you to judge how that will affect your interests before many days are out. That's the mainspring of it all, and I, forsooth, must be got out of the way because beneath a prude's face she carries a courtesan's behaviour."

Mrs. Bishop used a plainer word. She paused not, but flashed on.

"You may heed me little, Sir, because you, like others, was aware of my Lord Baltimore's relation to me. I care not, 'tis the truth. I own it painful to be supplanted and by so arrant a jilt. Therefore I go with pleasure. As to poison—for I suppose that's your meaning, I snap my fingers at so low a charge—so very much beneath me! you can't prove it, Sir, and there's a law of libel if you make the assertion."

"Madam," says Mr. Rich serenely, "I propose to let sleeping dogs lie, and you will do well to follow my example. I would recommend you on parting to keep your opinion on Mrs. Fenton to yourself. She has powerful protectors. Tomorrow, all money matters outstanding shall meet with due settlement. I have now the honour to bid you farewell."

He rose and bowed. She curtseyed, in a black suppress rage and moved towards the door. There it broke out in one fierce sentence flung at him—

"Look out for your favourite, Mr. Rich. I will have my revenge if I swing for it. And when the time comes, blame yourself and his Lordship. Not me.— Judas!"

She shot out of the room and flung the door to behind her, and her steps were heard along the passage. A moment, and his Lordship emerged, dusting his velvet cuffs with a laced handkerchief.

"What's the verdict, Sir? Guilty or not Guilty? In either case you carried it perfectly."

"I declare I know not!" replied Rich, with an anxious brow—"But I doubt we've seen the last of her yet. A violent dangerous woman. Look out, my Lord, and for Miss Polly too."

"A notable temper indeed. But I think myself not inexperienced with that charming sex, and I judge this a woman's violence come and gone like a cat's-paw. Good-night, Rich. You need be at no charges in the matter."

He departed with his usual easy grace, and Mr. Rich left alone, stared into the fire much perplexed.

"Damme if I understand the business!" he muttered to himself. "My Lord swears and Bishop subscribes, yet I would take the innocency of Miss Polly's face before them both. I think she's an honest girl in spite of them. But who shall say where a woman's concerned. 'Tis beyond me. Lord send she's on the mend tomorrow, be it as it will. Yet I think the jewels I have in charge to be his after all. Curse the women, and the men that won't let them be!"

# CHAPTER XI

FROM Miss Polly's troubles to Madam Diana's is but a step and not a long one.

She was took back in a coach to Queensbury House, and the Duchess being at Court heard nothing of the affair until next day, and then sent very obliging inquiries.

The girl lay very heavy and ailing all that day, not well able either to control nor examine the thoughts that roamed through her brain. She would have sent for her mother but Mr. Rich, on his guard against any attempts of Mr. Fenton's to make his profit out of Miss Polly, had advanced money to get him out of the coffee house, and put him in a fair way to pay his debt upon it, provided he would retire to the suburbs. Mrs. Fenton willing to be clear of the temptations of the town for her husband joyfully seconded him, and at present they had a lodging at Gravesend.

So 'twas a stranger who watched with Diana, and this gave her time to resolve on silence as to her suspicion of Mrs. Bishop though her terror of the woman was such as she knew not how to face the meeting with her. 'Twas a sensible relief when a missive from Mr. Rich bid her have no uneasiness about her part until she should be quite recovered, adding in a careless postscript that Mrs. Bishop on a better proposal had left him at short notice and Mrs. Parker would be answerable for Lucy Lockit.

"And let me beg my admired Miss Polly," concluded he—"to take the necessary rest and return to us in the bloom and beauty she alone is possest of in such abundance."

'Twas very kind and she was sensible of it and sent an obliging message in return. That day she past in solitude but for her attendant, feeling her strength revive at every moment, and the next morning was able to rise and walk about her room, but still unvisited. She received the Duchess's commands to attend her in the library in the evening of the next day. She could scarce believe so short a time could so have changed her looks when she saw herself in the glass before proceeding thither.

Pale and with purple shadows beneath the eyes, the dark hair piled about her face made it appear as though carved in ivory, and even the fresh coral of her mouth was faded. The white muslin folds of her *negligée* without a hoop fell loose and flowing about her and outlined her graceful limbs and bosom with an elegance which even she herself might at another time admire though now too wearied to give a thought to her looks. A tender and moving figure.

So she went slowly to the library, and, the door opening, was surprised to see her Grace magnificent in a white satin gown embroidered in silver, the petticoat covered with a trimming answerable, and a necklace of rubies like roses about her glorious throat. Lovely as when Prior wrote of her—

"Fondness prevailed, mamma gave way,
Kitty at heart's desire,
Obtained Love's chariot for a day
And set the world afire."

She swam forward to meet Diana and touched her kindly on the shoulder, motioning her to a chair.

"I would see with my own eyes how Miss Polly does," says she. "I was full of regrets to hear of so unfortunate an accident and was it not that the apothecary enjoined quiet, I had gone yesterday to enquire in person for Mrs. Diana. But my woman and your own obliging message reassured me."

"I thank your Grace," says Diana with the tears of weakness welling to her eyes, "and am your bounden servant to my life's end in gratitude for this and all your other immeasurable favours. If I could think I should live to testify it better than in words——"

"My dear, you repay me double in the satisfaction and pleasure you have bestowed on my good Mr. Gay and myself, and the delight your charming air must carry wherever 'tis known. This evening I receive company in the gold and white drawing-room and must leave you, but before I go would ask privately between you and me—have you any suspicions that there was any foul play with you that you dropt so sudden after drinking the wine from Lucy's hand?"

"Madam, to you I can tell my heart. I know not—how should I—but indeed that woman terrifies me beyond measure, though I can't believe that a mere stage jealousy could carry her to so fearful a length, and other grudge against me she has none."

"How know you that?" cries the Duchess with one of her bright rapid flashes. "Let me tell you, Mrs. Di, that I know better, and though I may not be more particular (for reasons) I entreat you to avoid all men at the playhouse, and keep yourself very secluded there. I had a word with Mr. Rich to that effect, and can assure you he thinks as I do. There's a better fate for you, Mrs. Di, than to be a playhouse trull, and since you are none by nature, close every approach that may make you one by force or persuasion."

Diana all but slid from her chair on her knees before the radiant figure that towered over her in so majestic a height.

"Madam—Your Grace, my heart beats responsive to every one of your words. I'm beset and persecuted at the playhouse, though not so much of late. And Mr. Rich himself is all goodness, but what can he do? Sure the place swarms with bold young men—so audacious as your Grace can scarce believe. Indeed, when the run of the piece is over I would give all but my life to retire from the stage and play no more. I hate the playhouse."

Now this did not suit the Duchess neither, for 'tis to be remembered, she desired the girl for the Polly of Mr. Gay's succeeding piece. She might not have said so much had she known the bitterness in her heart. She pulled a chair for herself.

"Mrs. Di, you make me bold to ask—Have you any other living than the stage?"

"None, Madam. So I see not how to leave it, yet loathe my living. And yet—the stage itself—the joy and delight to sing, to act—to attract kind looks and sunshiny smiles—how beautiful, were it not for the bad men and women that make it a torment!"

"My dear," says the Duchess, touched by this simple grief, "you are a good girl. So continue and fear not. You have powerful protection. If I say it of myself I say true, and I will add that his Grace the Duke of Bolton is, after his haughty fashion, your sworn knight. Mr. Gay also, and in the playhouse Mr. Rich is a kindly watch-dog. And I could name more. Whatever life you might choose there would be dangers and displeasures with your figure and lack of fortune,—and you would not there have the protection you have now. Be of good courage—and dispense not with the utmost prudence and I predict a shining future. And now must I go, but will return in an hour to see you for a moment."

She extended her hand graciously and Diana kissed it. She knew the words were truth. Then watching until the great lady swept out of the doors, she took a book of prints from Mr. Hogarth's pictures and supporting them on a table began to look them through. And time went by.

Meanwhile in the white and gold drawing-room lit up with the magnificent lustres and hundreds of wax candles, a minuet was dancing by fair ladies and four gallant gentlemen, and the rest sat by to see, the Duchess a little apart with the Lady Fanny Armine. 'Twas a scene from some exquisite French pastoral in delicate rose and blue—the ladies like Watteau shepherdesses in high-drest hair garlanded with wreaths of little roses on one side and hooped skirts disclosing miracles of small feet beneath them—the beaux, magnificent Damons and Celadons in pink and violet satin coats and breeches. The couples passed and re-passed, bowing, smiling, garlanded heads held high, swords, fans, all playing their parts in the pretty measure, a scene of grace and high breeding indescribable, and fitly set in the noble rooms.

"Fops! Fools!" said the Duchess suddenly—half laughing, half melancholy. "What a world do we live in, Fanny! Is there a touch of truth or reality in it all? See my Lord Govan there—you and I know his history. Should he be in any decent woman's house? Yet there he smirks and struts! See my Lady Deloraine. Is there a fish-fag in St. Giles's with a tongue as foul as hers? Shall I tell you the story of her speech with his Majesty at the last basset party at Kensington Palace?"

"You don't need! Sure I have nothing here to wash my ears with! After half an hour of Lady Deloraine I go home and make the attempt, but all the perfumes of Araby won't sweeten them. But is there none you can say a better word for? Look yonder, your Grace."

She motioned with her head to a corner where the Duke of Bolton sat in earnest talk with Lord Hervey—the Queen's faithful attendant—a pale handsome man, most sumptuously drest.

"Lord Hervey?" asked the Duchess. "No—I meant not him, though I think him a devoted servant. 'Tis Bolton you would say. A great and gallant gentleman, and not a day passes but I swear at Fortune that tied him to that toad of a woman and he scarce more than a child when 'twas done. You also respect him, Fanny? I like you the better for it."

"I love him," says the lady, softly beating time with her fan to the music.

"As how?" the Duchess swept one of her rapier glances at her.

"As I need not be ashamed to tell you nor all the world, Madam. As a true friend—faithful and kind. If I could see Bolton content and happy with a deserving woman I'd mark the day with a white stone in my calendar."

"Why, so would I! I did not think any woman but myself had plumbed his deeps. I sometimes think that excepting my poor Queensbury, he's the only man I know that in this gross age hath any respect or tenderness for women. Fanny, I knew one like him when I was a child—I have sat on his knee! And when I was a girl of fourteen I would tell Mary Granville and all my cousins, "I have seen the man I would marry, and if he'll wait two years more I'm at his service. I have not since seen his like—unless 'tis Bolton."

"Who was he, Kitty?" says Lady Fanny softly.

"Colonel Harry Esmond—and 'tis a long story, too long for a minuet. But he was the true Marquis of Esmond and—No, the story's too long. But the man himself—I dreamt of him as a girl. Dark, noble, with manners that did but reflect his mind, wise but with a kind of gentle humour that played upon the surface as sunlight upon the sea. Tender, and courteous to all women, young or old, high upon the point of honour, brave, proud so that none dare take a liberty with him more than with the King at his coronation.— O Fanny—there was none like him! He went to the American colonies—I think 'twas Virginia,—in 1715—but I treasure a little letter I had once from him and when I think of truth and honour I think of Colonel Esmond, who was old enough almost to be my father though I worshipt him as a girl does and forget him never."

Her beautiful eyes grew large and dark with thought. The minuet,—the white and gold walls lifted and dispersed like dreams. She saw the hero of her youth— Had he waited, had he understood, she had perhaps had a different life. So she dreamt, foolishly and fondly as women will.

Lady Fanny's voice recalled her.

"I saw him once," she said. "The Carterets knew him well. But I was too young. Duchess, in talking t'other day with Bolton I said I wished he might find a woman with all the virtues and graces that should fill his sore and lonely heart. Was I wrong? Do you blame me to turn an advocate for—what shall I call it?"

"Why, Fanny,"—says her Grace, with a shining smile—"How should I blame you? What choice has a man in Bolton's case? Either he must take the vile pleasures of the town, or sink into a soured loneliness, or make a home with some woman kind and tender that will keep youth and joy green in him. Can I trust you, Fanny—if I say something in my mind? I don't speak idly, as you know."

"You can trust me. I tell you I love Bolton—and—I don't wholly hate your Grace!" says Lady Fanny, smiling also. She stretched her hand behind her painted fan, and the Duchess quickly claspt and dropt it. Little did the Duke know what those fair creatures plotted as he glanced their way idly. How should he? But indeed like all men of his sort he had a great faith in the sex and was very amenable to the guidance of the good among them though he did not know this himself.

The fine couples past and re-past in their minuet, and the Duchess sunk her voice to a thread.

"Fanny, when you came in long since with my Lord—let us say Bas—you came very inconvenient, and I nearly tiffed with you that day. I wanted you gone."

"Didn't I see it? Didn't I go?"

"Yes, to both! I never knew you fail in tact and breeding. Well—was you surprised that day at my company?"

"Astonished. I could make neither head nor tail of it, and still less when I saw her on the stage as Polly. Lord, what could I think but that 'twas one of the Kitty escapades, and that her Grace was eclipsed in Kitty for the moment?"

"Kitty's not a bad sort neither when you know her," says the Duchess laughing. "At all events she has a certain method in her madness. Well, but to return. Fanny, I bid you disengage yourself from this mob for a moment and find your way to the library. There you shall find the woman I destine for Bolton. And, as you love him, so I bid you treat her. Now I can't talk with you longer. The minuet is all but over, I trust you, your Ladyship, and you shall be my helper if you will, though the Church will not bless our enterprise."

She glided off to receive a new entry of guests and Lady Fanny sat amazed. As yet the matter was not clear in her mind. She did not know whom to expect, nor what might be the Duchess's intention. But the curiosity of a true woman built on the foundation of her friendship for Bolton and the Duchess, made every minute seem an eternity to her as she gradually slid towards the door, dropping a word here and there to the gay groups she past, but permitting none to detain her. Lord preserve us! What could be the meaning?

So it came to pass that Diana, turning the leaves of her book slowly, heard a faint sound as one great wing of the carved door opened sufficient to admit a strange but shining lady, fair as a rose in her pink damask gown with stiff pointed waist and cut so low as to disclose a lovely bosom beneath a long throat with a black velvet ribbon tied about it and loops of pearls that were less white. So singularly clear against the dark doors, she might almost have appeared a celestial visitant were it not that angelic beings are allowed to be less modish in the pictures wherewith the artists favour us. Her ladyship's beauty was more on the sparkling order than the pensive and religious. She came gliding up to Diana with an easiness and grace all her own, and dropt the prettiest little curtsey;—nothing formal nor alarming, it exprest the friendliness it intended. Diana rose and curtseyed also, smiling, as it were, involuntary as she might at a child, a rose, a bird.

"Madam," says the newcomer, "I am commanded by the Duchess— Lord, 'tis Polly!"

The fine speech fluttered off into silence and Madam stood staring at the girl, with thoughts whirling like a windmill in her head.

Bas;—this was the woman. Then she must hate her. But no! Bolton vouched for her purity, for her terror of his pursuit. Then she should love her, if she could forgive her unhappy attraction for him. But a slut of a

Polly—in a Newgate rabble? Then she must despise her! But a girl like a lily—delicate and a gentlewoman, then sure she must admire her. Indeed 'twas a dance of contradictions in her head that turned Lady Fanny herself pale for a moment as she stared at her rival. Then, masking herself in her armour of high breeding, she sank easily into a seat, every sense on the alert,—every glance a weapon, every smile a shield, beneath the face that exprest a careless languor and pleasure.

Diana, fearing nothing, knowing nothing, and therefore the stronger of the two, awaited her Ladyship's pleasure. Sure all that came from the Duchess must be good.

"I knew, Madam, you were staying with her Grace but did not recall it at the moment. 'Tis indeed a distinction to meet in private the lady whom all the town adores. But I trust I see you recovered; for in common with all the world I knew you ailed. I hope a mere nothing."

"Nothing, Madam. I thank your obliging concern. I hope to resume my part tomorrow. 'Tis condescending in you to quit the company yonder to visit me."

There is no mistaking the tone and air of a gentlewoman. The girl possest these and my Lady Fanny noted it half angry. How dare she bear the mark of a class that should not be hers. And then her charming face so delicate and pensive. My Lady had seen her more than once on the stage, all winsome, pleading, sparkling, singing with voice angelic. She had hated her then, had watched her with a viperish jealousy. This pale girl in her flowing draperies did not resemble Miss Polly. 'Twas impossible to see her in the mind's eye with Macheath and his company. Sure that must be a dream and this the reality.

" 'Twas by her Grace's command I came to make your acquaintance, and my own inclination seconded it. If I speak as a friend—are you happy in your profession? You appear very young."

"I shall be nineteen before very long, Madam. Yes—I thank you—I am happy, though I must own that it has disadvantages not known across the footlights. But her Grace's goodness has smoothed my way. She is a wonderful lady."

"You say true. She has a heart as great as her face is beautiful, and knows not fear."

"O happy!" sighs Diana, "I would I were not afraid. But her Grace teaches me courage."

"You have met company here?"

"Very few, Madam. Mr. Gay, Mrs. Pendarves, Lady Granville. I think no more."

"You have not then met his Grace the Duke of Bolton?"

You'll allow 'twas searching, since the fair actress evaded the name. Lady Fanny's keen observation marked the change in her face,—a shade of reserve—a something difficult to record in speech.

"I have had that honour, Madam."

"He is a friend of mine also. A gentleman kind and noble in all his thoughts. His life more melancholy than his goodness deserves."

There was no reply, but my Lady knew she had a listener.

"You have heard the story of his marriage?"

"Save that he is married I have heard nothing, Madam."

"A singular case. You may turn the story into a play and act in it one day, Mrs. Fenton, but the lady concerned does not resemble you. At the age of fourteen his Grace was contracted by his father and hers to his distant cousin the daughter of the Earl of Carberry—a young lady of nineteen. He had not so much as seen her, and was then at school. Two years later he was sent to make the Grand Tour, and at the age of eighteen was recalled to marry,—she then being twenty-three. When he saw her he entreated his father to release him— You will not wonder if ever you see and know her Grace. He threatened to shoot himself sooner than marry her. At last he flatly refused. Finally my Lord Carberry waited upon him and told him that the best years of her life were gone waiting for him, that she was homely, had no fortune, that her only recommendation was her relationship to the Poulet family (his Grace's), that, in short 'twould be her ruin if he refused her now. Can you guess his reply?"

"Yes,—for I know the Duke," says Diana, lifting her head, her great eyes fixed like stars on my Lady. "He would say—'She shall not suffer for me.' "

"Exactly. I see you know him. He made it plain to her father that 'twould be a ceremony and no more. And so he carried the matter through but never lived with her."

Silence. My Lady proceeded.

"Later, when his father died 'twas known that had his Grace acted then it would have been possible to carry a bill through the House of Lords to dissolve the marriage. 'Twas known also that his Majesty the last King was favourable. His Grace was warned that 'twas then or never. He replied that the poor lady had never offended him, that she was his wife and to cast her off would be a dastardly action. So the chance past never to return. He has now been married sixteen years."

Silence still. Again my Lady Fanny spoke.

"Thus he has condemned himself to a life of misery lest another should suffer. I know not any man else who would do the like. Do you, Mrs. Fenton?"

A voice so low as scarcely to be heard——

"Madam, I know not any man who would do the like. I did not know such a man could be."

No more was said on that head. My Lady Fanny drifted the talk to Mr. Gay, to Diana's early days, and finally rose to leave her, satisfied that she had done her part. She said a cordial farewell and made for the door, smiling and waving her hand as it closed upon her. The grace of her manner was charming. Diana, who need envy none, envied that bright and harmless glitter like summer lightning in July.

But the smile fell from my Lady's face as she paused a minute in the ante-room to collect herself. So that was her rival. Surely an innocent one—surely trembling on the verge of an interest in Bolton, if not already over it. Yet who could tell? If she could but be certain!—If the girl were bound hand and heart to Bolton, might not Baltimore return to his old allegiance?

Who shall blame her if in speeding the Duchess's plot, she helped her own cause also. She was at that time neither wholly selfish nor unselfish, neither true nor false, half hating, half liking the girl, swayed with every thought that crost her brain. It takes a woman and a passionate one to be thus complicate, and 'tis impossible a man should write her thoughts. 'Tis much if he can record her deeds.

She looked at herself in a long glass that could not flatter the charming truth, and set a curl to advantage and re-looped the pearls. Then, going softly through the corridor, she entered the great drawing-room making as though to pass by Bolton at the door.

"I thought your Ladyship was gone on to the masquerade," says he. She smiled at him over her shoulder.

"No indeed, your Grace. 'Twas a work of charity. I sat awhile with Mrs. Fenton in the library."

She went lightly on. Presently he past out.

# CHAPTER XII

DIANA still bound by the Duchess's command sat where my Lady Fanny left her, her mind full of what had passed. So that was the story. 'Twas a chivalrous one to take a girl's fancy, it must be owned, and none the less if her fancy were already engaged by his chivalry to her. How he must suffer? Can such a woman hear of suffering without the desire to soothe it? She might well estimate the consolation of rank, wealth, health, youth at too low a worth in considering the trouble that obscured them all. But what indeed could she guess of a life that moved on an orbit so high above her own? This, she told herself and though her mind asserted it, her heart denied it, saying—"You comprehend him. And he you."

And even as she thought thus, he stood beside her. The door had unclosed so softly that she did not hear aught, nor yet the light step on the velvet piled carpet. She turned suddenly and her heart's sensibility rushed in a betraying wave of crimson to her pale face. But this he did not see.

She, woman-like, saw everything; his manly courageous bearing, his head held high, the splendour of dress, and the blue ribbon that crost his breast and exprest royal favour. It almost made her heart to die within her, so far apart it set him. What, save in the way of dishonour, could so great a prince have to do with a girl whose profession was the next thing to a woman of the town's,—to act, to simper, to win, attract and simulate. Perhaps, she thought with bitterness, that was why nearly all of them went the way they did—the step between the two being so narrow.

He bowed as he might to her Grace.

"Do I see Mrs. Fenton better? And may I have the happiness to call her by her true name, and hope that Mrs. Beswick's her charming self again? The Duchess has been in great concern and Mr. Gay well-nigh distracted. Not to speak of the whole town bereft of its idol."

"My Lord Duke, I thank your Grace, I am quite recovered. Tomorrow I return to my part. I would that you or any one could tell me how to express to her Grace my grateful heart for her unending goodness.'

"She is very little known even in her own world," says the Duke, leaning against the table, "for she is called cold, variable, proud, whereas I have never known her forget a friend or weary in a kindness. But I think in your case, Madam, it came very natural to her. This, however, is not what I would say. Mr. Gay hath brought a rumour from the playhouse that hath seriously disquieted him and all your friends. May I name it?"

She fluttered and bowed, pressing her handkerchief against her lips. Could it be of Lord Baltimore?

"Madam, the report is—but Mr. Rich said he knew nothing of it—that in a storm of jealousy the woman Bishop who plays Lucy hocussed your wine, and that you had an escape of your life. Certainly her dismissal gives some colour to this."

"Sir, I don't know!" cries Diana eagerly.— "But sure it can't be possible. I know her to be jealous of my success, but that's a poor reason for murdering a woman, and she has no other."

"Has she not?" he said, looking gravely down upon her. "You walk in the midst of perils and see them not. Mrs. Bishop has a reason far deeper than the one you name, and though I can't tell, I imagine this is why Mr. Rich hath dismist her. Be open with me, Mrs. Fenton. I am your friend."

"I know it—don't I rejoice in it? But I know nothing more. I think—I believe the wine was tampered with, but am not certain and may do her a fearful injustice. Mr. Rich tells me she left on a better proposal. And I know of no reason whatever for her hate."

There was a long hush, Bolton debating within himself whether he should or should not enlighten her ignorance. Would she walk the safer for the knowledge? At last, with a sigh, he broke the silence.

"Mrs. Beswick, I would you were done with the playhouse. You have won your laurels—I would you could rest on them. 'Tis no place for you. Do you love it very dearly?"

"I hate it!" she cries, with tears. "But what shall I do? 'Tis my living, and not only so but 'tis as natural to me to sing as to speak.— And further, her Grace and Mr. Gay talk of nothing but the new 'Polly' and my part in it, and how could I forsake them?"

"Will you permit a word of counsel from one who is your friend?"

"O most willingly and gratefully. I have none to counsel me in all the wide world. I have not a relation but my mother and she not in London now."

"Then, Mrs. Beswick, it can't but be that you have many offers of marriage. I hear of hearts by the dozen at your feet. I counsel you to take some good man for a husband and leave the stage for those who have a very different inclination from yours."

It stung her unbearably—somehow 'twas the last thing she expected. He was now pacing up and down, as if restless and disturbed, and as he came near her again in his turn, she commanded her voice sufficiently to answer:

"Sir, shall I tell you how many offers of marriage I have had? Not one. The other offers are beyond reckoning, but of these I need not speak. What then shall I do?"

He stood still, looking upon her in a kind of amaze.

"What—so much beauty and sweetness of mind and body, and not one to claim it for his own? My God, what are we men come to! Is't credible!"

"It is true. I might marry a man below me possibly,—but I was born a gentlewoman. The men above me, or my equals, will not marry me."

He took a few more turns, looking down. Then turned again.

"Child, I can't express the pity and interest I feel in you. 'Tis beyond words. You know me a friend. May I act as one?"

"If in any way possible to me I thank your Grace with a full heart."

"Thus then it is. I am a rich man—even burdened by possessions. If you would prove to me that friendship is possible between man and woman, permit me to place a yearly sum at your disposal, and to persuade you to leave this business that will be your misery and ruin. None but you and me shall know the matter. Let me do it as for my sister."

She looked up at him with a sweet kindness of gratitude, that expressed itself very sensibly in her face.

"Your Grace, 'tis very like yourself to propose this, and if I could accept it from any 'twould be from you. But I can't. What would the world say to see me living in comfort and not a stroke of work to show for it? My character would be sunk beyond hope. I thank you deeply, but must refuse."

He broke out into a kind of passion.

"Then I won't rest night or day but I will think of a way. Curse me, if I don't! What, shall a man see a woman's life spoilt—a woman too he honours and—regards, and stand by idle? I say no more now. I bide my time. Madam, you are all sweetness and goodness. You know not what is in my heart. You know not——"

He stopt as if distracted, looking at her. Then turned swiftly and went away, passing the Duchess at the door as though he saw her not. Her quick eyes observed, her quick brain drew its own conclusion as she closed the door behind her.

"Come, Mrs. Di, I was detained, and you should have been asleep long ere this. You have had visitors, child?"

"Two, your Grace." Diana furtively dashed the tears from her eyes. "May I ask who was the lovely lady that came on your command and spoke so kind.

"My Lady Fanny Armine—a beauty and toast; she is an old friend of mine, if so young a beauty may be called old in any sense. I would have you believe her a friend. She is to be trusted. And now to bed. Your work begins tomorrow and you must wake fresh as a lark."

She went obedient, and the fair Kitty returned to her guests, and was the shining centre of them all. His Grace of Bolton had slipt away, and my Lady Fanny in bidding her farewell whispered:

"Kitty, I'm with you heart and soul. The girl is as fresh and honest as a lily in a cottage garden. May the plot prosper! Do we do right or wrong? I declare I can't tell which, but will follow where you lead."

"We do wrong—very wrong in the letter of the law," the tall Duchess answered, looking down upon her, "but considering each so friendless—she by her profession and her nature, Bolton by his most miserable marriage, I think we may take what guilt there is on our shoulders if we throw them together. The world has a hard name for what we do, but I value not the world's judgment. Good-night, Fanny, and sleep with an easy conscience."

My Lady Fanny did not however sleep as well as could be wished. Her heart was away with one who had forgot her. Her thoughts worked restlessly, considering whether if deprived of his idol he might not turn again to her. She could not force herself to believe her image so utterly effaced—what woman can credit that she who once was All is now nothing?

---

Mrs. Bishop, in her lodging in Soho could scarce believe it neither. Since we are privileged to look into her mind and read in that chaste book it may be said that she had no notion to murder her rival, but merely to cause her such suffering as might perhaps injure her voice and disable her for her part during the rest of the run which sure could not be so far distant,—the success already having out-reached all expectation. Therefore none was more alarmed than this lady when Diana fainted and fell so sudden on the drinking. She had not observed her to be ailing already, or had deferred the experiment.

Now she sat, sullen, raging inwardly in such a room as may be seen in Mr. Hogarth's earlier pictures of the Harlot's Progress. 'Twas not beautiful nor desirable, yet well enough if the lady had brought content to it. She did not, however; her mind was all of a turmoil, and on the money side as well as the sentimental. For having lost her engagement with Mr. Rich she could not for the life of her tell how to procure another. He must of course be aware that the Lucy who succeeded her played the part very flat in comparison with herself. Perhaps she had not the spite, rage and jealousy to wing her words which seethed in Mrs. Bishop's bosom, but the town did not taste her so well and Mr. Rich knew it. Mr. Gay also. But yet she was dismist, and must stomach the knowledge that they could do without her.

The rain was falling outside in a muddy blur of London weather, and the women, between a mixture of gay and slatternly, that filled the neighbourhood, were hurrying home with draggled tails, when she heard a manly step outside her door, and a resounding knock.

"Come in!" she cries shrilly, adjusting her cap in the glass, and kicking a tawdry petticoat under the table with one swift motion.

"How can I when the door's locked?" cries a masculine voice outside. "Are you besieged, Mrs. Bishop, that you bolt yourself in?"

She guessed the voice and ran to the door, knowing it meant news like a cup of water to her thirsty soul, and throwing it wide, Macheath himself, Mr. Walker, marched in, a little ripe in liquor.

"A sight for sore eyes," cries she overjoyed, "come hither by the fire. The chair isn't damask but 'tis comfortable. And now stay!—the kettle boils. I have a drop of right usquebaugh, and a hot cup of comfort will do my Mr. Walker good this dreary weather."

She bustled about as she spoke, and he stretched out his long legs watching her. She was a handsome buxom woman, and it pleased him to see her minister to his comfort and her own, for she filled two glasses and they steamed very pleasant in the glow of the fire. She put a cushion behind his head and spared nothing to please him, not even drawing back when he cried:

"How many thousand of stage kisses have I not had from my Lucy? Why not one for friendship's sake and to sweeten the glass?"

He flung a careless arm about her and she bestowed the kiss laughing, then pulled up a lower chair beside the one where the Sultan sat enthroned.

"Well—how goes all at the playhouse, Macheath? Am I missed?"

"Why, yes," says he stirring his glass, "Mrs. Parker is as flat as a flounder. I don't say but what she has her merits in other parts. I have known her a passable Cherry, a decent Lucy in "The Recruiting Officer," and she wasn't a contemptible Parley. But Polly escapes her. Instead of glaring at my bride as though she could tear her limbless on the spot, she simpers and pouts at her.— No, 'twon't do by any means, and Rich knows it as well as I."

"What? Has he said anything?"

"Nothing. But don't we know our Rich? He looks at her furiously sometimes, then holds his tongue as if afraid to go too far and leave himself without even e'er a Lucy at all. That won't do neither, you know, Mrs. Bishop."

"Would he be glad to see me back, think you?"

"Why, yes and no. I should judge that Miss Polly doesn't like you, saving your presence, and Miss Polly's word is law in the playhouse, and so it ought! You won't come back while she's there, Madam."

"And I know," says Mrs. Bishop sadly, "that yourself values her as high as Mr. Rich. Alas! I have no one to take my part."

" 'Tis known to all the world that I love Mrs. Fenton, on this side marriage however, as much as any man may! 'Tis the sweetest, softest, most delicate little beauty that ever nestled up to a man on the stage. No offence to you, Mrs. Bishop. I don't undervalue your fine eyes, and if you've another kiss to bestow 'tis as welcome here as flowers in May."

'Twas bestowed and gallantly received.

"Let us toast your inamorata!" says the lady raising her glass. "Here's to the beauteous Mrs. Fenton and her success. But why won't you marry her, Mr. Walker? Sure no woman could despise a man whose handsome leg bears out his handsome face, and with a voice to charm the bird off a bough. Indeed I've seen Mrs. Fenton look at you so soft, so languishing——"

"Have you so? But alas! 'twas all in the part. I value not languishing looks that are shown off to the public for a weekly salary."

"No—no. But off the stage. In private."

"Well, 'tis more than I've seen myself, and her words are as nipping as a January day."

"You're too modest," says the lady. "You underestimate your person and qualities. Why not marry her?"

"Because— Have you another glass of the stuff, my dear? 'Tis main good, and goes like fire through the veins. I thank you. Well, because—I'm married already."

"Gemini! You astound me. And when, where, and how?"

"Years since when I was playing in Durham. I won't have her trouble me, and she keeps away—but here am I,—noosed, hanged, done for. Were't not for that curst blunder I might marry a fortune."

Mrs. Bishop mused a little on this bit of news. 'Twas to be considered how it might affect her views. He continued:

"If 'twere not so I had offered myself long since to the lady. Indeed she has a melting eye."

"For Mr. Walker. Not for another," corrected Mrs. Bishop. "I speak by the book, for I heard her tell Mr. Rich you was the perfect lover."

"Others have thought so also." Again he stirred his glass reflective, and threw up his head, expanding his manly bosom.

"If I was a man——," says the lady, and pauses.

"If you was, my dear, Sir Harry Wildair's self would fall behind you."

She laughed coquettishly—

"Well, I should at least know this, that a woman likes to be forced to compliance with her adorer when she's too mock-modest to speak for herself. You knew that once too, Macheath?"

"There's very little I don't know about your sweet sex, Madam. Yes, I know that. And what then?"

She drew her chair nearer, and leaning on the arm of his whispered in his ear. He listened, his face changing from curiosity, to doubt, to pleasure, to surprise—as the whisper went on. Then she drew back and looked at him.

" 'Twould suit us both. Putting her beauty aside and I own her a pretty girl, her voice is a fortune to the man that owns her. 'Tis to make your future at a bound."

Macheath stared at her suspiciously.

"You don't propose this for nothing, I dare swear. Where's your gain in it? I won't play any woman's game blindfolded!"

"You don't need to play mine. What I want is to get back to my part. I was making my name in Lucy and I like ruin as little as any woman. And if you can help me back and help yourself in doing it I'd as soon 'twas Macheath as another. I've a kindness for you. We've been comrades for many a day."

He filled his glass again absently, drawing near the sentimental stage in his cups. 'Twas a big fool of a man at best, born to be a woman's tool one way or another, and was besides in the melting mood.

"You think 'tis as easy as you say?"

"Easy as roasting eggs. And once she's yours she's the kind that will be all tears and kisses and obedience. She'll never look at another man, I promise you."

"Why then, my dearest, kindest of friends, 'tis worth doing, and I'm all but ashamed when I think how little you ask for yourself from the venture."

"Little!" says she, tossing her head. "I can tell you I value it high enough, Sir. It may be to reach the top of the tree if I get back now to the cast. And when you bring Miss Polly back all yours I'll warrant she'll thank me so sweetly for her handsome man that we'll live like two birds in one nest. Moreover, as you know well, Mr. Gay has another piece in hand. We stand to win or lose a prize indeed."

They talked long, compounding their plan, and she plied him with glass upon glass within the limit of safety, for his part was to be considered, and if a man's too maudlin the public objects. But when he left, tramping down the stair and whistling "Let us take the road," a pretty plot was hatcht between them. She could have wished a better instrument, knowing there was more swagger than strength about Macheath, but when a poor woman can't find what she would, she takes what she may, and there an end!

And when he was gone she sat awhile looking darkly in the fire, revolving matters that fell outside the knowledge she intended him. If my Lord Baltimore knew the girl unworthy—the self-chosen mistress of a man like Walker— Well, hearts have been caught on the rebound ere now,—and if the plot failed she could sell Macheath without mercy to his vengeance, and take the reward due to a guardian angel of injured innocence. If it succeeded 'twas very possible it might lead to Polly's dismissal with her Macheath. Good it could not do her. But in either case Mrs. Bishop saw the road lie open before her to the playhouse. A woman does not play in the plotting comedies of Wycherley, Vanbrugh and their like without learning a little contrivance at a pinch.

When the time came, she went out and lurked about in the rain to see Polly's departure after the play. She noted the Duchess's fine chair draw up for her, the chairmen wiping their lips with their sleeves as they came from the neighbouring pot-house where they waited.

She saw my Lord Baltimore stand in the doorway, his hat slouched forward and his cloak thrown about him. She saw Polly pass him with head averted.

And each item that she saw, she fixed in a mind wax to receive and marble to retain.

# CHAPTER XIII

THE greatest lady in England, Queen Caroline, sat in her apartment in Kensington Palace on Sunday night a week later, drinking her chocolate, with Lord Hervey and the Princess Emily in attendance, all three personages much at their ease in Zion and in a fine flow of gossip and reminiscence. Her Majesty could as little dispense with her dish of gossip as her dish of chocolate. 'Twas the relaxation of a truly powerful and commanding mind, and since 'twas a liking as common to her sovereign lord and master as to herself, she's the less to be censured for what is called a feminine failing.

In mingling and seasoning this delicate dish and serving it to her Majesty's liking, my Lord Hervey had no peer and was valued accordingly. There was scarce any hour of the day or night that the door was not open for him to the Presence, and he took the fullest advantage of his position. Nay, even in illness, he was not banished, having the honour to sit t'other side of the door that gave on the Queen's bed and there entertain her with the tittle-tattle, political or social, of the day. 'Twas more than was allowed to the Peachum and Lockit of the court, Sir Robert Walpole and my Lord Townshend.

Behold then a sombre room in the great red brick palace. The windows were narrow and high with small panes and richly draped damask, still further to exclude the light. Tall portraits of departed royalties and worthies or unworthies glimmering in massive gilt frames adorned the high walls and were lost in the upper gloom, and above the door leading to her Majesty's toilette room was the corpulent nude Venus beneath which the chaplain on duty for the day would kneel to perform morning prayers for the Queen's benefit whilst she and her ladies proceeded with her toilette within.

"And a very proper altar-piece!" cried the pious Dr. Madox, reviewing its contours and harkening to the chatter from behind the door. Indeed, with the exception of the Queen herself and a very few others, 'twas the patron saint of the courtiers of both sexes.

The lady who sat in her great armed-chair was a fine presence still, though her handsome features had lost the delicacy that was once the admiration of Europe. Perhaps there was the more majesty to take its place, but even this could be and was sufficiently laid aside in her hours of intimacy. You are then to picture a florid handsome woman,—the King's fat Venus, as Lord Hervey himself had audaciously described her with a side eye on the altar-piece aforesaid. Her stiff-bodied gown of velvet laced with gold could scarce contain her exuberant charms, and had it not been for the high brow and bright commanding eye a chance observer had said "Here's a fine ample housewife in the autumn of her days," and little suspected that here instead was the lady that ruled her husband through his vices, her country through its venality and her family through a lashing tongue and a hard heart.

My Lord Hervey perhaps understood her and was valued by her as much as she could value any one, which does not necessarily set his value high.

"But, Madam," he continued, "if the Prince of Wales is to be married 'twas plain he must part with Mrs. Vane, the present Sultana, the more so as 'twas your own opinion; and the matter was discust by him and his friends. I leave your perspicacity to guess whom your Royal son appointed as Ambassador to the lady to announce that he preferred her room to her company. In short, though exprest handsomely enough, that he was dog-tired of her."

"I should guess he chose to do it himself," says the Princess Emily, whose love for her brother matched that of his parents. "He would never omit so fine an occasion for brutality to a woman."

Since her Royal Highness was the softest-tongued member of her Royal family, so her speech must be read as gentle in comparison with others.

"No, Emily," says her Majesty, knotting serenely. "Your brother is a nauseous fool, but even to his purblind folly it must appear that the public expects a decency in such things. I wager he chose my Lord Bolingbroke as a polite letter-writer whoever he chose to carry it, but his choice was with his usual folly for Mrs. Vane has out-lettered him altogether. The imbecile must needs go about showing her answer, and I own I thought the gray mare by far the better horse. If indeed she writ it at all."

My Lord clapt his hands softly.

"Trust your Majesty's discernment!" he cried in a polite rapture. "Of course Mrs. Vane didn't write the letter. 'Tis much if she could write her own name with a row of crosses for kisses. No, Madam, here is the true and authentic history. His Royal Highness chose my Lord Baltimore for the messenger of doom, Baltimore being in all his secrets, and his master supposing that if ever there was a man that had experience of the sex, 'tis he,—but Mrs. Vane is somewhat of a virago and when Baltimore sounded the trumpet of parley, she respected not the flag of truce but sallying forth routed him with great slaughter and so returned him to his master."

"What did he offer her on the Prince's behalf?" inquired the Princess.

"Why, Madam, a mere nothing—a flea-bite. The virtue of an opera-singer might be priced more highly. Sixteen hundred guineas a year. I wonder Baltimore had the effrontery to run of such an errand."

"He's more princely in his own pleasures," cries the Queen. "I hear he has offered Polly Peachum two thousand guineas a year and a diamond necklace. But my son adds a disgusting avarice to his other virtues. However—who writ the letter for the Vane, Hervey? 'Twas excellently done."

"Madam, your humble servant!" He bowed exquisitely—his thin white hand on the embroidery above his heart.

"Aha! didn't I say 'twas a masterpiece of tenderness and diplomacy, Emily? When one of the Walpoles was spoke of as the writer, I said there was a finesse the Walpoles lack. It might almost be thought a woman's, and has certainly won the heart of that blundering fool, the English People," concludes the Mother of her country.

"It is happy in your commendation, Madam," says the author, "but indeed Lord Baltimore did his errand so cold and haughty as he might have been dismissing a cook-maid for indiscretion. Mrs. Vane virtually slaughtered him and sent a cartel of defiance to the Prince, and since I knew it would not be displeasing to your Majesty I put the salt and pepper—even a dash of mustard also, in the cartel, seasoned with sobs and tears. The poor afflicted lady is much commiserated by the public to whom she has published the letter; and the Prince's."

"Excellent, Hervey, excellent!" says the royal matron. "Disservice to the Prince is service to us. Call for more chocolate. But tell me, how is it that the little slut Polly refuses Baltimore's friendly offers? Of course he's more than half mad and wholly bad. Didn't I always say so, Emily? But she's not to know that, and sure she estimates herself very high if such a sum won't buy her. What's the reason? Is there a higher bidder?"

"Why no, Madam, but you're to remember the girl's at auction, and won't knock herself down to the first bidder. Is there not Sir Robert Walpole, that has a fine person and the finances of the country at his back?—(Her Majesty laughed with infinite relish at this description of her minister and his swollen body)— Is there not his Majesty the King? Mrs. Howard's charms are on the wane, and Miss Polly may hope for your Majesty's interest at Kensington Palace! Unfortunately she does not speak High Dutch."

He delivered this with a demure gravity, and the Queen laughed more heartily than before. The King's German favourites were a favourite subject of jest between her and her vice-chamberlain, and Princess Emily's. "Fie, for shame, my Lord!" did but increase the hilarity. The Queen wiped her eyes with her laced handkerchief.

"Is she so pretty a creature as they say? But for the follies of the Duchess of Queensbury that ought to have a whipping for her pains—making a mere play a political matter! I had been to the playhouse to see her. But is she the sort to take a man's taste?"

"O, a delicious wench, Madam. Were your Majesty a man, and I can figure none more gallant were your Majesty re-sexed,—you'd not spare the pretty Polly a day. She's so shy, so alluring, so dextrous with her crystal voice and wooing eyes and enchanting person that I swear the man who could resist her argues himself a——"

"Nincompoop!" finishes her Majesty, twinkling.— "But what is Baltimore about? Why don't he abduct the lady and carry her off to his wilds in Maryland? Sure if he cut off her head or bowstrung her there when he was tired of her the savages wouldn't interfere with their Sultan."

"Sure your Majesty mistakes," cries my Lord— "I'm credibly told that morals having fled from England have colonized Maryland, and that Lady Deloraine, Mrs. Vane, Mrs. Howard and our other Dianas would be sent to Coventry there without recommendation to mercy. But indeed 'tis a sad pity your Majesty may not see 'The Beggar's Opera.' I know none would taste its wit more highly, for your Majesty has the humour to laugh at your servants as well as your enemies."

"So I should but for that haughty fool—Queensbury. Emily hasn't yet heard of her vile indiscretion of yesterday. Tell the Princess, Hervey, while I finish my chocolate."

"Why, Madam, you was at Richmond and so missed all the to-do. 'Twas a prodigious court, and the Empress of Queensbury smothered in jewels—the fireworks at Bartlemy Fair nothing to the blaze. I noted her very busy about in the corners with knots of her friends and supporters and so drew up near, when, as bold as brass, she thrust a paper before me and told me here was my chance to subscribe for the printing of Gay's new play—'Polly'—the sequel of t'other. He's poor and we all know Kitty's too poor to pay for the printing herself! Well, thinks I—here's our enemy delivered into our hands, and off I went to His Majesty to ask if it was his Royal pleasure that subscriptions be demanded at the pistol's point in the drawing-room as though 'twere Hounslow Heath. He went up himself to the fair highway-woman and damme if she hadn't the effrontery to ask His Majesty's self to be a subscriber! It flung him into a raging fury and with twenty minutes the deed was done and her Imperial Duchess-ship was notified by the vice-chamberlain that her attendance at court would be dispensed with for the future, at his Majesty's order."

"A triumph indeed," cries the young Princess clapping her hands. "What an indiscreet fool the woman is! Sure she must know she has herself to thank. How did she take it?"

"With a pride that covered everything, Madam. She marched out like an Amazon without a soul to follow her, all were so amazed. 'Twas a complete rout. But shall 'The Beggar's Opera' be stopt, Madam?" He appealed to the Queen.

"Why, no. The people are so engaged with the trash that Sir Robert fears it might provoke a riot and I applaud his prudence. 'Tis enough to forbid Kitty the court and to stamp out the other. They'll take the hint. The people is a bull-headed beast, Hervey, and I have made it my maxim to run with them sooner than provoke their horns against me."

"Your Majesty's prudence is inexhaustible," says Lord Hervey bowing, "and Sir Robert makes a fine figure-head for its display— If——"

"Mamma! My Lord!" cries the Princess, "here's the King."

There was silence and a heavy step approached the door, the Queen sliding the talk off into the last sermon of Dr. Hoadly's, for she was a regular attendant at Divine Worship and could dissect a discourse like a divine. Lord Hervey replied in kind, and his Majesty opening the door roughly entered upon such a scene of domestic quiet as might make any man bless his household gods for a peaceable wife and daughter.

All rose to their feet, but at a wave the Queen and Princess resumed their chairs, whilst the King threw himself into his own. For a small dapper person 'twas remarkable how heavy and clumsy he walked and what noise he made, but the gout is no respecter of persons and an inflamed toe and bandaged foot are the sworn enemies of grace. The Royal brow was savagely clouded too, and the party of three quaked before the foreboding signs of storm.

"If ever I am guided by the Queen's counsel, especially if seconded by yours, my Lord, 'tis as certain as I sit here, to plunge me in difficulties," growls the Ruler—who knew not he was ruled. "Here's a to-do that a little patience and good sense had entirely avoided and we are made to appear ridiculous to the world. Had you, Caroline, the gift to preserve your temper, as I set you the example, and consider before acting, I should escape many troubles I scarce know how to meet."

The Queen bit her lip, knotting faster. The Princess sat mute as a mouse. Lord Hervey bowed, standing, and none dared to question.

"Here's this jade—this impudent woman, this Queensbury!" says the little light-haired Autocrat striking his finger on a paper in his other hand, "has the damned insolence to write to her King, and not only so but give it to the public—a letter such as——"

He stuttered off into rage almost unintelligible, and still the Queen knotted on, but tangling her threads. Some of his Majesty's remarks are best unrecorded,—but when he resumed to Lord Hervey his words could be understood.

"Let this teach such an officious busy-body as yourself, my Lord, to stand off in future and permit the King to form his own views. Hear what the curst jade writes——"

He unfolded the paper and read with some difficulty, (for her Grace had dasht off in a fury not less than his own) the following billet-doux:

> "The Duchess of Queensbury is surprised and well pleased that the King hath given her so agreeable a command as to stay from Court, where she never came for diversion but to bestow a civility on the King and Queen; she hopes by such an unprecedented order as this is that the King will see as few as he wishes at his Court particularly such as dare to think or speak truth. (Here the indignant lady slid from the third person to the first.) I dare not do otherwise, and ought not nor could have imagined that it would not have been the highest compliment that I could possibly pay the King to endeavour to support truth and innocence in his house, particularly when the King and Queen both told me they had not read Mr. Gay's play. I have certainly done right then to stand by my own words.
>
> "C. QUEENSBURY."[A]

[A] (This letter is authentic.)

---

"What say you now, Madam?" cries he ending— "Here are we made to appear ridiculous, whereas had my counsel of moderation been followed——"

The Queen, about to speak, checked herself and bowed submissively, hoping thus to make her court, for 'twas ever her maxim to be supple in inessentials, and conceal the steel hand in the silkiest of velvet. But 'twould not do this time.

"Can't you speak, Madam? You're voluble enough when 'tis mischievous to speak— What's your opinion of the woman?"

"What can it be, Sire? A female Yahoo!"

"What's a Yahoo?" inquires the Sovereign, blinking his little red eyes rapidly.

"A character in Gulliver's Travels," says the Queen—"and might have been drawn for the Duchess's picture—chattering, silly, an ape in speech and action——"

"I read that book or endeavoured to, and was of the opinion that some of the man's adventures could not altogether be true," says the Sovereign angrily. "What are books? Rubbish, no more. Leave talking of such nonsense, Madam, and as 'twas you and my Lord Hervey made this mess, get me out of it."

His Lordship now drew the fire on himself, willing to spare his Mistress, and the Defender of the Faith blustered and stormed for another half-hour till the Queen was near weeping with fatigue and annoyance. Her pride, however, bid her bide it, and she was supported in her resolution by a comical face Lord Hervey ventured at her when his Majesty turned on the silent Princess and rebuked her for keeping her mouth open like a butchered calf.

'Twas the happiest family circle and set an example to all others in the three Kingdoms. This must be owned. Finally the storm muttered itself away for the present, the Queen determining that a dignified cheerfulness was the best mode in which to meet the affront.

"In this Court,"—says the King, concluding—"there isn't an honest man nor a decent woman. I defy any good thing to come out of such filth."

"Why not, Sire?" says the Queen composedly,— "I am sure I have ate very good asparagus raised out of dung, and your Majesty will admit our eldest son is a compendium of all the virtues."

It sufficed. She knew well that that endearing subject would draw his Majesty from any other (and not infrequently used it for the purpose) as the sole one on which they were heartily agreed. He raged on ferociously on this and the Duchess was forgot. Indeed 'twas near midnight when he rose to go to his own apartment and the Queen almost dropping from weariness of mind and body. But before he departed his Majesty bestowed one piece of the news on his family—

"Since you love to be poking your nose into other people's business, Madam, instead of minding your own, here's a scandal for you. Berkeley, just come down from London declares Gay's Polly fled last night after the piece, 'tis not known with whom and is not yet found today. 'Tis a slap in the face for Gay and Queensbury and the whole malicious crew that I can't but rejoice in, but 'tis what all the world must expect from the Newgate crew that frequents that playhouse. If right had its own they should one and all stand in the pillory."

The door closed behind their Sovereign and the three looked upon one another.

"If 'tis true,"—said the royal lady—"it may be made an engine to hurt the Duchess that would have such a wench in her house. 'Twas worthy company for a Hyde however. What were the Hydes when all's said and done? Make it your business, Hervey, to discover the threads in the intrigue. The worst is, they have all the best lampooners on their side—Swift, Pope, and half a hundred more. I don't know how 'tis, but all the fools hang on to us."

" 'Tis because your Majesty has wits and brains enough to furnish forth your whole party and make it victorious. And to spare. Let 'em have all the others, say I, so long only as we keep your Majesty to counsel us."

'Twas said with a real touch of admiration and the Queen was not insensible of it. He assisted her to raise her wearied body from the chair and added,

"I know not, Madam, how you endure as you do. Sure 'tis either your sense of superiority or your fine wit that enables you to laugh where other women would weep and tremble. A Stoic might draw lessons in fortitude from such a spectacle."

She endeavoured to summon a smile into her face to match the laughter he spoke of, and faintly succeeded. He knew what disgust and suffering lay behind it and respected her the more in his infidel fashion for her contempt of her husband, and her resolution to hide it from the world.

" 'Tis a coarse, gross woman,"—he mused as he went along the corridor later,—"but the heart and brain and courage of a man. 'Tis she should have been King of England, and perhaps we had then matcht Elizabeth. The vicious fool she uses is a poor tool for such a hand. But where's Berkeley?"

He talked with that gentleman for half an hour before seeking his own repose. He saw the importance of any matter that might entangle the Duchess, and indeed Miss Polly's matters were almost become an affair of state into such high company were they got. The poor girl would never have believed her own consequences had she been told it.

As to Madam Diana—no one troubled over her at all. Dianas were not believed to haunt the playhouse in Portugal Street. 'Tis probable no one credited her existence but herself and one other. Let us charitably add the Duchess.

# CHAPTER XIV

IT was in the great white and gold withdrawing room of Queensbury House that her Grace discoursed that Sunday night to her friends and partisans on the insult received from the King.

"Lord!" says Lady Fanny, using her fan with as much energy as had it been a flail descending on his Majesty's back.— "Was ever such treatment known to one of her Grace's rank! These little Electoral Princes imagine they are to come over from their bear-garden in Hanover and insult the most ancient families of England. The Stuarts, who were at least gentlemen, whatever their shortcomings, had never attempted such insolence."

Indeed many of the company were at heart partisans of the exiled Royal family, and this was received with sympathy.

"And if rank was not sufficient one might suppose her Grace's beauty would secure her from such boorish rudeness,"—replies the aged Sir Temperley Harington. "But his Majesty's taste in women is merely lamentable. Ah, ladies, ladies—I am old enough to remember such beauties as can only be matcht in this room. I remember the exquisite Mrs. Stuart, later Duchess of Richmond, in black and white, her head and shoulders glittering like a January night with diamonds, and did I not see his Majesty King Charles the Second of blessed memory unable to take his eyes off that enchanting vision? I was but twelve years old, but she fixed my standard for all time. 'Twas at a ball at Whitehall. Had that sweet lady committed high treason he would have rather crowned her head than severed it from her charming neck."

Lord Carteret sauntered up in his white satin coat brocaded with gold, the plaits sticking out from his waist nearly as stiff as the farthingale of Queen Elizabeth.

"The beautiful Mrs. Stuart did commit a sort of high treason in refusing the King's advances,"—says he laughing, "and were I the King it should be at least petty treason. Yet he did but kiss the fair hand that struck the blow. Was Lady Castlemaine as fine a woman as our grandfathers tell us, Sir Temperley?"

"Infinitely more beautiful, my Lord. Such a haughty grace tempered with the most seductive languor might well excuse a monarch's subjection. Ah, Duchess, had you committed any crime with such a King on the throne he had but commanded you to an assignation for punishment. But the days when a woman was truly adored have departed along with the grand manner. Go to Hampton Court,—look upon the beauties pictured there and honour them with a sigh."

He himself sighed and snuffed,—a fine enamel set in brilliants of the divine Frances Jennings adorning his snuff-box. 'Twas whispered— But why revive ancient scandals laid in the dust with their owners?

"For my part!" cries the Duchess's clear ringing voice;— "I desire no monarch's attentions, and the corpulent German lady is welcome to such as can be spared from his German charmers. All I ask is common justice and civility, and depend on't Mr. Gay's new piece shall be printed if I pay the cost of every letter. But was ever such a simplicity as to let 'The Beggar's Opera' proceed unhindered that's as full of skits upon them as an egg is of meat, while they crush this new piece where there's nothing to hurt nobody?"

"They daren't touch it!" says Lady Fanny— " 'Twould be like when the Queen asked Sir Robert what 'twould cost to close Hyde Park to the public. 'A trifle, Madam. Only three crowns!' says he. No, she won't do that. But what to do next, Kitty? Write another letter?"

"Not I. But one, and that a masterpiece, was my motto. No—I have another card hid in my sleeve!"

"Lord, what's that?"

The company crowded about her chair. She waved her fan, imperial.

"To support the Prince of Wales."

A chorus arose—

"Lord, my dear. He's as bad as his father and mother combined."—"You don't speak seriously," and so forth.

"I'll have Mr. Gay introduce a new song in his favour tomorrow—'twill drive them mad. I'll see Polly on it this night. Lord, I forgot!" She stopt of a sudden.

"What, Duchess?"

"Why, she's not here. I had the prettiest note from her last night when the chair returned without her to notify me that her mamma was took ill at her aunt's house and she must go to her at once."

"The dutiful girl!" says Sir Temperley.— "I own she's as pretty as sweet Mistress Nell Gwynne, and a deal more innocent, if a face can be trusted. I wish I were her aunt."

"Aunt? She has not a relative in the world—so Mr. Gay said when I asked him,"—says Lady Fanny.

The Duchess, bewildered, felt in the silk bag she carried on her arm.

"Since you know better than I, hear her letter."

> "*Your Grace*, your humble servant presents her duty and ventures to inform you that my mother is come up to London very ill at my aunt Mrs. Webster's, and I am in duty compelled to wait upon her. Tomorrow being Sunday I will continue with her and hope to return to the playhouse on Monday. Your bounden and obedient humble servant to command.—
>
> "LAVINIA FENTON."

" 'Tis dated 'Saturday, After the Play,' and the chairmen brought it," she concluded. Lady Fanny was opening her mouth to speak when the door opened and the American Prince entered seeming pale, and disturbed, and the company parted for him to advance to her Grace's chair, some of the intimates looking at him in surprise. It was now a considerable time since he had presented himself in her presence where he had never been courted, he guessing, as is likely, that his welcome would be on the frosty side. She rose and dropped a curtsey now, very stately, yet with a cold smile.

"We were speaking of his Royal Highness the Prince of Wales but now, my Lord, and in a manner to glad the ears of his faithful servant."

This news and the smile alike astonished his American Highness. What! The Duchess hitherto had turned her beautiful back as impartially on the Prince of Wales as on his parents. My Lord's quick mind reviewed the situation. This then was the outcome of the *faux pas* made by the Royal party in insulting her. Her support was welcome at all times, but doubly so when Mrs. Vane was carrying public opinion with her against the Prince. He bowed and spoke with a becoming earnestness.

"I wish my Master were present himself to hear so charming a declaration from such lips, Madam. Even in a position so exalted as his, her Grace of Queensbury's approbation must be prized. A Prince of Wales must needs be dumb on many matters he may himself disapprove, but those who know him best know that his Royal Highness's sympathies are ever on the side of justice and merit."

A whispering flutter ran through the company. Was this the signing of a new protocol they witnessed? All heads turned to the Duchess. She looked my Lord Baltimore in the face.

"Not even the most exalted position can save its owner from misjudgment. But all must be judged by deeds, not words. At least 'tis thus I act."

So! It was to be a waiting policy! Sir Temperley and other ancients drew a relieved breath. My Lord Baltimore drew closer to the Duchess.

"Madam, may I beg your Grace for an audience of a few minutes on a matter entirely private? It is quite apart from any public matter, I dare assure your company in asking their pardon for withdrawing you a moment."

He gave her his hand to the ante-room, and to the recess at the further end. The courtier in him was still predominant for the first moment.

"If, Madam, I may convey to my Master what you have said, 'twill be a sensible pleasure to his Royal Highness.— I venture to assure you of his sympathy with Mr. Gay's genius and his horror at the insult put upon your Grace. He spoke of it last night so as I wish you could have been present to hear."

She drew back a little, but not ungraciously.

"I thought the business had been private, my Lord."

"Undoubtedly, Madam—but yet——"

"There can be no objection to your conveying my humble duty to his Royal Highness. There is not one of the King's subjects but should present his duty!"

Her smile however made the message particular and the courtier was content. He proceeded to the next item, but this time with a very different manner. Watching him closely she could perceive that his hand on the back of the chair shook a little. He might have laid it there to steady it.

"Madam, I appeal to you now as the kind protectress of Mrs. Lavinia Fenton. There's a rumour in the town today that she did not return to Queensbury House last night. That—in short—that the lady has been abducted or has eloped. (Suddenly his voice broke and quivered. He looked at her entreating)—Madam, I am very uneasy, dare I beg any information you have?"

The Duchess gazed at him in astonishment. Never had she seen the American Prince moved one inch before from his haughty or languid composure. She might have pitied him but for her knowledge of Diana's mind and his persecution of an innocent girl. She laughed coldly.

"Reassure yourself, my Lord. Mrs. Fenton writ me fully. She is in excellent hands—her mother and her aunt. Shall we return to the company?"

"But Madam—Madam!" he almost caught her robe as she turned—"Are you certain your information came from her? May I see the billet? I know her hand well——"

"And how?" asked the Duchess, stepping back and fixing him with her eyes.

"Because she has wrote often to me. Because she is mine—heart and body. Therefore you will conceive my terror to hear——"

"I don't believe it. You lie," she said, and there was a dead silence. What shall a man do when a lady and such a lady insults him with a word that only blood can wash out? His habitual composure stood him in good stead. White to the lips he faced her.

"It is a cowardice peculiar to your sex, Madam, to insult a man who can make neither return nor defence. I pass that by, however, until you shall appoint your champion. I assert that Mrs. Fenton is my mistress, and on that ground, request you to tell me what you know."

'Twas a bold throw. If he could alienate her friends—if he could leave her no refuge but himself, might not the terrified bird fly to his breast—her only refuge? And what matter's a player's reputation? She has none—'tis but a jest to laugh at. Who can destroy what has no existence?

The Duchess, now as cool as he, considered a little before replying.

"My Lord, I make no apology for my candour for I still believe you lie and partly see your motive, nor shall I show you the letter, neither. She's with her friends and will return tomorrow."

"This is Sunday and so a difficult day," cried he, "but I beseech you, Madam to hear me, even if you distrust me. 'Tis said all about Portugal Street and the neighbourhood that Mrs. Fenton entered her chair as usual after the play, and was carried off."

"She never did!" says the Duchess stoutly. "I have it here under her hand. She left a billet and my chairmen brought this with them instead of the lady. 'Tis all perfectly simple."

"Not so, Madam—not so!" he cried, almost distracted,—"for 'tis said she was only gone a few minutes when another chair exactly like the first came up, for which a man waited. He gave a letter to the chairmen and they went off as they came. 'Twas a trap—a feint to catch the poor innocent. Whose was that first chair?"

"Her mother's, man! Whose else!" The Duchess was growing impatient. She turned towards the door.

"Would her mother's chair be lined with red velvet and bear your Grace's arms?"—says he with fearful earnestness. "Why were there two chairs? We trifle with precious time and more than her life may be at stake. I must see that letter, Madam, if I force it from you."

"I dare you to touch me,"—she said tossing up her head. "Stand back. I believe 'tis all some vile plot of your own against the girl's honour. Leave my house and——"

The further door opened. A gentleman entered carelessly, looking about him and not for a moment seeing the two in the recess.

The Duchess sprang forward with a cry.

"Bolton—Bolton! Come hither. This man insults me. He would snatch a letter— You were never more welcome than now."

He drew his sword instantly and stood lightly leaning on it—the lady beside him.

"Give the word, Madam," he said, "and I strike."

But Lord Baltimore did not draw. He was raging, helpless before the pair, the victim of a dreadful anxiety that left him unable to resent what at another moment had sent him flashing against his former friend.

"Afterwards—afterwards!" he said fiercely—"I'll meet you anywhere. Was I ever backward? But now— If the girl is to be saved, show me the letter. Delay is madness."

The Duke turned calm eyes on the lady.

"What does he mean, Madam?"

" 'Tis some mad tale about Diana," she replied angrily, "and nonsense from beginning to end. He will have it she's carried off—I know not what all! Whereas I have it under her own hand, she's with her mother and aunt."

"May I see this letter?" The quiet voice fell like cold water on her hot anger and the man's. She took it instantly from the bag and laid it in his hand. He read it, Baltimore trembling like a leashed dog in his eagerness.

"I don't like the letter,"—said the Duke—"the wording is suspicious and she names no house. And I have it from Mrs. Fenton's own lips that her mother is her sole living dependence. Who is this aunt? Why do we hear of her for the first time? Have the goodness, my Lord, to repeat your story."

He told it rapidly, but more fully than to the lady. It is easier to deal with a man and he therefore told it better. She stared at him with widened eyes as he finished.

"The matter is serious," said Bolton, and stood looking on the ground considering.

"I might have believed him"—she cried,—"but that he lied in one particular and so may have lied in all! He asserted the girl is his mistress! A palpable lie."

"A palpable lie," repeated the man beside her. "My Lord, I repeat her Grace's charge. You have lied."

"I shall know how to defend my honour later," said Baltimore—a red fever-spot on either white cheek—"but now—I live, I breathe but to find the girl. Let us be enemies, but at this moment, man, help me to save her that is got into some villain's hands. Madam, will you not retire? This is a matter for men."

Bolton's eye seconded him. She curtseyed, and as the Duke held the door open for her she whispered low:

"Beware lest it be a trap of his own. Tell me all that passes."

They were alone, the Duke still leaning on his sword.

"I will be frank. I don't trust you. I know your pursuit of this poor woman to be most unmanly. It hath drove her almost to despair. Why should I believe a word you utter?"

"For her sake!" says Baltimore, raging yet subdued by this freezing contempt. He paused a moment—then added. "But I was a fool to come here. I don't want your help—yours least of all. I go my way and act as I can. My seconds shall meet yours later."

He made for the door, but the Duke was still beside him.

"We will go together,"—he said, and the two went down the great staircase, the grooms of the chambers and lacqueys staring after them, for there was a something strange and ominous in their looks and companionship that tinged the air with doubt.

In the street, the Duke halted.

"Your plan?" he asked.

"I know not—how should I? It's Sunday, curse it! Where does Rich go Sundays? The playhouse is shut. 'Tis impossible to find a soul."

"Whence then the rumour you heard?"

"My man brought it from Portugal Street."

"Then we go there."

In Portugal Street, the Sunday leisure set free groups of persons, slatternly women and half drunken men to talk over all the news of the day and of all the items the story of the last night was the most favoured. Under the stinking oil lamps, along the gutters, about the dirty cobble-stones the rumours, amplified now beyond recognition, flew to and fro.

Polly was muffled and forced into the chair. She had waved her hand for help. A man with his collar pulled up about his face was guessed to be Sir Charles Jermyn that had long loitered about her. So it raged on, and both men knew that 'twas all false and this but wasting precious time.

"Who shall say she did not go by her own choice?" mutters Baltimore at last—almost under his breath as if it was wrung out of him, as they stood by the corner to consider.

"If your Lordship had won her, yourself could answer that question," said the Duke. "She is no wanton."

"The Devil knows what a woman may be." Again he fell silent. Bolton turned from him to a little group of women clustered at a door.

"You all know Mrs. Fenton!"

"Why yes, your Worship. God bless her pretty face. We see her come and go daily."

"Do you also know Mrs. Bishop?"

"Why yes, your Worship. . . . Why not? We see her as often."

"Where is her lodging?"

"Turn up the corner, your Honour. Trenton Street, forty-five."

The Duke walked briskly off—Lord Baltimore hesitating an instant, then followed him. The lady in a wrapper and cap that had seen more coquettish days herself opened the door and received the salutations of the gentlemen with the utmost astonishment.

"You see me very unprepared for company, my Lords," says she curtseying and holding the door so as to bar entrance. "What's your pleasure?"

"A word with you, Madam," replies the Duke sternly. "We will follow you to your room if you will be so obliging as lead the way."

She hung on her foot a moment as if demurring, and glanced doubtfully at Baltimore. His face was a shut door, and seeing no help, she turned and preceded them.

The room indeed was little fit for such courtly company. Not, as I have said, that 'twas in itself despicable, but her belongings were littered about in most admired disorder. She must drag a satin manteau off one chair and a sprigged gown of handsome stuff from another before she could request them to be seated. They however preferring to stand, she begged to know their business, perplexed beyond measure to see them in company and striving to guess her course from Baltimore's face so resolutely turned away.

"My business is simple enough," says the Duke. "Be so good, Madam, as tell me what you know of Mrs. Fenton's departure from the playhouse, last night."

"I, your Grace? Nothing. What should I know? I would have you remember I was discharged by Mr. Rich upon some dislike Mrs. Fenton took to me. I thought it unjust, I own. I don't love the lady, to be plain with you. But what's come to her?"

"There is a doubt as to her present situation. You will be handsomely paid for any light you may throw upon it."

"Money? Take your money elsewhere, your Grace. And if you want news of Mrs. Fenton, there's one man can give it you better than any. He stands beside you." She pointed, like an actress, a tragedy finger at Baltimore. Sure a man of his reputation with women could easy enough stand a charge that would but add to his dazzle in the town. She little thought how she served his turn however by the assertion. He stepped forward instantly.

"My Lord Duke, this woman knows what she says. I am the man that has the best right to Mrs. Fenton's whereabouts. All the playhouse knows this. But I am at sea— She is robbed from me, on the very eve of her placing herself openly under my protection. For God's sake, Mrs. Bishop, be open if you have aught to tell."

'Twas partly real, partly acting. She saw her chance to wound and sprang at it.

"I will be open my Lord. 'Tis true she was your Polly. Your Polly, but other men's Polly also. And I can only suppose that she's now gone off with one of them. Yet 'tis possible she may take up with you again one day if you're prepared to share your interest in her with others."

"She knows nothing!" cried Baltimore. " 'Tis but her malicious anger."

The Duke looked at him in silence, then left the room and strode down the stair, leaving the pair together. For the first time he recalled the connection between them.

# CHAPTER XV

WHEN Diana left the playhouse on the Saturday, a heavy rain was falling through the grimy dark, and she muffled her head in her hood and stepped swiftly from the door into the chair, her little feet splashing in the puddled ill-lit gutter, the flambeaux dazzling in the rain. The men lowered the roof instantly and shut the door and set off at a swinging trot, eager no doubt to have done with the dirty night.

Her thoughts were strangely intermingled—the songs and laughter of the playhouse still echoed among them, the gay kindness of the good Duchess, the words of my Lady Fanny,—(" 'Twas strange she should tell me, of all women, that story of his Grace's marriage.")—all these things mixt with a deep content that my Lord Baltimore had been absent this night and indeed many nights lately. 'Twas like a cool lotion to allay a burn—this absence! Sure it might mean he was weary of a pursuit that could bring only rebuffs and contempt, and if so she could deal with others, less to be dreaded.

The play had now been playing two months to crowded houses and still there was no slackening in the rage to see it. Money was turned away nightly, and the rows of chairs on the stage were three deep and some of the boxes run into each other to make more room. 'Twas raging like a fever in the provinces also and a whole regiment of pretty Pollys had sprung up to follow her lead, but none, none like the fair original, so swore men and women alike. A triumph to turn any girl's head, and since the idol was but a girl, when all's said and done, it might easily turn hers were it not for a stronger passion than vanity that swept over it and submerged it and left it forgotten.

Love. What was it to be the adored of the town when the one man on whom her own eyes waited knew her very triumph to involve disgrace? Supposing, even supposing, that her birth equalled his own, that he were less than a great Peer of England and she more than a poor lieutenant's daughter, supposing she were lovely as the fabled Helen, with all the enchantments of Circe added, how could this or aught else rub out the blot that she was but a puppet at whom every rake might stare and form his loose conjectures? True, noblemen as great had condescended to the stage for their pleasures, but that served her nothing. There was a something in her heart that told her the man's respect for her girlhood would close that door for ever, nor could she wish it otherwise. While, as for anything more, she trembled with shame that even a regret for a thing so impossible should cross her mind. O that she had never seen him but eyeing her on the stage with cold admiration as she played her Newgate part to the life. Alas for the Duchess's mistaken favour that had taken her from her own humble sphere and set her in one in which however her own heart made her native, her circumstances made her but a tolerated intruder.

So far reason carried her, and then her thoughts were words no longer—but dreams, longings, griefs. Longings for a voice best forgot, for a face—better she had never seen it; for a friend high, gracious, endearing, that made all others as nothing to her and to whom she herself could be nothing but a passing thought. 'Tis the man should look up, not the woman. Before marriage, at least, hers is the throne, but here was this beggar-maid kneeling on the lowest step, her face hidden in her hands for shame, whilst King Cophetua gazed beyond her into regions she must never know.

And he himself so comfortless! There lay the sharpest sting. Suppose she could change places with the shining and lovely lady who had talked with her so condescending—Were she the Lady Fanny Armine—yet herself!—might there be more than a few words of praise? So in imagination she saw the proud eyes soften, the stern mouth relax,—the high courtesy break into the wonderment of passion. His arms—his lips—.

Thus lost in dreams unspeakable she past along the rainy streets, and never heeded how the time went by. At last the chair drew up. The men at the house must have forgot the flambeaux—so dark it was as she looked forth. The roof was raised and, sudden, a cloth soft and blinding fell over her head, and strong hands pulled it about her throat. In the dreadful surprise and alarm she screamed aloud, but the wild cry was muffled in her mouth and herself could more feel than hear it. Her hands were grasped in two strong ones and a man dragged her from the chair. There was a whispering, and then a door opened and in the darkness and terror she knew she was lifted into a house and the door shut behind them.

On the stage a girl must have swooned in such a terror. In life, her heart beat to burst her bosom, her body shook as with an ague, but she kept her wits, clung to them as a drowning sailor, that has but the one frail spar betwixt him and an eternity of horror, clings to the floating hope.

Stairs, and heavy feet of men who carried her, and now, stopping, they released her hands a moment, then bound the wrists together, making her captive indeed. Another door opened and she was laid on a sofa, still blinded, and heard renewed whispering and the chink of money and then retreating steps and the creaking staircase. Was it to be murder? She wore about her neck the Duchess's miniature set in pearl. But no—no! She knew a deeper dread; should she faint, she must be utterly at his mercy?—God forbid! She gathered every wavering sense into her agonized heart and waited.

Hands loosed the wrappage about her head, and a dim light dazzled her a moment till she put her arm before her eyes. It was certainly my Lord

Baltimore she thought to see, but no—a tall man of handsome person stood with his back to her, wrapping a bandage about his own wrist as though 'twas wounded. He turned—and a faint cry broke from her lips—Macheath—Walker! And by the fire a woman.

Her first thought was hope. For my Lord Baltimore she had nothing but deadly terror—the white mask of his face a language she could not read. But this man she saw daily, had laughed, had jested with him, half ridiculed his passion as a foolish calf-love that a girl may rally a little if she notice it at all. She slid her feet over the edge of the sofa, her mind clear as a dagger's point at once.

"Mr. Walker!" says she—"You've rescued me, and are wounded in my defence. Loose my hands instantly that I may help my deliverer."

"Your deliverer indeed, my angel," says Walker, turning very red and walking up to her. "Haven't I seen you persecuted night after night by that fop that would drag you in the mud for his own pleasure, and could a true lover like myself endure to stand by and do nothing? Not I! Here stands one that offers you his love and no dishonour with it.—There's a parson below will marry us in a twinkling, and I hope I'm a man can protect his own wife from Baltimore or any other scented essence in the town. I'll unbind your hands, my life, the minute I have your word to give me them for good."

She stared up at him incredulous. The woman had not turned nor spoke and her capuchin was about her.

"Sir, you're drunk or mad!" cries Diana with spirit. "What have I ever said or done to encourage you to such an insult! I despised you always."

"Your sweet eyes—your sweeter lips, Madam, are my best excuse"—says the outraged lover. "They spoke more handsomely than your tongue. And if you did despise me you take a foolish time to tell me so, for here you're in my power. But sure I know my Polly's little coquettish ways and take your pretty contempt for a lure the more."

He approached a step nearer.

"Madam—Madam!" screams Diana—shrinking back—"You've a woman's heart. You won't see a poor girl terrified to death. Help me, unbind my hands! O, Madam."

The woman by the fire turned slowly with gleaming eyes. Mrs. Bishop.

Then indeed for a moment the victim knew despair for there was that in the woman's face to make her tremble. Hatred, fury—every violent passion might have been depicted from her silent look and clenched hands. But not a word did she speak, and was the more dreadful.

"Hold your noise!" cries Macheath, very fierce and flushed with anger. "You do but hurt your own cause. 'Tis for me to command and you to obey and this lady is here for a witness. Hear then my purpose——"

There was a little of the playhouse rant about him as he stepped back and flung out his fine chest with the true highwayman's air. He was fool enough to relish his part in the acting.

" 'Tis my purpose to wed you immediately, Mrs. Fenton, and many an actor has played lover to his own wife on the boards, and 'tis that I intend. There's money and love and joy in the future I offer you and many a fine lady would leap at the chance. 'Tis perhaps unknown to you the love letters I have by the score from handsome heiresses that know a man when they see him. I wager yourself has not so many."

"Stow all this talk," says Mrs. Bishop, sharply. "Can't you see, man, what she needs is the whip not the honeycomb? She's in love with my Lord Baltimore. Is she likely to accept to be an honest man's wife when she can be a peer's Miss? and rob a better woman than herself!"

"Baltimore!" Diana could scarce articulate, so terrible was the woman. "Mrs. Bishop, you are most frightfully mistook. I loathe the man. His mere presence oppresses me. Is it possible— O how blind I have been! Yourself loves him? Then take him, and I'll bless the day that rids me of a man I hate."

She could not clasp her hands but stretched them forth beseechingly. How came it she had never seen nor suspected the true cause of the woman's jealousy? O blind that she had been! She saw Mrs. Bishop far more to be feared than the weak handsome fool that swaggered so big and loud before them. Her one aim must be to convince her. The man was the lesser danger.

"Mrs. Bishop—did I ever say an unkind word or look a hard look at you? How have I deserved this? Only—I see—because you was under a frightful mistake. I swear to you that my best hope is never to see my Lord Baltimore again. If he is pledged to you—but indeed that concerns me not, only rid me of him and I'll bless you."

"We'll rid you of him effectively, Madam," interrupts Macheath, very gloomily. "He won't interfere with Mrs. Walker, I swear!" But Diana did not heed him. She dragged herself to her feet and faced Mrs. Bishop.

"Madam, I now perceive I have stood in your light in more ways than one. For my Lord, be assured there's no effort of yours I won't second to escape him. For the stage—I'm sick of it. 'Tis no place for me. I'll throw up my part tomorrow, and earn my bread in any way that gives me peace. I swear it."

"Can you give me back my Lord's heart? Can you undo the disgrace put on me when I was kicked forth from the playhouse and all for your baby face? No, Madam. God himself can't put back the mischief you've done me. I live but to see you in the dust, and afterwards could be content to starve."

The duel was between the women. They scarce heeded Macheath and he stood watching with an imprecation on his lips. Once more Diana began the hopeless task.

"Madam, I have money and to spare. 'Tis all at your disposal and more if you'll aid me to leave this house. Set me but in the street and——"

A laugh was the woman's only answer, but no more was needed. So, seeing she did but beat on marble, she stood a moment despairing, yet entreating some unknown Power in her soul for courage, for understanding to protect herself. But it seemed none took pity. And as she so stood suddenly a thought flashed the blood along her pale cheeks and sent the light to her dimmed eyes.

"Have you thought, Sir, that I shall be missed? The hue and cry will be raised when the Duchess knows I am not come."

Mrs. Bishop laughed harshly.

"Her Grace's anxiety was set at rest by a letter under your own hand to say you was otherwise engaged tonight. No, no, Mrs. Fenton. Here you are, and make the best of it. You leave it but as the wife of a man so much too good for you as I wonder he honours you with the offer."

"Madam," says Mr. Walker with great state, on hearing this praise,—"Mrs. Bishop says true—My offer need certainly not go abegging when half the women in London would jump at it. I allow for modesty and coquetry, and a rake like myself loves modesty in his women but you've said and done enough now to prove you the possessor of both. Prepare for the ceremony. The parson is belowstairs."

He went and opened the door, calling aloud,—

"Mr. Evans, be so obliging as walk up. The lady and me are ready."

But Diana had slipt to her knees by the sofa, hiding her face against it, beaten down at last, hopeless of any aid or pity but what might come from her own helpless courage. What stung her most cruelly was the letter to the Duchess. Heavens! What might not such wretches have writ in her name,—and the Duke would hear it and know her utterly vile. In that moment she tasted more than the bitterness of death, and owned herself utterly overreached.

A shuffling step came up the stair and a man entered whom, had she seen, she must shrink from with loathing—a dull heavy-eyed scoundrel in a parson's greasy gown threadbare at the edges,—one of the unfrocked crew that hung about the Fleet, ripe for any mischief, with the smell of drink hot on him. He took notice of the young creature on her knees, and showed his gapped teeth in a laugh. 'Twas not the first and would not be the last in the way of his business.

"Drag her up, Sir,"—he says to Walker. "She must stand. Let the lady hold her up on t'other side. 'Tis the signature after that really matters. Come on, young Madam,—Time and tide wait for no woman. I'm due elsewhere in thirty minutes."

But Diana did not raise her head.

"Come along, my dear. You promised to make me happy. Be as good as your word!" says Walker, wheedling and laying hold of her arm. Then first the man Evans observed her wrists.

"You must untie them, Mr. Walker. Sure a lady can't take the ring with her hands like that, and besides I mustn't have it said I married any woman dragged bound to the altar— Free her hands, Sir,—she can't escape anyhow."

Walker seeing him in earnest took out his knife and cut the bond as her hands lay stretched out on the sofa. But still she lay as if dead, with her head upon them.

"Now we're nicely!" says the horrid man. "Stand up, young lady, and we'll proceed with the sacred ceremony. Dearly beloved——"

Diana sprang to her feet.

"Sir, I am a young woman under the protection of the Duchess of Queensbury and the Duke of Bolton. I'm the famous Mrs. Fenton of 'The Beggar's Opera.' And if I come to harm rest assured the doers will be hunted to the gallows. This wicked man and woman have dragged me here——"

"You came of your own free will"—screams Mrs. Bishop, but the girl continued—

"And be assured if I live, I'll drag my case before the King and have justice though I die for it."

'Twas gallantly said and she faced them now like her fighting father's daughter. A moment—and the fallen parson looked doubtfully to Walker.

"You kept this from me, Sir. I did not know the lady had powerful friends. I understood 'twas a poor orphan. If this is the distinguished Mrs. Fenton, the town will be up to protect her. I can't go further till I have satisfaction."

Diana, seeing she was on the right track, continued earnestly.

"Sir, if you'll take me to Queensbury House or to Mr. Rich's house in Bloomsbury you'll receive a hundred guineas. I promise it. Less it shan't be and more it may. This portrait on my neck assures you of what I say—'tis her Grace, the Duchess. Take it as an earnest."

She tore it off and thrust it in his hand. He looked at it doubtfully and in much fear. A small ducal coronet surmounted it, and all the town riff-raff knew the handsome haughty face beneath the pearls. He clutched a greedy hand on it.

"Madam, I can't break faith with my employer. One gentleman don't betray another, so you must not expect I shall take you from his care, but all the same I won't marry you, so I won't, for the Church requires the woman shall say 'I will' and mean as well as say it. But I'm convinced that a little private talk between yourself and the handsome groom will soften your heart, and then I'm your man. I recommend the lady to leave the young couple together also and descend with me, and I'll wager all will be well."

He looked with a leer on Walker, and on Mrs. Bishop, and the woman rising threw on her capuchin and pulled the hood over her head.

"The reverend gentleman says well," she cried, "and I'm much mistook if when we return tomorrow morning we find you not as keen for the ceremony as now set against it. That's the only salve for a woman's honour, Mr. Evans. Will you lead the way?"

Diana caught his arm, entreating, praying not to be left with Walker. He loosed her hands laughing—

"Why, Madam, you've your remedy. Let the ceremony proceed, and the veriest prude need not shudder to be alone with her husband. Shall I go or stay?"

Mrs. Bishop was already at the door, looking darkly back upon her.

"You've but a moment to make your choice," says she,—"Marriage or worse. Come, Mr. Evans."

He looked back, Diana made a spring for the door, but they thrust her back and Walker caught her.

“Choose!” cries the man, opening his eyes at her and laughing as if her pain pleased the devil in him. She drew away from Walker and faced them all.

“I choose,” she said with her cheeks pale as death and her eyes glittering. ’Tis then a woman is dangerous!— “Go. Since there’s no help for me in God or man I’ll protect myself. Go!”

“Take notice,” cries Mrs. Bishop shrilly, “that she requests to be left alone with him. Mr. Walker, I wish you a good-night. Madam, I wish you the same with your lover.”

“Madam and Sir, your Servant!” says the reverend gentleman. The door banged and their steps were heard descending. The hall door opened and shut. They were heard to pass along the street.

“Won’t my charming creature lay aside her reserve now?” says Walker, approaching her once more. “We’re alone in the house, and if ’twas necessary to mislead others my Mrs. Fenton can be at her ease with her faithful lover. Let me have the joy to announce at the playhouse tomorrow that we’re man and wife. There’s many a man would speak no more of marriage after your refusal and you in my hands, but I’m my lovely creature’s most devoted, and will be as ready to send for the parson tomorrow morning as I was but now.”

He made to put his arm about her gallantly but she sprang back, a pair of scissors in her hand that she caught up from the table. He laughed contemptuous:

“You don’t fright me with that toy, child. Put it down.”

She held it up.

“I’ll plunge it in my own throat if you come nearer,”—she cried—a white fury with a line of gleaming teeth showing through her white lips. A mask of hatred that struck him dumb.

Not a brave man, though a showy, he tried to temporize.— After a minute’s hesitation—

“Put it down, my girl—put it down. I won’t frighten you. You’ll hurt yourself.”

She said no more, but stood rigid. A moment and Macheath flung out his arm suddenly to catch the weapon from her. She sprang aside, and he tripped his foot on the claw of the table and sprawled over it. Like lightning she rushed to the window and flung up the sash.

“Help—all good people! Help a poor girl trapped and held here by a villain!”

Her screams rang through the street, and a kind of terror that was half hatred seized the man lest she ruin him outright. He sprang at her, and holding her with the strength of fear and fury, bound her wrists once more, and when he had her helpless, bound her ankles also, and lifting her, flung her on the sofa.

"Lie there till I loose you," he cries. "Hunger tames beasts and may tame a wild cat like you. I leave you here till tomorrow, and if you come not to your senses when I return with the parson, 'twill be the worse for you."

He took a third strip of stuff and bound it over her mouth, then stood a moment looking at her.

"You've yourself to thank for this rough usage. I would have dealt otherwise with any but a fury. Learn wisdom now, before 'tis too late."

He extinguished the light, leaving her in darkness and went out, locking the door behind him, to seek counsel of Mrs. Bishop. The affair had reached a point that terrified him, and he knew not how to go back nor forward. Flight, not love, was his present inclination, and he thought never to return.

So she passed the night of Saturday and the day of Sunday.

# CHAPTER XVI

THE Duke, on leaving my Lord Baltimore with his former inamorata, strode down into the street, and stood for a moment in deep thought. 'Twas Mr. Rich was in his mind—that and the resolution to have done for good and all with his former friend and follow his search alone. The woman Bishop sickened him—Baltimore scarce less. 'Twas such a bewilderment of lies and intrigues as an honest man scarce could cut his way through. Better act alone, and if more slowly more certainly.

So standing a minute, he called a chair and directed the men to Rich's house in Bloomsbury. He had never entered it—their meeting being at the playhouse or other haunts of amusement, and certainly this occasion on which he made his bow there was the last he would have chose. To speak of Mrs. Fenton to any man was as distasteful to him as if she had been his sister—or his wife.

The comparison was strange and tingled along his veins like a draught of strong drink. His wife. O thought undreamt of and mad! Sure it should have been impossible for his idlest fancy to present such an image to his mind even for a moment! He dismissed it and returned to consideration of how he should open the matter with Rich.

The fine house astonished his Grace first as he drew up at the portico—a portico with pillars, forsooth, and extinguishers for the link-men to thrust their flambeaux. He knew Rich prosperous but had not expected this.

Strange days!—When a Harlequin and a man that adventured his luck in a playhouse could live so! We may thus observe the Duke haughty in spite of his contempt of many of his own company. He smiled a little sarcastic as a well-laced lacquey opened the door to the chairman's thundering knock, and, not knowing his visitor, announced somewhat supercilious that Mr. Rich was private in his study.

"Take this"—says the Duke briefly, writing his name on a paper, "and I'll follow you."

He directed the chair to wait and went with his quick step after the lacquey.

Mr. Rich flew to the door to receive him.

"My Lord Duke! The joyful surprise! What kind wind brings you to my poor shanty. 'Tis an honour I often wished, but dared not propose. The claret, Jenkins."

"Why, I thank you, Richie," says the Duke, as easy as any Lord Foppington and his levée, "You'll welcome me the more when I tell you I come as an ambassador of the greatest lady in London."

"The Queen?" cries Mr. Rich, trembling with excitement. "Doth her Majesty, honour us at the playhouse? Indeed I never dreamt— We must soften the allusions, your Grace."

"I forgot the Queen!" says the Duke coolly. "No, I meant her Grace of Queensbury. She's certainly *your* greatest lady, Richie, if we consider what she has done for your play."

Mr. Rich bowed assenting, pushing his cravat into place and wishing the Duke had gave more notice of his coming.

"Well, but it's thus," continues the visitor, stretching out his long legs easily in his chair,—"Mrs. Fenton did not return to Queensbury House last night, but sent a billet in place of her charming self. Her Grace commissions me to ask if Mr. Rich knows aught of her doings."

"Why, yes, my Lord Duke, and was more than a little overset for the moment, but on consideration can't see that 'twill affect the piece. If she turns a stage lover into a real one 'tis the lady's pleasure, though I could wish she had chose better while about it."

"We play at cross-purposes, I perceive!" The Duke sat up straight in his chair.

"Did the little minx not tell her Grace?" Rich was fumbling in his pocket.— "Why—where is it? O, here 'tis. I suspected nothing, being too busy a man to watch the flirtations of my pretty players."

Constraining himself to quiet, the Duke took the paper coolly and opened it.

> "Will my indulgent Mr. Rich forgive his Mrs. Fenton if she tells him that when she returns to the playhouse on Monday his Polly Peachum will be the bride of her Macheath in earnest as in play? 'Twas not necessary to trouble Mr. Rich with the affection that is sprung up, but his worthy heart will sympathise. Indeed I'm so persecuted with men as I must needs have a protector to stand between me and their insults, and Mr. Rich will own I have chose a stout one.
>
> I present my duty and my husband's to Mr. Rich and assure him he shall find us as ever (united as apart) his most faithful humble obedient servants,
>
> "LAVINA (FENTON) WALKER,

"FREDK. WALKER.

He laid it down.

"Of course the girl's a fool for she might have done much better!" continues the worthy Mr. Rich. "Walker's a loose fish, your Grace, and apart from all this, his reputation at the cards and bottle is none of the most unsullied. More than once I told him he plays Macheath so well because he hath a bit of Macheath under his own skin. But what would you? He hath a fine person, and the women look first to that on and off the stage. There's a postscript—did you observe?— ' 'Tis a brief honeymoon, for we return punctual on Monday.' "

"Read this," says the Duke and hands him the letter to the Duchess.

Rich's eyes all but started out of his head reading—

"The little liar! She judged her Grace would be offended at her secrecy. Well, why not be candid, say I? I thought better of Polly than to deceive her noble friend."

"I judge not so," says the Duke, rising. "Mr. Rich, both these letters are forged. Neither was writ by Mrs. Fenton. See for yourself that both could not be!"

"Why so it is!" Rich stared confounded at the Duke. "But what then—Lord! You fright me, Sir. Polly's more precious to me than diamonds. What's in your mind? My Lord Baltimore?"

"I know not. What's your own opinion of Baltimore?"

"Why—I'm bewildered. She gave me a necklace he gave her, because she would have none of it. Yet my Lord tells me and Bishop seconds him that she's his mistress. How shall a plain man tell what's the truth between them? I thought she scorned him. I have the jewels upstairs in keeping for her, but am not certain 'twas his gift."

It began to puzzle Mr. Rich's brain that the Duke was himself so earnest now. He had dropt the screen of the Duchess of Queensbury that he began with and his careless ease went with it. 'Twas a very anxious man that looked Mr. Rich in the face now, and cared not to hide his care.

"I begin to think we wade in deep waters," says he. "With your kindness we may swim ashore. Alone I cannot. My Lord Baltimore was with me today and made the assertion you speak of, but I believed him not. I propose now to follow all the clues given in these letters. They may be blinds only. They may be more. Where does the player Macheath lodge?"

"That story I reject entirely—now I see the other letter," cries Mr. Rich. "Indeed I could but half believe it before. I never saw a sign or token of the girl giving him a look more than needful on the stage. He moved his lodging two days ago and I know not the new one."

"Who should know?" asked the Duke.

"Scawen—old Scawen. She knows all the players' business, even to which has herrings for breakfast and which beef and ale. Let us to Scawen, my Lord Duke. I'm with you heart and soul. I would not lose my Polly for anything in earth or heaven."

"I thank you, Sir," the Duke said briefly. He stood while Mr. Rich was cloaked by his lacquey and another chair spoke for, and then the two were off, swinging down the street, each secluded from further conversation.

'Twas not far from the elegance of Bloomsbury to the somewhat sordid respectability of Mrs. Scawen's house, and at the window,—it now being six of the clock—they espied the good woman preparing the table for her Scawen's supper, with a steaming dish of stew before his place and a tankard of home-brewed. She opened the door in the utmost astonishment to see her visitors, wiping her hands hastily on her apron and dropping almost as many curtseys as words in her agitation.

"Why, Mr. Rich, why, my Lord—anything I can do—indeed it's an honour. Won't you please to be seated? Scawen will be in any minute. Sure a glass of home-brewed, though but a poor offering, won't hurt either the one or the other of you."

The Duke put his lips to the tankard sooner than disoblige the good lady. Mr. Rich came straight to the point—Walker's new lodging.

" 'Twas but two days ago he moved in and the landlady and husband went off junketing for a week to her mother at Hampstead village," cries Mrs. Scawen, who indeed knew everybody's business.— "Like a good-natured gentleman, which I always found him, Mr. Walker said he would eat at the coffee houses till they returned. Number 4, Wooton Street, ten minutes from here. Take the first turn to the right and to the right again and there you are. But what's this about my dear Mrs. Fenton, Mr. Rich? I hope no harm——"

For these questions however they could not stay and told her so, leaving her curtseying still like a puppet and with one eye on the couple of guineas Bolton left on the table.

Outside, Mr. Rich halted.

"Your Grace, I had best not go with you to Walker's, for this reason. I believe the man's name has been traded on as well as Mrs. Fenton's. He dare not meddle with her. Depend on't 'tis my Lord Baltimore, and you're on a wrong scent. Now I don't want to quarrel with Walker unless needs must. Look how my company's melting away! Mrs. Bishop gone, Walker hanging in the balance, if he don't hang in a worse place, and my Polly—the Lord knows where! Ask yourself how I'm to face the public tomorrow, and spare me Walker if you can."

The Duke acknowledged it reasonable.

"True. I'll see him alone,— But, Rich, I tell you this for truth also. If I find him mixed up in this scoundrelly business you may whistle for your Macheath, for I'll deal with the villain."

On this they parted.

During the ten minutes of his walk to Wooton Street, Bolton turned the question of Baltimore over and over in his mind, but could see no light—so dense was now the maze of intrigue and falsehood. He suspected all about him—only one person stood clear above it. Whoever he might doubt he never doubted her. There was a look in her honest eyes that spoke for her as true as a dog's speak when he looks up in his master's face, and he could as soon suspect her of windings and treachery. But his thoughts were bitter. What a world for honest men and women to move in! Did the great Dr. Swift say too much against the race of human beings when he depicted them as foul and filthy Yahoos in his terrible book that Bolton had read from cover to cover, finding food in it for his own scorn and melancholy? Diana—yes, but she moved like the Lady in Mr. Milton's "Comus," a virginal figure solitary amid the rabble rout of lust and hatred. And he—what could he do for her, but drag her down as low as any of them in their basest will? God in Heaven!—what a world! And still he strode on, and the women in the street fell back from his set face and wondered.

Arrived at the door, the house was dark but for a faint light on the first floor, where a rotten wooden balcony hung against the wall. There was no knocker. Clearly those that went in and out had their own keys. He stood dead silent listening. A man's voice he could not distinguish in the distance. Now a word from a woman equally indistinguishable. Growing impatient, he shouted aloud.

"Mr. Walker. A word with you on Mr. Rich's behalf," and repeated this twice in vain. The street was empty and quiet on the Sunday night and the people at their suppers, but he spied a big hulking fellow at his door, watching him with some curiosity and the Duke marches straight up to him.

"My good sir, I want that door burst in, and there's a guinea for any man will help me to do it. Are you that man?"

The man grinned and slowly detached himself from the door post.

"What about the watchmen?" says he.

"Why, that I take on myself. 'Tis for the rescue of an innocent young woman."

"There's no young woman there. But I'm your man. Come on."

They set their shoulders and knees to the door that offered but little resistance from age and bad hanging, and in five minutes the way was open. Bolton, halting with the utmost punctilio, pulled out the guinea.

"I recommend you, Sir, to keep a close tongue and prop the door so as it shan't attract attention. I am the Duke of Bolton. Five guineas more are at your service if you are at mine."

'Twas agreed, and in the dark he felt his way upstairs, till a rim of light beneath a door stopped him. He put his hand on the catch and walked in.

My Lord Baltimore faced him.

For a second he saw nothing else than this crowning justification for hatred and suspicion, and then became aware that Diana, her hands and feet bound, lay on the sofa behind. Like lightning his sword flashed from the sheath and he advanced on Baltimore.

"Liar! Villain!" He said no more, for his enemy's sword leaped to meet his, and the two clashed in air as each man put himself in the fighting posture.

"Twice you've insulted me. It's death for you or me!" cries Baltimore, and then, their teeth grinding, their eyes wild with hate, the battle began. The woman's voice, for she could move neither hand nor foot, came between them.

"Your Grace— You're mistook. O, cease—cease. He did not bring me here. He did not bind me. O, hear me, I beseech."

She wept and entreated, but still the fierce swords thrust and parried. As soon stop a tiger in his leap.

"A hit!" cries the Duke, red for joy and fury,—his sword had slipt through Baltimore's right arm,—the springing blood dyed the gay velvet and gold. He raised it frantically and thrust once more at Bolton, but his heart was stronger than his arm. It dropt and the sword fell clashing on the floor useless as a child's toy. In bitter rage and shame he flung himself into a chair and covered his eyes with the other.

"Liar! Coward!—Trapper of women, you have your deserts," says Bolton, in a voice the more awful because low as a woman's. He turned then to Diana almost fainting on the sofa.

"Madam, I can't decipher the story, but I know you pure as light. Have patience till I unbind you."

He knelt by her, with gentle and skilful hands unknotting the cruel bandages that had left great marks about her wrists and feet. He supported her in his arms, and, white as a ghost at cockcrow, she sat up leaning perforce upon his shoulder, half-dead from terror and long fasting.

"Don't speak!" he said tenderly. "Rest. 'Tis all over now, and you are safe. I beseech you, don't speak."

"But I must speak! O hear me, I implore you. This gentleman is innocent. He came but ten minutes since and would have released me. Indeed 'tis true, your Grace. 'Twas Walker and Mrs. Bishop misused me. I have told his Lordship that I have been bound here all night and this day. O let me rise that I may bind his arm. Look how he bleeds."

"If his attention is more welcome to you than mine——." The Duke was stiff and haughty once more, bewildered to the last degree.

"Pray, Madam, incommode not yourself for me. 'Tis but a scratch. A flesh wound!" cries Baltimore. "Curse the blood! Reach me that bandage, my Lord Duke."

His Grace pushed it with his foot and a look of scathing contempt. My Lord picked it up and kissing it with gallantry because it had bound Diana's wrists, proceeded to knot it, one-handed and holding it in his teeth as best he could.

"I can't see that!" says Diana, rising, wavering with weakness, to her feet. "Your Grace, you are a Christian and a gentleman. I tell you he is innocent. If you won't bind it, help me to him that I may bind it myself."

"You shall not need, Madam. Your rebuke is just,"—says the Duke coldly. "I will do it, and will then leave you to his Lordship's company."

Dead silence while he knotted it dexterously about the arm, first slitting the sleeve and cambric shirt beneath, my Lord submitting in silence and with something of a smile in his eyes. This done, the Duke wiped his sword, took up his hat and bowed to Diana.

"I leave you now, Madam, to the fate you have chosen for yourself. We shall not meet again. I wish you happy."

Diana looked despairingly at him, but was silent. My Lord took up the word, sitting very much at his ease in the chair—the Duke pausing to lean on his sword, looking on the ground.

"Your Grace, I will be the lady's spokesman. She is overwearied. I have pursued Mrs. Fenton for many weeks with intentions the most dishonourable. To my fire she opposed frost. I have made no way with her. She is chaste as ice and pure as snow. I have lied like a poltroon in saying she favoured me, and entreat her forgiveness for this and all else. Also your Grace's. What mad schemes I have had to bend her to my will I need not tell, for they have all come to nothing. This day I heard she was gone, and of all that circumstance your Grace knows the truth. I swear it on my honour as a peer, as a gentleman. We sought her together, and you left me with Mrs. Bishop. Your Grace knows her for my cast mistress, and 'twill explain her rancour. Left alone with her, with alternate threats and promises, I dragged out the truth of Walker's plot against the lady's honour. I know not how far she encouraged it, but it seems Walker came to her in terror, too frightened to proceed further, and for all I knew they might leave this innocent here to die that they might save their skins. I have my own methods with Mrs. Bishop and she gave me the keys. She will not offend again. As for Walker, I know not where the base scoundrel is fled. So I came here on Mrs. Bishop's guiding. This is the whole truth. In this I have done honestly. In the lie I told, I have done so as I can neither forgive myself nor expect forgiveness."

Silence. Diana looked steadfastly at the Duke, her heart all but pausing, as it were, to hear. He came slowly forward to my Lord.

"Though I think your pursuit of this lady execrable, knowing her what she is—and at present can in no way bring myself to pardon the lie that has smirched her fame to another as well as to myself, I have in this matter done you an injustice, and therefore apologize and bitterly regret that I was mistook."

My Lord raised himself in his chair, with something of dignity.

"Your Grace, I forgive you freely and again ask your pardon and better opinion. Your censure is most just. In your presence I will amend my crime. I have aspersed the lady's honour. I put mine in her hands." He rose and advanced towards Diana, pale as death, but stately and beautiful, a touch of triumph in his aspect.

"Mrs. Fenton, I entreat your forgiveness for the sufferings I have caused you consciously and unconsciously. I honour the ground you walk on, for there is no purer woman in all the world. And because this is so, I ask you before this gentleman to be my wife, and I swear that I will hold you as the light of my eyes until death darkens them for ever."

'Twas a fine motion and my Lord knew it, though at the moment he was sincere. He stretched his unwounded left arm to clasp her hand, but she shrank away from him toward the Duke.

"Madam, you must answer," says he briefly, still looking on the ground, and at this command her voice broke very low and trembling upon the room and her two hearers.

"My Lord, I thank you. For the honour you do me I thank you. And I refuse it though I forgive and will forget your aspersion on me."

Amazement, incredulity on my Lord Baltimore's face. The Duke had turned aside; his was hid.

"Madam, you surely have not considered. I repeat my offer. The marriage shall take place tomorrow."

A pause, and then—

"Madam, you still distrust me. I swear amendment. Cannot you love me a little? In offering all, do I offer nothing? Have you no forgiveness?" 'Twas the bitterness of wounded pride. The real man spoke at last through his formality. To have stepped down so far and to be scorned! He held his arms to her as if they were alone. The blood stained his bandage.

She uttered a little womanly cry.

"Your poor arm! O, Sir, pray be seated. Don't ask me any more, I beseech you. I like you better than ever I thought to do. Indeed I pity your wound—indeed I do, with all my heart. But I don't love nor esteem you. Marry some great lady that can. This is my last answer. Press me no more."

He frowned and flushed, turning to the Duke.

"You have heard. Tell it to the town, your Grace, that Baltimore was rejected. I see not that I need be ashamed."

"I shall tell nothing to the town, my Lord, save that you are a man of honour. You have done right,—and for the step you have taken now—were my hand as free as my heart I would lay my own name at this lady's feet, so do I love and honour her. My case is hopeless. This being so, yours is a happier one and may one day meet its reward. But if you shall one day succeed——"

His voice broke on it, Diana speechless between the two and Baltimore staring spellbound. The Duke recovered himself first from this strange scene. He spoke hurriedly!

"She's half fainting, and we think but of ourselves. Stay with her, Baltimore, while I get a coach."

He sprang down the stair, and Diana, slipping back upon the sofa, covered her face with her hands, Baltimore almost as white and stunned as she.

# CHAPTER XVII

IN Queensbury House, the Duchess sat that night in her library to hear the story from Bolton. Diana slept in her own room, worn out and wearied beyond all power of speech or even of thought.

In his splendid rooms in the next street my Lord Baltimore lay in solitude, considering the past, not entirely unhopeful for the future, and as the Duchess heard the story of his offer, she sent a kind thought to him, winged above the grimy house-tops that might well help to assuage the sting of his wounded arm.

"Good blood doesn't lie," says she in her bright sententious manner—"A haberdasher hadn't acted thus, and especially before a third person. But he made his amend like a gentleman."

"Like a gentleman!" asserts the Duke. "I never liked him so well. But a good woman makes men better, as a bad one drives them to the devil."

"And which am I?" says she with her smile that none other ever matched.

"You are Kitty. There's none like you. Nature broke her mould after she made you, Madam, and so did she also—with another. One other. I thank God I know the two women I love—one as a friend, the other as a lover—incomparable."

She prest his hand softly,—nay, even touched his face,—brushing it like a butterfly's wing for gentleness. There was a minute's silence.

"I knew long since you loved her," she said, "And indeed 'tis a fair creature in mind and body, and, as I think, a spotless heart. What shall her future be? Baltimore I dare swear she will never have— She's so simple that unlike the women of our world she thinks love the only wear! and to be my Lady Baltimore nothing to the purpose. The little sweet fool! How shall it end, Bolton?"

He made a gesture of despair, but said nothing.

The Duchess continued:—

"I shall hear her tale tomorrow, and perhaps decipher her heart in it, but what then? Shall she continue at the playhouse?"

"Not if I die on the threshold. I sent a message to Rich on coming here that I would wait on him in an hour. My way is dark before me—I know not how things shall be, yet know certainly that on those boards she shall never set foot again."

"I think you in the right," says Kitty softly. "Yet—our poor play!"

"Madam, consider. Consult your own noble heart—you that was her first friend and she so forlorn. I know what it will reply. And consider this also,—we know Congreve said, '’Twill either take greatly or be damned confoundedly.' Well—it has took. It has played now for fifty-eight days—a thing unknown. ’Tis Gay's own counsel to withdraw it soon and hope for a renewal next season. It flies all over England like thistle-down on a wind. What you set out to do is done. Never was such a triumph. Spare her then, Madam, who has made it so. She is all genius, fire, and light, yet as little fit for the grossness that must meet her there as your own sister. Yet if you command her to continue she will, so deep is her gratitude to her kind protectress."

His voice, low and pleading, the care and trouble in his face, moved his friend. She looked at him with exquisite gentleness. The world had not known the bright cold Duchess then.

"My friend, would I add one trouble to your troubles? And I think you in the right. After all—the play's but a play—the girl is living flesh and blood, and I know in any case she could not return for many days. I'm sorry for Rich, but again—what is a Harlequin manager to the pleasure of noble persons? Go to him. But before you go, once more tell me—is there no thought in your mind for her future? Return to her mother she cannot. The husband will use her worse than the playhouse."

"It drives me near distraught that I can think of no outlet. Were my wife other than she is—perhaps as her gentlewoman— But ’tis impossible."

"Impossible, and can't you hear the town's chatter? Besides, as soon shut a swan in a poultry yard as make a waiting-gentlewoman of a girl that can sing and play and look like this. She has her own throne, Bolton. How ask her to hold her lady's fan and gloves? Not but what I believe she would do that also, for she is all sweetness, but ’tis a thing unthinkable. Well—I must consider of it. Go you to Rich."

He kissed her charming hand, and went his way, and the Duchess, whistling her Pompey, despatched a word to the Lady Fanny Armine.

"Come to me for a council of war tomorrow morning. Great events."

’Tis needless to describe Mr. Rich's consternation and frenzy when the Duke made him acquainted with the circumstances. But to do him justice, his first thought was pity for the poor girl so cruelly trapped and used.

"Why, my Lord Duke, if I had Walker here at this minute, I'd run him through the body,—Stap my vitals, if I wouldn't,—the gross cowardly lump of flesh! Never again shall he play in company of mine, and as to meeting

Mrs. Fenton—why sure the poor Polly would die of terror at his feet. 'Tis to be supposed he's in hiding. The hue and cry shall be sent after him."

"Why no, Mr. Rich," says the Duke, very composed and resolute. "We choose not so. The lady's name must not be dragged in with so vile an adventurer, nor mentioned in a breath with a woman like Bishop. My Lord Baltimore has dealt with her. She's the worst offender, since she confesses she made the fool believe that Mrs. Fenton was taken with him. These two will trouble us no more. But—there's a further matter. Mrs. Fenton is very ailing with the shock and horror. Her spirits are sunk very low. The Duchess judges as do I, that she could not return for a fortnight or more."

"Lord bless me—here's a stew! What shall I do? Why the business fell off to half when she was absent three days not long since. A fortnight! Lord! The poor child. Well, but—we must publish a part of the story without names, and her return in a fortnight will draw the whole town if but to look at her! Tell her this, your Grace, and beg her to give her adorable self all due rest."

"You are all goodness, Sir, and your sensibility and justice are known to us, but I regret very sensibly to tell you that Mrs. Fenton returns no more. 'Tis fully determined and can't be altered."

'Tis well to draw a veil over the next ten minutes and Mr. Rich's agonies,—waves breaking against a rock. The Duke was patient, he sympathized, he deplored, but held to his point immovable. Indeed it took Mr. Rich more than ten minutes to realize his fate, and he then sat with his hands on his knees, the very picture of despair.

"What in the devil's name shall I do?" says he— " 'Twas too good to last. Well—there's no more to say. I beseech your Grace to leave me for I'm a sore bewildered man. It all comes together like, for the sequel—"Polly" is forbid to be played and I counted on this. She hath had two Benefits, your Grace. Indeed I have treated her well."

"All know it," says the Duke soothingly, "and a grateful heart is your reward. Further, Sir,—if—(and I know you are an honest man)—you can demonstrate to me that you are at a money loss in this regard you shan't be the loser—no, nor the other patentees of the playhouse. I'll see to that."

Rich looked at him astonished,—then a smile more knowing than beautiful overspread his features.

"Your Grace, I say no more. I'm answered on all points. I can but wish my Mrs. Fenton well and happy whoever she may bless with her society. I don't give up hope that we may see her again one day and she as welcome as sun in winter."

But Bolton had marked the smile. He spoke very grave.

“Mr. Rich, I treat you as one gentleman another when I say that no conjectures must be made, that this whole story is private to your ear alone, and that the lady’s honour is and will be unsullied as snow. There the matter must abide, and in your hands I know it safe, and that your voice will repel any insinuations.”

Rich promised eagerly. What would he not have promised such a patron? But he meant and kept his promise. Future events took the matter out of his hands, and set loose circumstances he could not control, but so far as man can be true, he was true.

They parted with courtesy and mutual respect and liking, and the Duke returned a solitary and wearied man to the unloved splendours of his dreary and empty palace. Why had she refused Baltimore? That was the question that tormented him. Sure none but Love the almighty—the Lord of all, could determine a poor girl to refuse a coronet, the handsomest and most followed man in London—a man also who must adore her since he broke down his pride and laid his all before her.

As for Mr. Rich, he plunged into affairs with all but frenzy, determined to pull triumph from the wreck if possible. But his soul was sad too for his Polly with her great sweet eyes. This girl had the gift to make all love her with what love they had to give, maternal, friendly, sisterly—manly, adoring. Excepting only a rival, she had but to smile, and hearts were at her feet. Possibly the charm might be her own loving heart exprest through those clear mirrors of her violet eyes. ’Tis much to be beautiful, but goodness and beauty together, must sure be a love philtre irresistible, and if genius be added—the lady, like another Helen, fires another Troy.

With the morning my Lady Fanny’s chair, lined with puckered satin like a jewel-case to hold its jewel, stopped at the door of Queensbury House, and dainty as a newly burnished bird of paradise she alit, leaning her arm on the footman’s, and went tripping up the great steps in the early sunshine. A smile hovered like a sunbeam on her rosy lips—she palpitated to taste the mystery the Duchess exprest in her letter, and the more because her thoughts were sweetened with hope. The straying sheep might sure be reclaimed to the fold of her heart if Bolton— But who could tell? She tript the faster up the great shallow stairs scarce touching the gilt balusters with her gloved hand as she went so light.

The door opened, she ran straight into the Duchess’s arms and bestowed and took a warm and friendly kiss.

“What is’t, Kitty? Great events? I tore myself from my bed an hour early and drove my woman crazy and here I am. Don’t delay for chocolate, but speak. I die of curiosity.”

But Pompey and the chocolate must be waited for before the Duchess would speak. She then commanded that none should be admitted on any pretence, and drawing her chair to my Lady Fanny's poured forth the story, concealing nothing.

He who had watched,—were any man thus privileged, might have read the progress of the story on the eager listening face. It darkened with anger, it softened with pity as Diana's misery, bound, fainting, helpless, was disclosed before her.

" 'Tis a cursed thing to be a woman!" she cried—"The world is against us. What are we but a prey from beginning to end—in love, in business, in everything. But go on!"

She struck her hands together, at the player's insults to his victim. "Were I a man!" she cried. Indeed 'twas a quick generous soul and the friendship between those two women easy to understand while the one talked and the other heard. But 'twas when the Duchess came to Baltimore and his part in the story that a darkness clouded her bright face and her hands claspt hard in her lap.

Not a word—not a word did she say, only listened, listened. He was wounded,—she winced as if the sword pierced her bosom. Diana entreated to bandage his arm—she half drew back in suspense and doubt. But 'twas when my Lord laid his great name and person at the girl's feet that the beating heart sent its tide of crimson over the face, that ebbing left it white and blank. The Duchess either not seeing or judging friendliness lay that way, continued with her story, but 'tis doubtful if my Lady Fanny heard for a few bitter moments.

Suddenly, the tale done, the Duchess slipt on her knees by her friend's chair, and put her arms about her, silently. So they continued for some minutes, and a hot tear trickling down Lady Fanny's cheek fell on the Duchess's, and yet neither spoke, only the kneeling woman's arms tightened about the other, and the room was still. At last, the blackbird in the gilded cage sang loud and sweet in the sunshine, and Lady Fanny started and looked down into the Duchess's wet eyes.

"My dear, my dear, don't cry for me. I'm not worth your tears,—A dream is broke, no more! The sun shines, the night flies and its dreams with it. But indeed my other Kitty, my Lady Desmond herself could not be more true and kind than you. I thank you, my dearest, kindest Duchess, with a full heart."

"Fanny, my dear, have we not warrant to say a prodigal son may return?" says the other very low.

"But not a prodigal lover! They never come back. The swine and the husks and the harlots—God forgive me, I mean not the poor ill-used girl, but we all know Baltimore's former life,—and he would have used her the like way had she consented."

"Yet, Fanny, he made amends. Bolton hath told me he meant his offer in more than words. There must be goodness in the man, and had you but patience——"

"I have had longer patience than I would even own to myself, much less to others. But 'tis done. Besides, Kitty—'tis a horrid shock that he should thus trail his name in the dirt. A player! One may comprehend an intrigue, but this is a million times lower!"

"If you say this you never loved him, my dear, and I rejoice with you that you have found the heart you did but mislay. For love, they say, seeks not its own, rejoices in goodness—and sure that was a good motion in a man sufficiently worthless. If indeed he meant it."

"Passion—no more!" says Lady Fanny, her fine lips hardening. "Bas would give the world in haste for any trinket he wanted, and repent at leisure, and his victims with him. Pity me no longer, my dear. I think my tears were the distillation of anger, though indeed I scarce know my own heart yet. Give me time to consider, and tell me what you have in view, for surely the world turns topsy-turvey when— Heaven help us!—I can scarce believe it! Bolton also! Do the men run mad? But he was safe in his offer. That woman, his wife, will outlive us all."

The Duchess resumed her seat, but took her friend's hand.

"I had rather hear you own you loved him—I can't tell why, but 'tis so. Better pain than self-scorn."

Lady Fanny laughed as sweet but not as true as the bird's song.

"What use to give a diamond when a string of glass beads would be preferred? And if lost, they matter much less. Rejoice with me, Kitty, since the beads are lost, that they were glass and never saw Golconda. Now spare my pride, and let us speak of Bolton. What would you have?"

"I would have a good man and a good woman made happy," says the courageous Duchess—"and if not after the world's way, then after their own. Bolton's life is like a wasting river lost in the sands, Diana's is one of such danger and dread as I don't like to consider."

"Well, since rank is nothing, and good blood but to be puddled with base, and honour a mere jest, would you have him marry her? But sure you know he lost his chance to have the marriage dissolved, and a man that's *your* friend has little chance with the King at present."

"True for you, Fanny. No hope that way. Then I would—don't so stare at me! I would have them live together as man and wife and trust to the future with hope and love to gild it."

"A thing often done!" says Lady Fanny bitterly—"and you and I—we know our world and how it ends. Two years at the most, tears, regrets, a pension, and then the woman takes up with some one else. Look at Mrs. Oldfield. First Mainwaring. Then Churchill."

"My Lady Fanny little understands either Bolton or his Diana in speaking thus, and I thought your wit sharp as a diamond. She is no wanton, and he—. His heart is aching, dying for love and a home and a fond woman to welcome him in it. He has tasted the pleasures—Yes, Fanny—but with weariness always, with sick distaste. I know not a man more to be pitied. And he loves this girl. He is true and tender—he would repay no love with pain. Least of all hers. Consider! You must help me judge. You half thought me jesting t'other night. I am in sober earnest."

"And this lady who spurns coronets—will she take up the position you offer, Kitty? Will he offer it? I think you talk wild. Will he bear to see her scorned? O, let me go home! I'm sick of the world we live in—mortally sick. A fine task for us truly to help a man to his mistress!"

"Who was it said t'other night—'The day that saw Bolton content with a good woman I'd mark with a white stone in my calendar'? I think 'twas you!"

"True. I said it. I meant it. But what part shall I play?"

The Duchess looked at her composedly.

"If she should do this, your Ladyship, would you still be her friend,—Would you treat her as his true wife, defend her name, honour her?"

"Would you?"

"Very certainly. But from me she has stolen no Bas."

Lady Fanny laughed sadly.

"How well you know me! You play me like a puppet. Yes—because she has robbed me, I'm to act the noble part, am I?"

"She did it not willingly."

"True. Well—you pull the string that makes me dance. You mean—why should I revenge on the girl what she could not help? You ask something of a man's greatness of soul from me when I would hug my own little petticoated rancours. But I'll respond. Yes, I'll help you to make her the fashion and know herself not despised."

"She cares not for the fashion. She cares for the friendship of women she can honour."

"And she would honour me?"

"She does."

"O Kitty, you wheedler! You roll the bolus in honey. But I'll swallow it from your hand and Bolton's. As I said t'other night when I little suspected what 'twould cost me—I'll follow where you lead. You may use me as you will with Bolton. After all—the Queen receives Mrs. Oldfield on the sly."

"My Lady Fanny is more than the loose-tongued Queen and she will receive Mrs. Fenton openly," says the Duchess gravely.

"She will!" cries Lady Fanny— "O Kitty, tell me to dance on the tight-rope at the Fair, to grin through a horse-collar, to do anything in the wide world you bid me—and if your Grace does it, I'll do it unflinching also. Let us court ridicule and worse in common!"

They kissed one another on it—the Duchess very tenderly. She knew the sore sting at her friend's heart, for if not love in the highest, still, love is pain and hurt pride a bitter salve for it. She knew also the fine high-bred generosity that rings responsive when the steel of a high call is struck upon it, and in all London there would be no aid like Lady Fanny's and her own for the poor lovers she would help.

"We will make them happy," says she, "Bolton is singularly helpless where women are in hand;—Diana but a trembling girl as yet, but will be a fine woman. Come hither and see her soon, and be her judge—and her angel."

They parted on this, my Lady Fanny carrying her hurt under a gay cover, as many of her ancestors had done a thrust through flesh and blood. Well—shall a woman fail in courage that heeds it a thousandfold more than any man—she that must oppose a tender unarmed bosom to the thrust? She knew not her own heart yet—'twas so sudden a downfall.

"When I see him I shall know. But he'll avoid me. He has not even pity—

"I have asked grace at a graceless face

And there was none for my men and me."

she said to her own heart. Words she often used since she knew my Lord Baltimore.

She took her pen when alone, and wrote thus to the cousin of her love:

"*My Kitty*, I have had a blow that leaves me bewildered. I scarce can tell whether I'm alive or dead. As a man falling from his horse picks himself up stunned and bruised and cannot say at first whether 'tis he or another—so am I. 'Tis either death or a cure, and for the life of me I know not which. When my eyes can see you shall hear. But pity me, my Kitty,—I would ask no pity but yours on whose faithful love I have reposed since I was a child. Love me also, for I am solitary. Fie, this soft self-pity—I loathe it. And I am embarked with Kitty Queensbury in an adventure so odd that sure 'tis one of her oddest, and I know not what your sedately married Ladyship would say to it or to me. Farewell, Kitty, for today. My little painted boat is run on the rocks, and I must try to drag her off and set my idle sail again and salve what I can of the wreck. She was called 'The Hope' and I know not whether my heart was the cargo or no. Again, when I know, I will be open with you.

"I send you my heart's love—*that* love at least I can never doubt of.

"From your affectionate humble servant and cousin,

"FANNY ARMINE."

# CHAPTER XVIII

TWAS a se'nnight later and Diana, recovered but pale enough still, sat in the Duchess's library and tried to read in a book but could not, so pressing was her own history.

For, it had been notified to her by her Grace that the long run of "The Beggar's Opera" was over. With the three leaders changed it struggled on a few nights as on crutches, but a meeting between the patentees of the playhouse and Mr. Gay had decided it should now be laid on the shelf till the next season. So the walls that had echoed so often to her voice were now unfaithful and echoed as blithely to others and the fickle public laughed, applauded and forgot her.

'Twas a wounding thought. However she might dread certain things the playhouse brought her it had been her grand triumph, and re-made her life into a marvel she herself could scarce understand. Wonderful figures, the Duke, her Grace, my Lady Fanny Armine, and many more now walked in her world familiar and kindly. While she lay abed weak and sad, my Lady Fanny visited her, sometimes alone, sometimes with her friend, brought her posies, rare fruits, talked with her softly, surrounded her with delicate cares, until she won Diana's heart and her languid eyes brightened when she heard the little high-heeled step come tripping to her door.

'Twas very wonderful. Wonderful beyond all speech that these great ladies should so obligingly bestow any of their time and thought upon a stranger whose fate had drifted her into their sight as the sea drifts its weeds, to be borne away on the next tide.

For the hour was now arrived when she must bid farewell to Queensbury House that was grown so dear to her heart. As she lay in the red velvet bed gazing upon the room grown so familiar, she had spent much time considering in what most dutiful and grateful terms she must take her farewell of the Duchess.

Her Grace being absent at Kensington that day and my Lady Fanny entering unexpected, she resolved to consult her Ladyship. She now sat in a great library chair with the Duchess's paper-cutting in her hand, a pastime all the mode and introduced at that house by the gifted Mrs. Pendarves, cousin to her Grace. With pointed scissors Diana snipped the paper into little rosy figures, urns, and temples in the Greek taste for decorating mantels and boxes in colors on a black background. Mr. Pope himself, the famous poet, had been pleased to direct the production of certain of these scenes from his own rendering of the "Iliad" and "Odyssey," and to commend Diana's skill.

"Our device shall be joyous, Madam," says he. "You are too young and fortunate to represent the grief of Andromeda and Hecuba, or the rape of Helen. No,—Mrs. Fenton with her little sharp weapon, shall depict the Princess Nausicaa playing at ball with her maidens, or the divine Calypso singing as she speeds her golden shuttle, till all the woods ring to that celestial harmony. And, if you please, Madam, I would have the Princess to resemble the lady who reproduces her features, since no more youthful and lovely model can be. And Calypso also, since her melody cannot excel Mrs. Polly's." For even Mr. Pope diluted his venom when he spoke with her, and gazed with pleasure on a creature of such obliging sweetness.

She rose and curtseyed to my Lady and drew a chair, and presently displayed her little works to the critic.

"But you haven't obeyed Mr. Pope, Diana. This Grecian Princess is more like Mrs. Pendarves than the model chose by Mr. Pope, and Calypso—who is she? I suspect this Hermes to be——"

She stopt suddenly, a little confused, but Diana, untroubled by knowledge of her thoughts, replied calmly.

"Madam, I thought of my Lord Baltimore in snipping it. My kind wishes attend his Lordship. I hope his wound heals."

'Twas said with such a complete serenity and absence of any second meaning that my Lady could accept of it with the same tranquillity.

"You think of him then kindly?" says she. "I have heard the story. Don't fear to speak."

"Without doubt, Madam. I feared his Lordship at one time, but 'tis long past, and he hath made amends so generous as blots out all offence. What!—do not we all err? and shall we not ask pardon? He hath a generous heart that would pay a debt with interest."

"And if you think thus, is your forgiveness not akin to pity and pity to love? Did he not swear to wait until all hope was past?"

"Madam, give me leave to say I think your Ladyship does not wholly understand him. I judge that he is one who pursues with such ardour that he will not be hindered. Let any obstacle be in his way and it shall be destroyed. But gained—the dust is then bruised on the butterfly's wings and he will cast it aside and chase another. When his generous heart made that surprising offer 'twas because he saw his poor prize torn from him. At that moment the world would not have been overmuch to give. But supposing my vanity believed him stable there would be a rude awakening. If we could read now his Lordship's thoughts I doubt not but he rejoices at his escape. He is one whose mind and inclinations will ever be stronger than the motions of his heart. He will not again risk refusal."

"You are a philosopher in hoop and gown, child. Will you not allow him a lover?"

"A lover of the chase, Madam. I think no more where I am concerned. Whether one day he shall meet his true mate, 'tis not for me to say. But I doubt."

"You don't trust him?"

"With me, Madam, trust and love go hand in hand. I don't love my Lord Baltimore, but wish him extreme well. I am willing to have hopes of him however if he find the lady I imagine."

"Describe her, child."

"She should, Madam, be beautiful of face and person, swift-witted and therefore able to meet and counter him on all points. He must not have any superiority allowed him. Her parts must out-top his, so that at all times he knows her superior though he won't admit it. Yet must all this be tempered with a charming sweetness, with gentle glances and endearing approaches, and over it must be thrown the veil of dignity and modesty. See the drawing the gifted Madam Pendarves hath made of the chaste Penelope. That is what my poor words would express but cannot."

She unrolled a classical drawing of Penelope confronting the lawless suitors, and Lady Fanny gazed at it.

"She moves a goddess," said she. "But where are these paragons, Diana? Sure my Lord must go unwedded to his grave if he waits for this!"

"No, Madam. My Lord has not eyes to see and he will marry as most men marry and be the worse for it. 'Tis only such a woman could endure and temper his failings. Another were mad to attempt it."

"I think, child, you say very true," replied her hearer and fell into a musing. Presently—

"Diana, have you ever loved a man? What is love?"

"I know so little that my thought is not worth words."

"Then you have thoughts?"

"Yes, Madam. Sure every woman must."

They were both silent. Her Ladyship then resumed, not looking in the girl's face.

"I heard the whole story, child, and with me 'tis safe. Dare I say that what touched me the most sensibly (next to your own sufferings) was my Lord Duke's? Sure he spoke from his heart! He can do no other."

"His Grace spoke on a very noble sensibility, Madam. 'Twas designed to comfort a poor distrest nearly-undone girl with the thought that she might still hold the respect of a man of honour. I took it no other. Your Ladyship will remember 'twas a scene very moving, and such draws words that overtop the more sober judgment."

"You are wise, Diana, as your sister goddess Minerva, yet I think you mistook here. Suppose, however, his Grace might mean to the full what he said, what would your heart reply?"

"That, Madam, I could only tell to his Grace," says the girl softly, " 'twould be dishonourable else. Shall I drape Calypso's robe from the right or left shoulder?"

Her gentleness was a rebuke, and my Lady admired and wondered at the grace and dignity that gave it. Indeed she had learnt much and swiftly in the society of such perfectly well-bred women and men as she lived with in Queensbury House. Good manners are an infection not to be resisted by gentle and pliable natures and they were native to her inclinations, and did but adorn a fine heart.

"Your Ladyship," says she presently, "I beg your counsel. I must leave here very shortly and I would do all in the way that best should testify my grateful heart to her Grace. What should I say? or write?"

"Who can teach you, child! All you do must be pleasing. But I think she will not have you go. What are your hopes?"

"I shall play no more. I could love it if men and women would let one be, but this they will not. I have spoke with Mrs. Pendarves and 'tis her opinion I could teach singing. Her goodness has promised me pupils."

"Yes—but, child, when you leave the Duchess—I would have you visit with me for awhile."

She looked up with the glowing smile that won all hearts.

"I thank you indeed, Madam, though 'tis of a piece with all your kindness in my sickness. To be with you cheers the heart like sunshine,—and how shall I merit such goodness?"

"But 'tis for my own selfish sake!" cries Lady Fanny. "Mine is a solitary life, and I think I could comprehend a friend. Yes—*friend*, child. Don't look so frightened. We are both women and young, why may I not choose a friend!"

She had not intended it. She was not easy won and her Ladyship's pride was a fortress, but at this silver summons she surrendered like others, and indeed forgot the grand scheme. She desired Diana about her very earnestly, and the Duke's advancement slipt from her thoughts.

"If her Grace will part with you, come to me!" says she eagerly. "I will do my utmost for your happiness, and you shall set my posies for me, sing to me, counsel me, for indeed I see you very capable of it. What say you?"

Diana would have spoken, but for a moment astonishment hindered her, and ere she could reply the door swung open and the Duke of Bolton entered. He had not seen her since the dreadful Sunday that even now poisoned her dreams.

Curtseys from the ladies to his Grace, bows of the courtliest ere he would seat himself beside them. Her Ladyship's dream blew away like a gay-coloured bubble in a breeze that must shatter it. A dream indeed. There was another future in store for the young creature beside her and she herself was pledged to it.

"You come very seasonable!" says she, gathering up her fan and gloves,—"for I am expected at my Lady Carteret's for basset and scandal. At least four reputations will escape with scarce a scratch if I am absent. 'Tis me for the death-blow!"

She drew her gay glitter over her face as quick as her capuchin over her damask gown. It needed the time and the place for my Lady to disclose the unmodish truth that among her other possessions she ranked a heart and a true one. Bolton however needed not testimony.

She kissed Diana on the cheek at parting, and turning on her little heel, made to go. At the door she paused, Bolton leading her.

"Diana," says she, "for a moment I will play Mr. Pope's oracle at Delphi. Happiness has wings. When she alights, capture her that moment. Cage her, close the door on the lovely thing, for if she flies she flies for ever. Be wise in time!"

She curtseyed once more and tripped downstairs all gaiety, touching his hand with but the tips of her fingers. As he handed her down the great steps she paused a moment more, and said softly:

"Were I a man and such a woman within my reach, I would win her if I died for it."

"And I," said he, "if I did not bring her dishonour for my first lover's gift."

"I think—" says my Lady deliberately, "that honour and dishonour are words we play with. Honour is a thing of the soul. It resides within and none but ourselves shall judge for us. The world cannot."

She looked strangely at him, and was gone.

"I have done my part by Kitty, but how about Diana?" says she to herself, watching him reascend the steps.

Being much at his ease in that house he went up again unannounced and Diana, thinking him gone for good, was still in her chair, snipping away patiently at the Duchess's little figures. She spent much time in catching up with her Grace's cast needleworks and others, for 'twas Kitty's way to snatch at a pleasure and forsake it almost instantly for the next, Diana or another following in her wake to gather the fragments.

So he found her, leaning pensive over her paper gods and goddesses.

"I rejoice I find you alone, Madam," say he, standing very tall and troubled before her—"I would hear how you do. You are still pale—almost as when I saw you in that cursed room. O, 'tis too much to think on what you suffered. But are you indeed well?"

She looked up and would have spoke, but he was instantly at her feet.

"If to have dreamed of you nightly and thought of you the live-long day deserves compassion, grant it to me, and answer me one question—one only!"

Does a woman think in these moments of sweet madness? Not she—how should she, with the one voice in her ears, the one face pleading, quivering before her. In that sudden passion she could not speak nor look. Her hands clasped in her lap, she gazed down on them and all her being was to hear.

He did not touch her, but leaned from his chair so that he appeared to kneel. Certainly the man's heart knelt as before a shrine.

"What I would know is this— Why did you reject Baltimore? I know no other woman that had done it. Is your heart so hard? Could you not forgive the man? Men err and women should pardon."

She never raised the veil of her lashes, only her hands trembled a little. Was he pleading for the absent?

"Since I saw you this question hath torn me. Is your chastity so cold, Diana, that you only cannot pity the flame you inspire? You saw him falsely changed, wounded, repentant, and yet you refused him. Tell me why, I beseech you."

"I pitied him. I would have bound his wound," she said at last, very low.

"Then why—why?" says he urgently. "Pity is near love, they say."

"I cannot love him, your Grace. You counselled me once to marry. I could not. My heart spoke for me and refused."

He considered on that a moment, then continued.

"You know what followed. You heard me, and now I ask a question so mad that you'll do well to kill me with the scorn in those large eyes— But answer first. Could I have said what he said—had I been free and not a fettered slave, would you have dismist me also?"

Then, in a quick revulsion—"No, don't answer, for I have no strength to hear."

He hid his face in his hands, propping them on his knee. So, quivering in every limb, she laid hers on them and drew them gently away until his eyes looked into hers.

"Let me answer, my Lord Duke. 'Twill ease my heart that answered for me when you spoke. Had Lord Baltimore been you, I could have loved the very ground he stood on—but refused."

"And why?" Their hands were claspt now each in each, their pulses beat one measure.

"Why? because if a woman loves her lover she will not ruin him, and I am what all the world knows me, and you a great Prince."

"Had I been free," he said in a hot whisper, "and you had said that folly I had crushed your sweetness in my arms till you had no strength to speak, to whisper, but only to love."

He made as though he would have done it, then dropt her hands.

"But I am not free," he said with an infinite melancholy. "You do well to be silent."

"I love you—I love you," she cried. "Is that to be silent? When you spoke this before that man I was like to have died for joy and sorrow. O heart of my heart, you suffer and I with you."

She threw her head back with closed eyes, the tears slipping from beneath the long lashes,—a pitiful fair face indeed for a lover to see. He knelt now and gathered her in his arms with a tenderness unspeakable.

"My true love, my heart's delight—not a look, not a word of yours now but shall live in my soul for ever, for this hour is the first and the last. I will not risk my treasure on the edge of a precipice. Dear, could I make you mine tonight, could I share my dukedom with you in open honour, it is yours as I am your man to my life's end. But since this is impossible put your beloved arms about me this once and then bid me go. Drive me from Paradise into the wilderness and shut the door upon me and forget me."

How could she speak? She claspt her arms about him as he knelt and these two unhappy lovers clung together in silence, with the salt of tears in their kisses, the passion of parting to redouble the passion of love and make it terrible as when death seizes life at its fullest and drags it down into the dark.

She knew so little of his life—of his will, that she could plead neither for herself nor him. If he willed it so it must be. Yet every pulse of her beating bosom pleaded for her—and as her arms relaxed his heart followed them.

"But let my girl hear me," he entreated. "You shall be my care though we may not meet. All I have is yours, and we will find a home for you. You shall not play. You are mine always—mine only. Promise me this, my beloved, my worship! Sweet."

"I promise."

Again a heavy silence. Then again he looked into her eyes—

"And if the day should ever come that death releases me from a bondage unbearable, then I swear that before God and man you shall be my Duchess—my Queen. And because I believe that this day shall and must come, teach me to have courage. With your own beloved lips bid me spare you and myself, and go."

She clung the closer to him now.

"You will not bid me. Then where shall I find strength? In this thought only—that if I stay I plunge my treasure into ruin. The Duchess, my Lady Fanny,—all the chaste women you love will shrink from you, and the day come when you could loathe me for the wrong I did you. Tell me, is it not so?"

She could not answer. 'Tis impossible to measure the future by the present. She too had no courage for this. Let him judge and break their life or save it. But 'twas all shot with joy like a gold thread running through a black warp, for her head lay on his breast, his face touched hers, his arms encircled her. O exquisite pain,—O cruel joy—how do creatures of mere fallible flesh and blood endure these transports of the spirit and survive them?

"Diana—speak!" he entreated.

Still lying against his heart, she spoke at last,

"I cannot judge. I am too weak. I am in your hands for I am dearer to you than I am to myself and as for you—I love you. But this I know for true, that to the last hour of my life I shall remember this and be proud that my beloved judged me worthy—were it but for this happy hour."

She drew herself away that she might look at him—their hands still claspt, and as they so stood, the door opened softly, and the Duchess came in and stopt a moment and then came forward, treading very softly.

# CHAPTER XIX

CATHERINE QUEENSBURY was near beside them before the two looked up from their transport of joy and grief. 'Twas in Diana's character that she drew not her hands from him away as though ashamed or fluttered, but stood a moment, then dropped her curtsey to the great lady that never looked greater than then. Her tall stature—her fine commanding face, a something soft yet proud, set her off almost to majesty. 'Twas natural she should speak first, and she addrest herself to the Duke that saluted her and waited her pleasure in silence.

"I met my Lady Fanny a street hence and she told me you sat with Mrs. Beswick. It hastened my return for I would speak with you."

"Shall I go, Madam?" asks Diana gently, with a motion to the door.

"No, child. I would have you hear all I say. It concerns you.— Can you endure that his Grace, if he will, shall tell me what hath passed between you?"

"Madam, there is not a word hath been said, but I would gladly have you know it. Could my thoughts be laid bare, these also should be yours."

"I rejoice," says the Duke, very grave, "that your Grace has had the goodness to put this question. You shall hear all."

He placed Diana in a chair before the Duchess and stood behind her.

"Madam, you shall know that I have repeated to this lady the words I spoke in the infamous room where she was trapped and a prisoner. I have told her that my heart is wholly hers, that she is so unspeakably dear to me (as knowing her worth and honour) that were I a free man this day, she should be my Duchess as surely as I stand before your Grace."

"You have done well," says the Duchess, holding her head as though it wore a crown.

"But, Madam, since that is not my happy fate, I have said that, should that glad day ever come, she and she only—be it today or many years hence—shall be my wife. To this I pledge my honour, and I call your Grace to witness."

"And meanwhile?"

"Meanwhile, Madam, we part. It can't be otherwise. I hold my love as high as your Grace's self. Shall I exile her from the company of good women?— I will not have her at the playhouse for the men and women that are about her there. Shall I drive her back into that society again and have the door shut upon her that your Grace's goodness opened to one most fit for it? No. We must part, but through your hands—my friend's—I will guard her future life."

"And you, child?" The Duchess turns to Diana. With a tremble in her voice but steadfastly, she answered.

"Madam, I love him. Could I do other than this? Look how he has chose me—so all unworthy, for a love so great as I think never was its like. Indeed I can scarce believe it, though told in your gracious presence, did not my heart know it true. What my Lord Duke says I say also. Only less dear to me than he is your Grace and my kind Lady Fanny. Madam, in my short life I have seen so many bad women that my heart clings naturally to the good ones. I can say no more—" her voice broke there.

"And 'twas for this love you refused my Lord Baltimore?"

"Not wholly, Madam. I could not love him."

"His rank, his riches did not tempt you?"

"No, Madam, since they carried the man with them. They are well enough otherwise."

"And since you refuse my Lord Baltimore and cannot have the Duke, what will you do?"

"I think to teach singing, Madam. I love my art."

There was silence—Bolton regarding Diana with a tenderness inexpressible. He looked up then at his friend as though to say—"You see?"

"I see," says she, replying to his look, and continued with composure.

"Were I to say to you, child, that the circumstances of your lover's life are so extraordinary, so pitiful as ordinary codes and morals scarce meet them, and were I to add to this that if a good woman sheltered him in her heart and could restore somewhat of the happiness he deserves, I, for one, would never forsake her, what would your answer be then?"

"I think it would be this, Madam:— There is still his wife." The Duchess continues:

"If to that, I replied that 'tis not a mere distaste keeps him from her but a circumstance he learnt on his wedding day that he knows not I know——"

"Stop there!" commanded the Duke, "I hold not the lady my wife, but she is Duchess of Bolton, and I hear no word against my family honour. You should not have known, or knowing should certainly be silent."

For a moment she flashed one of her dangerous looks at him. This lady must not be thwarted. Then halted, as if recollecting herself.

"You are right. Well, Diana,—but as I said, supposing the conditions extraordinary beyond belief, so as I who know them, acquit you of any crime against her Grace; supposing I assure you that my friendship and countenance cannot fail you, and that my Lady Fanny holds with me, do you still value your reputation higher than your love?"

It must be admitted an awful choice for the girl. Not only had she the pride of an honest woman, but 'tis to be remembered she had lived in the playhouse. She knew the men and the women, the foul jests, the contempt for women's virtue and men's fidelity. A virtuous woman that is sheltered may hoard her reputation as gold, but 'tis the very life-blood of a virtuous woman that lives in the midst of rank corruption and loathes it. That they should say she was one of them—that an affected purity covered a venal heart—'twas bitter! What should the world know of love? It will say, "A rich man—a Duke offers to make her his mistress and she accepts joyfully. The little base prude that held her skirts away from women that did no worse!" She could see, could hear it all.

"Madam, I know not if I have the strength for it," says she, looking not at her, but Bolton. "I thank you for an offer most generous of your friendship. O how to know right from wrong! If it were to be mocked at myself I could do it for love's sake. What shall I do? What would you have me do, my Lord Duke?"

"Let us listen to her Grace!" says he, catching her hand—a pale gleam of hope breaking through the darkness of his face. "Do you say, Madam, that we should have your countenance? Why then, the world would know 'twas not effrontery and intrigue. If I could trust my girl would still be honoured—Judge for us,—my brain whirls."

Catherine Queensbury bent pitying eyes on the two before her. She saw the situation strained too high, she took it in hand with her own bright logic, and condescended to earth from the heights.

"Were it myself—I can but speak from myself when all's said and done, I should not trample two lives with misery. I'm as chaste as other women, I hope,—I love my husband unfashionably. My tongue is as two-edged as another's where women are frail and men dishonourable. But though the case is not my own I know it unusual in a high degree. I would not have the thing done in a corner. I would have it announced to your wife and openly to the world as though a thing—not to be flaunted, no!—but to be done after consideration and openly. And I believe this done and with my own unfailing friendship and that of others I could name, 'twill pass for a left-handed marriage as it ought. For yourself I can't doubt. 'Tis only on Diana I hesitate and will persuade no woman to what she may consider her own dishonour."

He stared at the Duchess with a kind of amazement struggling with joy. She continues.

"Why, Bolton, you and I know such things are done every day,—and I have loathed them like another and could give excellent reason for my loathing. I know your heart and hers.— The case is not ordinary. Check me if you dare when I say I know your story from first to last, and acquit you of any obligation to your wife. The case rests with Diana therefore, and there I won't persuade her. With all I can do for her, she must still face contempt and cold-shouldering and sneers and misjudgment from many. Her life will be uneasy and the brunt will fall on her. I love and admire her, but know not if she has in her the stuff to face such hardship as this. Child, I will say no more, but leave you. Choose how you will I am your friend, and none shall say a harsh word of you in Catherine Queensbury's presence. So now I leave you."

She rose from her chair and left them without a look behind. The Duke closed the door as she went, and returned.

"Beloved, you have heard her. No man hath a right to ask such a sacrifice from any woman. Especially if he knows himself unworthy of such a purity and sweetness as yours. I have seduced no woman from the path of virtue. I have kept my hearth from such as would dishonour it, but short of this I have lived as a man amongst other men and what that means you know. The Duchess would not fail you, but she says true— Yours is a heart to suffer when they pierce it as they will. The case is now before you. I counsel you to dismiss me and I will make no complaint."

He dropped her hand lest even the touch should move her, and went away and stood by a great window, looking down upon the people passing. In all his life he was never to forget the sight of the budding lilacs in the courtyard, and the faint spring sunshine. It seemed he stood there long—he knew not how long, and then she came softly up beside him and put her hand in his.

"For life and death," she said, and turning he caught her in his arms, his stern face broken up into such joy as seemed a foretaste of heaven.

There is no pen can write of such joy. 'Tis only known to God and to lovers—lovers also who must catch it from the heart of pain.

That night he wrote to his Duchess—

> "*Madam,*
>
> "I wish to acquaint you before any other shall know it that I have determined to take into my house with all the rights of a wife but only not the title, Mrs. Fenton,—whose name will be known to you. I would not you should hear this from another.

My heart is hers. Our union will be such as God knows I wish yours and mine could have been but is not. In entering upon this new life I desire to ask your Grace if I can in any way contribute further to your comfort than I have already done. I shall esteem it a favour to be at your command in this respect and in any other conformable with the honour and love I have for Mrs. Fenton.

"And remain,

"Your obedient humble servant,

"BOLTON."

A strange letter, but the man himself was not ordinary, and so 'tis to be supposed his wife knew him, for she replied strangely also—

"*Your Grace*,

"Your letter lies before me and I have the honour to reply. 'Tis the last time you will see my living hand. I think you do right. I wish you happy. I thank you for many benefits—so great as there is nothing more I can ask but an occasional thought not wholly unkind. We cannot die when we would, else I think you had long ago been free and I also. I ask your forgiveness.

"Your obedient humble servant,

"G. BOLTON."

He read it thoughtfully, then carrying it to the fire dropped it in and stood until the last ash fluttered away.

"The poor woman," he said.

Diana remained with the Duchess until such time as her Grace judged proper, and Bolton saw her on the foot, as it were, of a betrothed lover.

On a certain evening her Grace commanded the attendance of certain of her own friends near and valuable—my Lady Fanny among them—she only knowing what was intended. The Queensbury clan was a large one, especially if we count among them her own numerous cousins. The white drawing-room, stately with wax lights, therefore accommodated a large company of men and women that night, each a little centre of power and influence. Among them was Mr. Gay, and Mr. Rich, much surprised to find himself in such excellent high company, stood at his shoulder, and 'twas noticeable also that some of the best pens of the Duchess's party were present—I name Dr. Swift, Mr. Pope, Mr. Thomson, and there pause, having given the best.

The Duke of Queensbury received the visitors with his Duchess and noble refreshments were served and music winged the hour.— So the time went by, and at last she moved to a gilt chair at the end of the room, and behind her stood her lord and the Duke of Bolton, both very splendid in star and ribbon as indeed were many of the men. Diana trembled and waited in her far-away chamber. So rising, her Grace addrest her company—with all her own composure:

"My friends, for such I count each and all of you, there is a thing I would say. I know well I am accused of whims and caprices and possibly of too great a courage in flying in the face of hypocrises and cant. I know not. I am what I am. But tonight I think there is none here will misjudge me whatever the world may do. Hear my story. I know a man known to you all and most unhappily wed. Call it a marriage I can't, nor can you. I know a woman young and beautiful, gifted beyond the common with perfections of mind and body, alone and unprotected. These two may live apart—and none will notice or compassionate them. If they live together, all the hounds of scandal will drive their fangs in them. Well,—I, Catherine Queensbury, have counselled the Duke of Bolton and Mrs. Fenton to trust the goodness of their friends and forget the malice of their enemies and make such a marriage for themselves as the cruel law will admit, for marriage I must and do call it though the law and the Prophets call it none. In Queensbury House my friends will be ever welcome."

Astonishment held the room breathless. Of all the mad Queensbury freaks this sure was the maddest. In her own drawing-room! A Duchess! A player! Lord help us! to what is the world coming? But hush!—the expectant left-hand bridegroom speaks, laying his hand on the back of the Duchess's chair.

"It is to be judged how I must thank this lady that has the soul of knighthood and chivalry with the face of an angel, for her protection and countenance. In this matter I would have nothing done secret, so do I honour the woman who consents to share my loneliness. To the ladies here I say, the circumstances being so strange, I can expect nothing but from their goodness and favour. To the men—I shall regard Mrs. Fenton as my wife,—attention to her is shown to me, and for any insult I have my sword. And now act as you shall determine right."

He passed down the room and all crowded about him as he went out. There was not one there but knew his story—perhaps very few but pitied him sincerely. But 'twas not that. 'Twas the suddenness of the attack, the daring, the oddness, the—what shall I say?—the insolent gallantry of the Duchess that would uphold her friend if she died for it, that won all hearts. 'Twas a tumult of recognition. My Lady Fanny's clear voice raised itself like a bird in a storm.

"For my own part, I side with her Grace. I think the Duke and Mrs. Fenton do well, and I shall esteem it an honour to receive her in my poor house. Those that think otherwise (and have a perfect right to their judgments) can stay away."

To be bidden to my Lady Fanny's house and stay away was unthinkable. Had she proposed to present to them Messalina, Aspasia and other celebrated demireps, they could not for the life of them stay away, and knew it. No, not even if Miss Sally Salisbury herself had met them at the door. And here also the girl's character spoke for her—all loved the charming Polly, her voice of silver, her obliging and modest behaviour. "One could not in a general way condone such things, 'tis true," say the ladies, "but this is an exception that makes no rule. It cannot so happen again. She is a good girl, and his Grace much to be pitied." So the talk buzzed in corners, and at the card-tables where the game was scarce heeded, and about the Duchess. But with no dissentient, for none dared raise her voice, 'twas virtually agreed that the Duchess could do no wrong and if she vouched for Mrs. Fenton, Mrs. Fenton was endurable. Besides this was certainly better than a misalliance, take it how you will!

Dr. Swift drew up to her when the way was clear.

"Your Grace hath courage," says he, "yet not so much as they grant you, for had you thrust a Wapping wench on them they had kissed your hand and taken her. You can't however expect the blessing of the Church on your enterprise."

"I never did!"—says the Duchess with one of her tosses. "I asked Dr. Swift's blessing that reads human nature like a book. And I think to have it, though not perhaps in public."

"I don't withhold it. On conditions, however. You are not to make such alliances general, Madam; I confine you to one. Or in default, I condemn you to give the example yourself and set up house with Sir Robert Walpole, the Queen's consent granted."

She laughed her clear hearty laugh.

"I promise, Doctor, I promise. And, in return—no sly allusions to my pretty bird and her man. And if any lampooner thrust at them from some dark corner I require that you pierce him to the heart with an epigram so pointed and terrible as Jove's own thunderbolt is not so sure."

Sudden she changed her tone and spoke low that none might hear.

"Dr. Swift, the world that is all lies, says that you have no heart. I know better. For the sake of one I loved and honoured, be good to my poor young girl."

A terrible spasm crossed his face. Of all her daring this was the greatest, for 'twas the year before this that Stella died, and all his joy with her. He did but look in her eyes and turn away, but she had won him—she knew it.

Mr. Pope later in the evening waylaid her.

"Madam, what is there your Grace cannot accomplish! You have made adultery a sentiment as well as a fashion. The ladies of London should tear you in pieces as the Mœnads did a far less offender, for there is not an erring husband but will run to Queensbury House to ask the Duchess's protection. You shoulder a heavy responsibility. Here's an opening for epigram!"

"I bespeak yours, Mr. Pope!" says she. "Your pen won't desert me, and 'tis more powerful than any sword or Act of Parliament. 'Tis so known to be employed always on the side of virtue and weakness that when it defends my lovers (should defence be needed) detraction itself will run to cover. Have I your protection?"

The word delighted the Wasp of Twick'nam. He bowed in the Versailles manner.

"Your Grace needs no assurance. The town will buzz with this tomorrow, but I'm ready, and 'twill be a delight to see what can be said in defence of a position that cannot be defended on any pretence whatever."

"No more it can! But it will," agrees the Duchess, dismissing him charmingly.

When all were gone she turned to my Lady Fanny, the sole survivor.

" 'Tis done, my dear, and I know not whether I have damned them or myself. But I'll never do it again. No, not even for my Fanny. Therefore be circumspect."

"You're a brave woman. I never admired you more!" cries Lady Fanny. "I could not myself have done it. But you have secured them from much grief, and if you've opened the way to more, 'tis not for any one to blame you. Come up and let us tell Diana what hath past."

They did so, and she kissed that generous hand with love and gratitude, and trembling hope.

# CHAPTER XX

THE town rang and buzzed to some purpose next day and the wits were busy indeed. 'Twas an opportunity to be clever they could by no means miss and some of the lampoons might have been writ by the Yahoos themselves had they turned their talents that way. But the Duchess's party was not silent neither. Dr. Swift took pen in hand and writ a paper that assailed the lampooners with a virulence not inferior to their own and a wit so far superior as left them gasping. This heavy artillery was followed by Mr. Pope's light skirmishing tactics, which harassed and annoyed the enemy beyond bearing and strewed the field of battle with moribund and slaughtered reputations. Had the two gentlemen been so minded they might have adorned their wigwams with more scalps than any Indian brave, and indeed their war-whoops were terrific.

In a while they penetrated even the chaste precincts of Kensington Palace where her Majesty followed the attack and defence with most searching interest in hopes to find the Duchess of Queensbury among the slain, and had instead the mortification to see her enthroned sublime on the piled fragments of her enemies. 'Twas only the Queen's high gust of humour, that laughed at all wit no matter the source, which softened the blow.

"That woman has the good fortune of her father the devil," says she to Mrs. Howard at the toilette—the chaplain at his prayers without her door. "Had I undertook to protect a common little wanton like Polly, Swift's bludgeon had been on my head and Pope's rapier through my heart ere I could cry for mercy. 'Tis as much as I can do to make our Kensington amours pass muster."

She shot a side-glance at the unfortunate Mrs. Howard who between the brow-beatings of her Sultan and the darts of the Queen was more to be pitied than envied on her glittering eminence. The lady curtseyed meekly. 'Twas not a subject she could handle with freedom. The Queen continued:

"But is't not a scandalous business that a person of her rank should announce her protection for a libertine and a——?"

The chaplain's loud Amen drowned the epithet in sanctity, and her Majesty and the prayers pursued their respective ways.

"A bishopric would buy Swift,—he was always for sale in the late Queen's day, and were it not that the man, though well enough as a lampooner, turns my stomach as a divine I would buy him tomorrow. But though not too squeamish myself I protest I can't swallow him. This paper he has writ on Bolton is as fine as I have seen anywhere, if 'twere not disgraceful a man of his cloth should further such an intrigue. 'Tis plain he hath abandoned all hope of a bishopric or he had not done it. The raillery is excellent."

She picked up the paper from her table and read aloud—

" ''Tis to be sure an unpardonable proceeding and an affront to all religion that this love matter was not conducted with the decent slyness befitting the humour of a chaste people such as inhabit these Isles. Had the Duke of Bolton concealed the lady in such a bower as the Fair Rosamond's and visited her by stealth (as indeed the example of a noble reticence is set us in the highest quarters where the very names of such ladies are unknown) there had been nothing but applause on a gallant freedom. 'Tis his Grace's lamentable sincerity that is the rock of offence and may lead to disastrous consequences. For suppose it incumbent on great sovereigns to go with flourish of drums and trumpets to the ladies they delight to honour, to pension them from the public purse and what not, where shall it end? We may yet have the chaste names produced to the world that are whispered only by Princes in their hours of relaxation from the burdens of state, and the delicacy which now surrounds our court and others entirely disappear.' "

Her Majesty read this with malicious enjoyment to see the colour mount in Mrs. Howard's face.

"The whole is worth studying as an example of irony," says her Majesty, "and I commend it to you, my good Howard. Had Swift not chose the profession he has, he had been at the top now. I know none more neat in his sayings than— 'A very little wit is valued in a woman as we are pleased with a few words spoken plain by a parrot.'— That's one I recall daily."

"It can't appear reasonable to your Majesty," says Mrs. Howard endeavouring to make her court and hide her vexation. The Queen laughed aloud.

"O, I can talk as foolish as another when I have a mind, and 'tis the reason why I can endure the follies of others as I do daily. See—my neck handkerchief, Howard. Here comes the King."

Indeed his Majesty entered at this moment, and swore because the chaplain's mumble outside prevented his hearing the Queen's remark.

"When will that intolerable snuffling cease!" cries he. "You should give directions that he lower his voice."

"Lord, Sir,—how can I?" says the Queen. " 'Twould be all over the town next day. I ventured once to have the door closed instead of ajar, and 'twas said the Queen had the door shut as knowing she was past praying for."

"The dirty buffoons!" says the monarch. "What is that handkerchief doing about your neck?" He snatched it off and flung it on the floor, crying roughly to Mrs. Howard, "Because you have an ugly neck yourself you hide the Queen's"—the poor mistress curtseying as she picked it up.

His Majesty next snatched at Dr. Swift's paper and failing to read it ironic was much gratified at the Doctor's seeming censure of the Duke until he came to the passage read by the Queen. His remarks at this point must be reserved for the two ladies, who may be said to be seasoned so far that their palates could bear more than the reader's; yet even the Queen put up her fan at this; and thus we leave the happy party.

There was a grand masquerade that night at the Haymarket, when all the high world was present. 'Twas a scene of extreme splendour, the walls adorned with emblematical devices illuminated with thousands of lamps of various colours, and elegant transparencies at either end. The ladies blazed resplendent and the men not less so, the brocaded coat of the Duke of Devonshire being valued at five hundred pounds independent of the jewels and this only one amongst many. But of all, my Lord Baltimore was the most magnificent, in white velvet and gold brocaded tissue. His arm was healed now, but an interesting pallor set him off in the eyes of nearly every lady present. He danced little, waiting, as it were, for some one not present.

At last she came, brilliant and beautiful,—my Lady Fanny, dressed as a Fair Persian in a sultana's robe of pale lutestring and a short velvet bodice so hung with jewels as almost to dazzle the eyes. She had a small gold cap with a veil of gold gauze dependent and my Lord thought he had never seen her so beautiful as he stood watching her charming face all smiles and gaiety and never a look of care to tarnish it. He longed to read her thoughts beneath that fair mask, to know if there were hope of forgiveness—of friendship, for his own wound was so recent that he scarce aspired to more.

Indeed his Lordship was sore and angry. Calmer reflection had made him something of a fool in his own eyes, and 'twas a frame of mind much assisted by the publicity of the Duke's engagement with Diana. His friend had obtained on easy terms what he had offered his name and title to purchase in vain. 'Twas then a plain case of love and he slighted almost openly, for though his offer was unknown, his pursuit was talked of all over the town. His first failure, and a public one, it galled him more than a little. 'Twas not perhaps surprising that his hurt pride considered where it might turn for solace, and what success might re-gild his faded laurels.

To this there was but one answer:—No beauty so brilliant, so modish as my Lady Fanny, could he renew his interest in her heart.

'Tis to be easily understood how his thoughts went. With a doubt very well hid, he asked her to favour him with a minuet, and she accepted with a smiling coolness that said nothing either way. 'Twas exquisitely performed and every eye on the charming pair and predictions flying from lip to lip as the reconciliation was noted. My Lady Fanny knew this well, and repelled all conjecture by her gay good humour, inscrutable as the famous Sphinx of Egypt of which travellers tell us.

The dance over, he led her to an alcove covered with greenery and flowers, a little retreat where they could be as private as they would, and there fetched her a glass of lemonade and taking her fan all painted with nymphs and loves, fanned a cool air to her glowing cheeks. He was disposed to believe the past was past and no harm done, and adventured as a man may on safe ice, his head in air.

" 'Tis a marvellous gay scene, Madam, is it not? And of all the beauties here I hold the most beautiful beside me in this little bower which Love's self might have contrived."

"I think my dress is very well!" says Lady Fanny smiling. " 'Twas designed for me by Zincke who had seen a dress in the Persian taste in a picture at Welbeck when painting her Grace of Portland's portrait. The cap I thought alluring with its demure veil which I can draw over my face when I will. Pray hush, my Lord—I know exactly what you open your mouth to say."

"What, Madam?"

"O, it runs thus— "Don't veil that lovely face which like the sun—" Sad stuff! I'll give you no more of it."

It piqued him for 'twas true to his intention and not only so but she mimicked his manner excellent well. Perhaps the ice was a little more slippery than he had supposed. He fanned her diligently and changed the subject.

"I see Bolton is absent. No doubt more happily engaged with his pretty Polly. Is she still at Queensbury House?"

"By all means. There are alterations making at his house to please her taste before he makes her mistress of it."

"And of him. 'Tis sure the oddest flight in all this world so to announce a thing that others keep decently private."

"Its oddity is but its honesty so far as I can see," says my Lady Fanny yawning delicately. " 'Tis surely more convenient to know how our friends are situate and 'tis their advantage also that this sincerity permits us to keep a friend we value."

"I yield to none in respect for Mrs. Fenton," says my Lord angrily—"but at the same time would certainly forbid my wife her acquaintance now she has chose to ally herself openly with a man she can't marry."

She looked at him with eyes provocative.

" 'Tis known your Lordship respected the lady."

How much, how little was meant? Impossible to say, but it left him confused and angry, and he therefore struck wild, as the men in the ring have it.

" 'Tis only a man can judge these points. The delicacy and weakness of the female mind are liable to gusts of sentiment, and your Ladyship's ardent and generous nature——"

"I have not found my nature ardent," says the lady.— "Rather, I am given to judging men coolly—and women also. I have seen Mrs. Fenton in trial and prosperity and I judge her a woman of sense and spirit. I shall always esteem her friendship, and fortunately have no dictator to say me nay."

"Fortunately?" He raised his eyebrows a thought. "If your Ladyship says this in earnest it puts a period to all I would say."

"And what is that?" says she, softly. "I never held an opinion so savagely but what it could be changed by argument."

If my Lord had but guessed it, the ice was thin indeed now, and the Siren beckoning beyond, but vanity is blind whatever love may be, and he went onward with a smile of confidence very thinly veiled by a lover's enforced humility.

"My Lady Fanny, 'tis not so long since I believed I might flatter myself that you condescended to a little pleasure in my company. Was I wrong?"

Her eyes, large and sweet, looked at him above her fan.

"Indeed, no! 'Tis very true."

'Twas so softly said that the colour kindled in his pale face. He drew his breath somewhat quicker.

"A shadow—I scarce know what—fell between us, and by no will of mine I have not had the happiness that was once so often mine. We have been much apart the last weeks."

"We have been much apart," she echoed, in a voice scarce audible.

"It has been a trouble to me. I revolve night and day how to regain my lost ground and once more be acceptable to the only woman whose liking or distaste can make my heart to beat faster."

Her soft and pensive silence was an invitation to continue. Gentleness itself was the charming face now looking downward as though unable to meet the fire of his eyes. Sure my Lord knew all the symptoms of surrender!

"If I confess"—he said gallantly, "that I was turned from the course of true love a moment—a moment only—by a wayside flower, my Lady Fanny, who knows the world and the thoughts of men she rules, will not think the crime unpardonable, since 'twas a fancy that never for a moment touched the heart where she only is secure."

He laid his hand on hers—it was not withdrawn,—and continued:

" 'Twas not inconstancy indeed—I durst swear it. 'Twas trifling of the lightest, yet had its use, for it taught me that I was but a captive sporting at the end of my chain. Your fair hand holds it, and your heart is my prison. Never will I seek for freedom. Can the loveliest of charmers, the most desirable of women make me a return?"

She did not look up. In a voice sweet as honey, she whispered:

"Indeed I have waited for this moment, my Lord."

He had her hand now in a firmer clasp. They were as solitary as in a wood though the company passed their bower, as they came and went.

"Then may I believe that this dear hand is mine? That my beloved will give me the day and make me the happiest of men?"

"You would have me marry you?" says she, raising her eyes to his. Even then her tone might have warned him, but he rushed on his fate.

"I would have it beyond everything in the world. I desire it with all my heart and soul, and now that your radiant eyes, your melting mouth give consent, at last I kiss this soft hand and claim it for my own—my beloved Lady Baltimore's."

My Lord was a finished wooer. His tone might have melted marble. It did not however melt my Lady Fanny. Her moment was come. While he spoke she had weighed her heart in the balance, had tasted every emotion he roused in her, and (to pursue her own comparison of the man fallen from his horse who knows not whether he is alive or dead) she knew now once for all that this gentleman was of no mighty concern to her, and that she lived and need fear his power no more. In short, that her heart was whole and at her own disposal.

She disengaged her hand with such infinite delicacy that the action appeared a caress, and entrenched it in her own lap.

“My Lord, you have spoken. Hear me in turn. I refuse your offer. No—’tis no coyness that asks to be conquered. You shall know my reason. Awhile ago you courted me. That cannot be denied. Yourself owns it. I, in my turn, own that I think you might then have won me, had you cared. ’Tis so long ago now that I remember not how much my heart was yours, but you certainly had an interest in it. Then—you left me. Do you think in this town of tattle I didn’t know it! Do you think your sudden silence and aversion passed unnoticed? You exposed me to the laughter and comment of the world. You——”

He tried to check her eloquence.

“My beloved, don’t I now make rich amends? Won’t all the world see the one sovereign of my heart? What more is in my power?”

She never heeded him.

“That the woman you attacked was worthy, was a mere chance. For all you knew and hoped she was the worst of her sex. And for this I was thrown aside. I will be frank with you, my Lord. It wounded my pride and I thought ’twas my heart but could not tell. You have offered yourself to another and was rejected— Why should I spare you now? And yet, remembering the past,—indeed I scarce could tell. I was resolved therefore that I would see you and hear your protestations that I might judge whether ’twas the one or the other. I know at last. My pride was hurt, but never my heart.”

He gazed at her transfixed. ’Twas the first time in his life he had seen the lady in earnest. It could not but appear extraordinary to him that a creature so airy, so sparkling—let us say so trifling, should now assume a superiority he must needs acknowledge. His silence gave her the final opportunity, and she spoke once more.

“So my Lord, we part. We shall meet often, but yet we part for ever. I thank you that you showed me what you really was, for I have now nothing to regret. I am saved from an unhappy marriage. You are no respecter of women, and deserve my scorn.”

He summoned himself for the defensive. The lady must not carry off all the honours of war from my Lord Baltimore.

“My dear creature—what is there to respect in them, I ask your sincerity? Here’s yourself has trained me on to make a declaration that you might quote to the town that I was at your feet and you spurned me. Indeed I have not much cause to honour your sex.”

“Fear not. I shall not quote it to the town, my Lord, for I don’t feel it a distinction,”—says the lady coolly. “I would not have it known that the Grand Bashaw believed he might throw me the handkerchief when another had refused to stoop for it. No,—the comedy we have played is over—here is the epilogue. You may find a slave, but never a wife, and your contempt of my sex shows an ignorance that deserves no better. There are few women but might despise you if they knew your worth and their own."

She rose, performed a magnificent curtsey and left her Adam to an Eve-less Paradise.

Rage and unbelief struggled in my Lord Baltimore's mind. Rejected a second time and where most he thought himself secure! It appeared an evil dream from which he must presently waken though the lights shone and music filled the air and the faces of men and women known to him passed the retreat where he sat alone in a very fever of thoughts he never supposed possible for his triumphant self. Sooner than be remarked, he rose presently and went out into the near dancing room where the first to catch his eye was my Lady Fanny with his master the Prince of Wales.

The Prince laughed heartily in answer to somewhat she said, and my Lord could hear his words:—

"Why, Madam, indeed I deserve your pity. I know not my fate as yet, but that she is some little German lady in her pinafore in the nursery! What is the use to be Prince of Wales if they don't let me choose among the beauties I see about me?"

"Because,"—says her Ladyship laughing, "your Royal Highness's admiration might make them Vane!"

'Twas known she was not enamoured of the reigning family, but this bold allusion to the name of his discarded English favourite was so daring as to terrify my Lord Baltimore and excite mingled laughter and fright in all who heard, and they were many. No one but she had dared it.

The Prince, a fine fair young man, stared doubtful a moment, then burst into a great laugh clapping his hands and applauding.

"Excellent, my Lady, excellent! If my heartfelt admiration would make them vain, I wish to God I might begin with your lovely self. My admiration is at your feet."

She disengaged herself all laughing, her eyes sparkling, her cheeks like living roses beneath her gold cap and veil,—the Prince catching at her hand would have detained her, but she joined the Duchess of Queensbury.

Baltimore looked after her with a sickening anger and regret. They had parted indeed.

# CHAPTER XXI

TWAS a moving day for her Grace of Queensbury and Diana when the Duke removed her to his fine house in Pall Mall, for not only did it cause both a pang to part after so many months of mutual kindness, but in such a case must be many misgivings however courageously hid. That he should regard her as his wife was much, and it seemed each day that past added force to his tenderness, yet it must be allowed that her position at best was beset with thorns he could not blunt.

If such a case be taken lightly and gallantly—the bond of a summer's day to be broke at nightfall—the world will laugh and let it go by with scarce a censure, but if any bold persons, breaking this rule, succeed not in getting the laugh on their side it will certainly be much against them, and they will be confounded with persons with whom they have nothing in common.

So Diana must reflect that the time might come when this situation would gall the Duke and she be the cause of it. The rude familiarities, the railleries provoked, he could deal with with his sword, but there are pangs subtle as air that cannot be so warded. He was not plagued himself with such considerations for, as men are used in love, he saw only the present deliverance from loneliness, the comfort he expected in her sweet society and all the delights of her beauties of mind and person.

'Tis to be owned that the brunt falls always on the woman. Whosoever's was the crime of Eden, our first Mother's daughters are reckoned the defaulters and must pay in heart and body.

Diana writ dutifully to her mother, now removed with her husband to Maidstone in Kent, and had a letter in return beseeching her rather to return to her stepfather's roof than so involve her good name.

"Bethink you," the letter continued, "that with the reputation you have made at Mr. Gay's playhouse, you'll never lack for bread and plenty and may hope an excellent marriage one of these days. 'Tis to be allowed the stage has its dangers, but prudence and courage (which your father's daughter should not lack) will bear you through as it has done to the present. Marriage is and must ever be your object."

And with much more to the same purpose did the mother instruct her daughter,—thus concluding:

"I would have you build no hope on the Duke's promise to marry, for when men have attained their wishes by an easier road, marriage is the most nauseous word to them, and furthermore his greatness and riches make it an impossibility from which reason and all his friends will turn him. If you hold out against him your chance is the better, as things desired and withheld grow the more valuable. I would therefore have you by no means break with him but observe a careful chastity that shall enhance your worth, and if, as I hear, her Grace's health be infirm, your constancy may meet its return. A waiting patience is therefore what I would have you practise."

There was a further suggestion that if, in all honour, his Grace should settle an income on her, on her concession of giving up the playhouse to please him, it might well be accepted as a return for her sacrifice.

And so ended. The writing was the hand of her mamma, but she knew the sentiments for those of Mr. Fenton and liked them the less. 'Twas obvious he had no expectations from the Duke's bounty. To her this must appear base and ungenerous and tinged with a low cunning she could not commend in herself should she follow it.

But lest this be partiality she laid the letter before her Duchess, on the day of their parting.

"Pah!" cries her Grace, flicking it on the floor. "Take it away, Diana. It reeks of—I won't say what, because your mamma writ it if she did not think it. If virtue is to be a marketable commodity let it be open dealing, say I, and not served like a French ragoût with a sauce of cant. By these few and simple prescriptions you may become as cunning and accomplished a little wanton as lives in Drury Lane, and this even within the bounds of marriage. I protest I know women honourably married in the world's eye that I hold contemptible for the very ring's sake that shields them. O child, we know much of what our teachers tell us in these matters and on the other side have nothing but the promptings of our own love and honesty, and 'tis hard to choose for very fear's sake."

" 'Tis very hard," agrees Diana sadly. "Indeed, Madam, love and trust are all my thought and to make his life more cheerful. As to marriage 'tis not to be thought on, and if I know my own heart, I may well bear censure. But once more I entreat your Grace to tell me before I go and the last step is taken, is it truly for his good? For, if you hesitate, I will not do it, though it cost me my life to refuse him. If I injure him I am undone indeed."

The Duchess for the first time put her arms about her and drew her to her embrace.

"My dear," says she, "if you desert him I know not where he shall turn. 'Twill break his heart. And this I would say for yourself. Let us suppose (though I believe it not) that like all men he is inconstant and leaves you for another, yet may you yourself be faithful, and looking back remember with joy that when he asked for mercy you withheld nothing but gave all. On that record, and knowing that it wrongs his wife in nothing, you need not fear to face either life or death. It may bring you sorrow, but I think no shame that need trouble you."

This she said with a certain solemnity of bearing—Diana looking up with awe. They clasped hands and she replied very simply:

"I thank your Grace. I will do my part whatever may chance. I have no words for your goodness and condescension to one so far beneath you, but my life shall be answerable to your expectations."

She went downstairs alone and entered the chair that should take her to her new life, the Duchess remaining lost in thought.

'Twas an ardent lover indeed that met his love in Pall Mall, that commanded his servants to obey her as though she was the Duchess herself, that surrounded her with such indulgences as might befit a princess. And thus the step was took and she entered upon her new life.

'Twas marked by a strange circumstance, for on her reaching the house, her woman put a small box in her hand most carefully folded and sealed with the Bolton arms, and on Diana opening it alone, what must she discover within but a cross of brilliants, beautiful as that which adorned the gifted Mr. Pope's Belinda. Indeed when she put it about her neck and so descended to Bolton, he gazed on her enraptured and quoted with delight the celebrated lines:

"On her fair breast a sparkling cross she wore

Which Jews might kiss and infidels adore."

adding—

"Who gave it to my love?"

"Was it not you?"—says she in quick alarm— " 'Twas in a box and I thought it one of your numberless generous gifts."

He shook his head smiling—

"Some less happy adorer. My girl shan't wear it until we know its history."

He sent for the wrappings and she stood at his shoulder to see. Presently he looked up gravely—

"I know the sender. You shall wear it. 'Twas a generous motion."

"May I know, your Grace!"

"Better not," he says sighing. " 'Twas a lady of my family, Di, I say no more."

She also said no more, but claspt her hand about the cross.

Was their life happy? The Duke declared to himself and to his best friend that he had never known happiness before. The uncertainties and doubts past, Diana's youth and joy overflowed the house with sunshine. Her voice filled it with harmony as of the crystal spheres, her beauty bloomed like a summer rose.

When "The Beggar's Opera" was revived with the new season, Mr. Rich and Mr. Gay, at a supper the Duke gave, declared his Grace deserved assassination for his selfish policy in robbing the world of such a Polly as if she played now would eclipse her former self as that self eclipsed all others. His Grace laughed:

"As soon hope for the Crown jewels, Richie, as one note of Mrs. Fenton's voice in Portugal Street. By the way, where's Walker? Have you heard of him?"

"Not a word, your Grace. He disappeared as if the earth had swallowed him. Doubtless with a new name and a new face he plays somewhere in the wilds with Bishop to keep him company! But shall Mrs. Fenton not give us a song here and now?"

"She must and shall!" cries the Duke, all pride and fondness, and so leads her to the harpsichord and sits enchanted to hear the notes of which he can never weary.

The Duchess came often and my Lady Fanny would trip in as light as air, and as had been the case with Mrs. Oldfield, yet with far better reason, the great ladies of the Duchess's party made it their business to exalt Mrs. Fenton and require her presence at their houses when company was expected. If herself she shrank at first from such attentions, when she saw it pleased the Duke she went contented and afterwards was the happier. Indeed he was her whole study and knew it, and she his. There was not a day but made them more valuable to each other.

Was it then happiness entirely flawless? Such cannot be on earth—'tis reserved for a better world. Let us enumerate.

It severed the Duke from some of his friends both of the austere and rakish order. The former because the connection stopped short of the ring, the latter because 'twas too faithful, too sincere to meet aught but their ridicule. Had the house been one where a fellow could come and toss off his bottle to a stave of Mrs. Fenton's with his own lovely Thais beside him, all would have been well, but this could not be, Bolton exacting as great deference in the lady's presence as had she been the Duchess herself. Indeed, from anxiety, he might be a little more particular than needful. So this would keep away my Lord Baltimore (who had besides other reasons) and many more. He swore he regretted none of them and perhaps did not, yet might wish for the power to dispense with them rather than be dispensed with.

It pained him if a word or a breath of censure passed on others which by any stretch his beloved might apply to herself. If he saw the colour rise in her cheek on this it paled in his own, so much did he fear a sting to that tender bosom.

It pained him that her foot should be insecure in the world. True, by his testament he protected her future with every affluence, yet he must know that with his death consideration would forsake her, and so clung feverishly to life.

'Twas not until one day he came unexpectedly upon a little book wherein she writ her private thoughts ('tis to this I referred in my second chapter) that he could believe her unwounded by darts he could not shield her from. They read it together, her cheek against his, and he was the more easy because she expressed therein the most unclouded contentment, and he never guessed 'twas writ for his reading. Did I not say—such a woman can't tell the whole truth if she would? But the crowning pain to both was when his first-born son was put in his arms,—the child that should have carried on the pride of his house and been the glory of his own declining years, and yet was nothing. He took it in his arms with a tenderness and pain inexpressible—the more so that to the lovely mother he must show nothing but gladness. Diana wept to see them thus. Who shall disentangle grief and joy in a case so singular? It is certain that those who censured might hold that hour a punishment sufficient for the two, if punishment they deserved. Would the child himself judge his parents one day? That also might come. Her thoughts of this she writ not in her book, but locked them in her own bosom.

So four years went by, and instead of wearying them, each day drew them nearer.

'Twas in France the news reached them that changed their life once more. 'Twas brought by a mounted messenger riding hard from the English Ambassador in Paris and reached the Duke late at night while Diana slept upstairs, the child beside her.

Little knowing its content, he opened and read.

"Her Grace the Duchess of Bolton died Wednesday was a week. Inform his Grace that he may return as is necessary."

He read again and, folding it, slipped it into his breast, and went up the stair to the great room curtained with velvet and a dim light burning in a silver lamp beside the bed. She lay there in the sweetest sleep, the image of youth and innocence, one soft hand flung out over her child that slept in a bed beside her, the other across her breast. Some happy thought passed through her dreaming mind as he stood looking down, for a smile flitted across her lips and vanished leaving its pleasure behind it. Indeed for all her twenty-two years she seemed but a child herself, save for the attitude maternal of the guarding hand. The two pulled at his heart-strings now he was at the moment of decision whether to cut the bond, to leave things as they were, or to make them his own irrevocably. Stooping, he kissed her on the cheek as light as her own smile. Drowsily she woke, as held in the arms of content,—he could see the glimmer of her waking eyes through the dark lashes. Almost before they opened her arm was about his neck—as he knelt beside her.

"What does my darling standing there alone? I'm too sleepy to talk. Come and rest. It grows late."

"Wake, Di," says he, "There's a journey before you. We leave in an hour for Paris."

She turned on her elbow trying to read his face—

"Beloved, why? What is it? Good or bad?"

"As you shall take it. For me wholly good. We go to the Embassy. By this time tomorrow you will be my wife."

She stared at him with great eyes as he put the despatch in her hand, but could not read it. She clung to him trembling like an aspen. Then, gathering voice, she whispered with passion:

"I will not. I will not. O have I not thought of this day—have I not told my heart again and yet again that you shall not ruin yourself for me. You are free now, O dearest and best. 'Tis for you to marry some pure woman and have noble children that may bear your name before all the world. I will not spoil your life. I utterly refuse."

"There will be no purer woman than my Duchess in all the world—I will not have even you slight her! Child, what is this? If I did not talk of this day 'twas for pity of the poor soul that's gone and has ended a life sad enough. But I have never wavered. You have been my wife, tender and true, for four years. More so you cannot be. This ceremony is not for you and me. 'Tis but for the world."

"Then leave it so," says she, clinging yet closer, "that if at some future time you see your duty or happiness requires it you may marry as you should. Consider, consider, my heart's Dearest. You may live to curse me otherwise. I took you when you was lonely and could do no better, though even then a queen might have envied me. But now the darkness is over and gone, the time of the singing of birds is come."

"There is only one bird shall sing for me," he says, fondly clasping her yet closer. "Shall a man have the greatest treasure of the world in his hand and let it slip? Say no more, beloved, but rise and dress that we may go."

Still with her face hidden, she stretched one arm to the child.

" 'Tis too late for that—too late! Nothing can give him his birthright we took from him. Marry some happier woman, my heart's dearest, and I will bless your first-born as though he were my own."

"He is yours," he answered steadfastly—"for this is he. We shall have others, and though this one cannot bear my title we will love him most of all. Speak no more of such idle words, my love. What are such things between you and me that know each other's heart? Rise now and lose no time for I would have all done lest I die and leave it undone. For very love's sake I fear."

What more could be said? She rose, as in a dream and before the morning dawned over the hills they were in Paris, driving hard.

For great princes the way is made smooth to their desire, and that day with all due witness and ceremony were Charles Duke of Bolton and Diana Beswick made one in the presence of the Ambassador and his suite and others, all still as death to watch the haughty bridegroom and the pale and lovely bride who moved as though she saw none on earth but he. And when the words were done and the rite ended, the Ambassador himself came forward very stately and bowing to the great lady:

"Madam, I congratulate your Grace and wish you many happy years with your lord," and so kissed her hand, the Duke smiling beside her.

'Twas when he himself kissed her hand in homage to the Duchess and her lips in homage to the wife, that her heart swelled almost to bursting with joy, and she looked up at him speechless, yet her whole soul speaking from radiant eyes.

Shall one say more of such happiness? No, for 'tis in its nature sacred and secret, and even to that dear ear she scarce could tell her rapture of content that he who knew her best should judge her worthy of the double crown of wifehood and duchess-ship. For him, eager as a boy, he never doubted, and he to whom his own rank was a trifle loved to call her "your Grace"—to see others make room for his lovely Duchess. Indeed she shone like a star released from clouds in those glad days. Himself had not known how beautiful, how glad and gay she shone to lighten all dark places.

So by easy stages they returned to London and to Bolton House and as he led her to the great drawing-room—her undisputed kingdom, a stately figure advanced to meet them and Diana curtseyed low before her Duchess.

She also sank in a most splendid curtsey as when one sovereign salutes another.

"I welcome your Grace to London and to our society!"—says she formally—and then, throwing off her state and clasping and kissing Diana, was overbrimming with joy and friendship to see her.

"Why, Bolton, the duchesses will never pardon you that have brought us one so lovely as puts all of us in the shade. Kneller shall paint her portrait and Zincke her miniature and the poets write her praises, and neither poet nor painter give us her own fresh beauty. For they can neither paint nor sing her golden heart that inspires it."

"Ah, Madam, you talk of duchesses," says he, holding her fair hand, "but I think 'tis none but the angels can praise one another without spot of human envy as you do. Did I not say long since that my friend and my wife were both incomparable, and seeing them together again I know it true a thousandfold."

Afterwards, they sat together in great content, for to this lady they owed their happiness and their all.

---

'Twas some weeks later my Lady Fanny wrote to her cousin my Lady Desmond, and this may fitly end the story of two noble hearts:

> "*My Kitty the kind and true*, your questions I will answer as best I may, and the rather that I have no subject more ready and agreeable to my pen than our new Duchess. 'Tis impossible I should describe her Grace's person for this I have done before, but I will say she hath put on a thousand new charms since her happy marriage in France, together with such splendours as can't be described, and in sober truth is a radiant beauty with none to peer her but my other kind Kitty. Yet such beauties do not compete unkindly—they shine like twin stars, each lighting the other.
>
> "Kitty, you preach often on the superlative advantage of birth, then tell me how comes it that this girl from Lord knows where, for I never judged well to enquire too curiously, moves with a tranquil grace that nothing can ruffle or confuse. You say 'Bolton's a man high-bred beyond the common. 'Tis from him she catches it.' I grant you his breeding, but can say that from the first time I saw her at Queensbury House, I saw her simple and joyous and sweet-natured and judged her simplicity the highest breeding, for it can never fail being very nature's self. You should

have seen her at a rout t'other night aglitter with the Bolton diamonds, and you know them fine,—yet still with a half-Quakerish air of quaint innocence under their weight of splendour that takes all the men by storm and makes all the women appear brazen. Excepting of course your humble servant whose air of innocence is art's perfection and in much request.

"But you ask—'Is she received? Is the past condoned?' 'Do my Lady Grimalkin and Madam Prude condescend to know her Grace?' No, Kitty, they don't, and were I she, loud would be my thanksgivings on that head. But all the young and lovely and kind and generous flock to her and make a charming society indeed. As for Bolton, he's transfigured. I never saw a man so youthened (forgive this new-coined word).— He will never cease to be a lover even when the days come of gout and penitence and regret for the pleasant sins one might have committed and did not. The pair shed goodness and charity and happy thoughts about them as natural as flowers.

"Is it then all a blaze of pure unmitigated joy, my Kitty asks dubious? Ah no! In looking at their little golden-curled cherub I guess their pang and my heart beats responsive. And other women less kind, less virtuous than she, have it in their power to send a shaft deep in her tender heart from which wound the blood wells to her cheek and dyes it crimson. What then? Shall presumptuous mortals hope for the happiness of angels? It cannot be, and, such as her lot is, few but must envy it.

"You ask also of my own future, my kind Kitty. Enigmatic, my dear, enigmatic to myself. I see Bas often and speak with him lightly and pass on with never a regret. He can hurt me no more. 'Tis all as dead and gone as the Pyramids. Did I ever love him? I can't tell. 'Twas in a former life if so. Did he ever love me? He never loved or will love any but his charming self, though I hear of attentions to the rich and handsome Mrs. Janssen that may end in wedding favours. Let them! I will dance at his wedding with the lightest pair of heels there, and thank Heaven for my deliverance.

"I writ you some time since—'tis good to be a widow. So good that I purpose to remain a widow indeed. You can't dispute my wisdom since the Apostle himself commends the State and recommends it in preference to marriage, his Sanctity forgetting, as I think, that one must endure the tribulation of the one to attain the tranquillity of the other. Well, I have endured and attained and there I leave it. If for a moment I wavered I love my widowhood the better now. Says the Prince to me the other day—'When shall we have your wedding favours?' Says I—'When I learn to love trouble better than ease and prefer discomfort to comfort. And that won't be till I lose my senses in dotage, Sir.' There's many a true word spoken in jest.

"Well, farewell, my kind Kitty,—but throw not a dart at my dear new Duchess. I name her the chaste Diana, and hold her so in word, thought, and deed. I fling down my glove as a challenge to man or woman who dares dispute it. And if even your dear self picks up the glove, I will fight to the death.

"And now the lights burn low and I am for sleep. I make you my curtsey. Good-night, Good-night!"

THE END

CPSIA information can be obtained
at www.ICGtesting.com
Printed in the USA
LVHW011241061021
699678LV00001B/56

9 789355 116956